FATHERS AND DAUGHTERS

FATHERS
AND DAUGHTERS

Anthea Fraser

Severn House Large Print
London & New York

This first large print edition published in Great Britain 2003 by
SEVERN HOUSE LARGE PRINT BOOKS LTD of
9-15, High Street, Sutton, Surrey, SM1 1DF.
First world regular print edition published 2002 by
Severn House Publishers, London and New York.
This first large print edition published in the USA 2003 by
SEVERN HOUSE PUBLISHERS INC., of
595 Madison Avenue, New York, NY 10022

British Library Cataloguing i

Fraser, Anthea
    Fathers and daughters - L
    1.   Romantic suspense no
    2.   Large type books
    I.   Title
    823.9'14 [F]

    ISBN 0-7278-7189-7

Printed and bound in Great Britain by
MPG Books Ltd, Bodmin, Cornwall.

Content

Family, Friends and Acquaintances

1973

Phyllis Marlow
Hettie Freeman, her companion

Gordon Marlow, Phyllis's son
Rita Marlow, his wife
Eleanor Marlow
Fay Marlow

Jeremy Page
Patrick Nelson
Andrew Bly, Patrick's dental colleague
Danny Martin, Jeremy's housemate
Bruce Taylor, Jeremy's housemate

Roger Hastings, friend of Patrick's
Pammy Hastings, his wife

Jess Ridley, Ellie's friend
Mark Ridley, Jess's brother
Alice Ridley, their mother

Mel Patterson, Jeremy's girlfriend

Plus, in 1994:

Laura Nelson
Christa Nelson
Jenny Nelson
Claire Nelson
Ed Marshall, Jess's husband
Dominic Marshall, their son and Ellie's
   godson
Matthew Marshall
Lucy Marshall

Plus, in the present:

Adrian Crawford, in love with Laura
Roy Delamere, Claire's partner
Oliver Drake, married to Jenny
Neville Henderson, Christa's lover
Lesley Kirkham, book-shop manager
Georgia Prentiss

Prologue – The Present Day

Every year, Fay Nelson wished – uselessly – that her family would ignore her birthday, and each year they insisted on celebrating it. Even worse, this year they were sure to invite Roger, which she certainly didn't want, though there was no way of saying so. No doubt she was being difficult and ungrateful, as Ellie didn't hesitate to point out, but she resented having to feign appreciation year after year, when she would much have preferred to opt out of the whole thing – as Ellie of all people should have realised, Fay thought crossly, closing the front door behind her: she'd told her often enough. But here, as so often, her sister put the girls' wishes first.

'It's because they love you,' she would say, when Fay protested. 'Anyway, why this hang-up about your birthday, when all the rest of the year you thoroughly enjoy socialising?'

Surely you remember? Fay wanted to scream at her. *It was on my birthday that Jeremy left me!* But that was something else she couldn't say. Jeremy's name was never mentioned these days; even Laura, with whom there'd been so many scenes in the past, had stopped talking about him. Yet it was through Jeremy that Fay had acquired Sandford Lodge.

At the gate she turned to look back at it, serene and unchanging through all the vicissitudes that had taken place within its walls. She and Ellie had loved it all their lives.

'It was built for your great-grandfather,' Gamma would tell them on childhood visits. 'When he died, it came to Grandpa and me, and in due course your parents will live here.'

Though they never did, Fay thought now, starting down the hill. During those last weeks of Gamma's life the atmosphere at home had been strained, her mother moving about tight-lipped, her father stubbornly silent. There had been low voiced discussions behind closed doors, and she and Ellie, shamelessly eavesdropping, had been appalled to discover that their mother had no intention of moving to Sandford.

It was the same summer that Fay had met Jeremy. 'Damn!' she said aloud, startling a boy who was cycling past her down the hill. This was another problem with her birthday: as it approached, so, inevitably, did the memories, as sharp and painful as if they'd happened yesterday instead of – incredibly –

twenty-seven years ago. Handsome, charming Jeremy, the all-round sportsman: county cricket player, tennis ace, and – most glamorous of all – silver medallist in the '68 Olympics. No wonder that, at nineteen, she'd fallen hopelessly in love with him.

Had she known what the future held, would she still have married him? Come to that, would she, later, have married Patrick? How could she have known that both her husbands would leave her, without so much as a word of explanation? That one of them would later be murdered, and the other disappear without trace?

'Oh, *damn!*' she said again, more forcibly, feeling for a handkerchief. She was coming to the foot of the hill, and across the road the river, glinting in the sunlight, blurred before her eyes as the old, painful questions, never far below the surface, reared up at her again. Was there any way she could have stemmed the course of events? Was she personally responsible for all that had happened?

But this was no time for hypothesis; she'd be late for work. Fay wiped her eyes, blew her nose, and set off purposefully along Riverside Walk.

Rushyford was an attractive town occupying both banks of the river Rush, which threaded its way alongside the main shopping street, crossed by a series of stone bridges whose single traffic lanes caused frustration to both residents and tourists. In a comfortable mix of old and new, the town boasted a Norman church, a market whose charter dated from the twelfth century, a theatre and concert hall, several good restaurants and a plethora of specialist galleries and boutiques. In the last year, it had also acquired a state-of the-art shopping mall.

The book shop where Fay worked part-time was tucked into one of the older alleyways between a delicatessen and a flower shop, but since it was on a short cut from Waitrose to the car park, business was brisk. She had never had what her daughters referred to as 'a proper job', having given birth to her first baby at nineteen and to the next three at two-yearly intervals. Looking after them and her beloved house and garden had kept her fully occupied, even through the traumas that had beset her. In fact, their unremitting demands had more than once saved her sanity.

She turned from the sunlit thoroughfare into a side street, catching sight of her hurrying figure in a shop window. Her hair, she noted, was already escaping from the knot she'd twisted it into. Left to itself, it fell below her shoulders, a ridiculous length for a woman of her age; but she coaxed it into a variety of styles – chignon, French pleat, topknot – none of which, admittedly, held for more than an hour or two. Much less trouble, she'd decided recently, to wear it short, like Ellie's; but when she'd mentioned her intention to Roger, she'd been surprised by the force of his objection, registering only later that his unpinning of her hair had become a prelude to their love-making. She should have presented him with a *fait accompli*.

Which brought her full circle, back to Roger and the fact that she didn't want him at the dinner. Christa considered them 'an item', she remembered with amusement, but although the girls brought current boyfriends to these occasions, Roger's inclusion would, she felt, place too much importance on the relationship. She wasn't ready to consider him in a permanent light – might never be – and the invitation might lead him to make false assumptions. Or, she thought with a wry inward smile, to panic, as she was doing.

There had, inevitably, been other men. She was a passionate woman, and when Patrick had unaccountably left her after twenty years, she had been bereft physically as well as emotionally. Though there'd been no shortage of would-be comforters, she'd had the sense to be discreet; the family was well known in the area, and during those anguished weeks she had been the subject of enough gossip and surmise without adding to it. Husbands of friends, though several approached her, were definitely out.

At that time, though, Roger had been in a different category, and the comfort he offered purely platonic. He and Patrick had met at dental college; Patrick had been his best man and, later, they had gone into practice together. Fay had liked both him and his wife, and the two couples had become close friends, spending weekends away together, going to the theatre and regularly dining at each other's houses. When Patrick had left so suddenly, Roger and Pammy, almost as shocked as Fay herself, had been there for her, punctiliously including her in invitations when other friends found her newly single status an embarrassment.

Then, two and a half years ago, Pammy had contracted cancer and died within six months. Reeling from the loss of a much-loved friend, Fay had attempted to comfort Roger in his grieving, as he had helped her. It was only in the last month or two that, almost without their realising it, their friendship had deepened into something more.

She started guiltily as the door of the book shop burst open, and Lesley's voice demanded impatiently, 'Are you going to stay out there all day? I've been watching

14

you for the last five minutes.'

Fay flushed. 'Sorry.'

'You were miles away,' Lesley added accusingly, following her through to the back room, where she hung her jacket on a hook.

'Just taking stock of my life,' Fay said lightly, repinning her hair in front of the spotted mirror. 'Not, I admit, at the most appropriate time.'

'Your birthday cometh,' Lesley commented resignedly.

'Exactly. As you know, it always affects me that way.'

Lesley Kirkham was the manager of the book shop; since they spent three days a week in each other's company, the two had become friends and, to a certain degree, confidantes. Fay knew, for instance, that Lesley's husband Paul was threatened with redundancy and as a consequence had started drinking; that her elderly mother was dropping hints about going to live with them – not an option in their small house – and that their eldest son was unlikely to pass his A levels. And she thought she had problems! Fay told herself.

As she turned from the mirror, her eyes fell on a stack of books against the wall.

'The new Carl Clifford?' she asked.

Lesley nodded. 'It's out on Thursday and there's bound to be a rush. Waterstone's are expecting an overnight queue.'

'We've a list of reservations ourselves, haven't we?'

'Yes, the names are in the book. Could you start setting copies aside, while I put the coffee on?'

'Sure.'

The book shop, aiming to give more personal attention than chain stores could offer, had recently introduced a coffee stand flanked by a couple of sofas, so that prospective buyers could browse in comfort. The policy seemed to be paying dividends, and sales over the last six months had shown a marked increase.

'Pour me a cup before you take it through,' Fay requested and, bending down, picked up a pile of books and put them on the desk. With her working day at last under way, there would be no more time for brooding, and she was grateful.

Ellie Marlow sat in her study at Rushyford High School for Girls, tapping her fingers absent-mindedly on her desk. It was the last week of term, and she had the reports to read through and initial, making a general, overall comment at the end of each, as befitted the headmistress; but although she had picked up her pen more than once, each time she'd laid it down again, to sit staring through the window to where, across the river, Sandford Lodge could be seen on the skyline.

She sighed, running her fingers through her short, curly hair. Easter holidays were synonymous with Fay's birthday, and every year Ellie had sulks and general bolshiness to contend with. Why did Fay have to be so ungracious, when the girls were planning a treat for her? But she'd always been supremely self-centred, as Ellie knew to her cost.

'You don't look like sisters!' people always said.

True. Fay was taller, fairer and prettier. They had the same grey eyes, inherited from their father, but Ellie's curly hair was chest-nut – a richer variant of her mother's ginger – while Fay's, pale gold, hung straight as a curtain. Their characters were equally dis-similar. Though the elder by four years, Ellie had been a timid child, eternally seeking her father's approval, which was seldom forth-coming. At school she'd been quiet and studious, working partly from the love of it and partly to please her parents, while Fay, totally self-confident, had had no need to strive, and though she had a good brain, seldom put it to use.

The gulf between them had increased as they grew older. Fay was continually sur-rounded by boys, while Ellie, though pretty enough, had lacked that magic spark that was sex appeal – all of which, she thought now, had resulted in Fay marrying at nineteen, moving into their grandmother's house, and becoming a mother six months later. The other girls had arrived in quick succession and, occupied with looking after them, her husband and the house, she had never gone out to work. Only when the last of the girls had left home had she finally, to fill in her day, taken the part-time job at the book shop. And now that Christa, after breaking off a long-term relationship, was back living at home, Ellie daily expected her to throw it in.

Did the exasperation she felt mask jealousy? she wondered, not for the first time. She hoped not. True, Fay had had two husbands and four children, while Ellie, though she'd had the chance, had never married. Instead, she had a fulfilling job, a comfortable bank balance, and the company, whenever she wished it, of Mark, her long-term friend and occasional lover. With wide-ranging interests and a large circle of friends, hers was a full and rich life by any standards, and if there was sadness at the heart of it, no one had ever suspected, and she intended no one ever should.

As for Fay, they'd irritate each other less if Ellie moved out of Sandford, as she should have done long since. It was supposed to have been a temporary stay, to see Fay over

Patrick's desertion as, years before, she'd moved in to help her over Jeremy's – though on that occasion, Ellie reflected bitterly, she'd not been needed for long. But she had now been at Sandford for over six years, and though there was nothing to stop her giving notice to the tenants in her own house, she'd been reluctant to do so. The trouble was that, though she loved her little house, it was Sandford that felt like home – as it always had.

Perhaps Roger would prove the catalyst. Fay had had several relationships since Patrick left, but Roger was different. He'd been a friend long before deeper feelings developed, and Ellie was pretty sure he was serious. Fay's intentions were, of course, anyone's guess, but this could yet provide the nudge needed to enable Ellie to move home.

Thinking of Roger reminded her that she really must phone him about the birthday – it was short notice as it was – and she jotted a note on her pad. That would bring the numbers to ten. Christa had booked a table at the new and very expensive restaurant that had opened in the converted watermill just outside town.

'Should be up to Laura's standards!' she'd said with a smile. Laura ran her own high-class catering company in London, supplying directors' lunches and private dinner parties with haute cuisine, and had built up a lucrative business for herself. *If only the best is good enough, Page Laura* ran her slogan, a play on her name. For Laura was Jeremy's daughter, and although Patrick had adopted her as a baby and she had been Laura Nelson throughout her schooldays, when she'd left home to start work, she'd reverted to her original surname.

Ellie's brows drew together as her thoughts moved to her eldest niece. The most difficult and prickly of the girls always, Laura nevertheless had a special place in her affections. During those early months, it had been Ellie who got up to her in the night, while Fay, face buried in her pillow, had sobbed for her errant husband; and as Laura grew up and acquired half-sisters, Ellie had suspected that, smaller and darker than Patrick's tall, fair daughters, she had felt something of an outsider.

Fathers and daughters, she reflected ruefully; what a fraught relationship it had proved in their family: her own father's blatant favouritism of Fay had led to a long-lasting sense of inferiority, which still, on occasion, returned to haunt her. Years later, Jeremy's desertion of Laura, almost at birth, had undoubtedly had an effect on the girl as she grew up and began to ask questions. And finally Patrick, father of Christa, Jenny and Claire, had, in his turn, also deserted his family, with God only knew what damaging results.

Ellie's eyes filled with sudden tears and, hastily picking up her pen, she at last reached for the pile of reports.

'You're already perfect; why gild the lily?'

'In other words, get a move on!' Laura interpreted, leaning over the dressing table to apply her lipstick. She could see him in the looking-glass world behind her, his hair parted on the wrong side, the light glinting on his spectacles as he glanced at his watch.

Not, to give him his due, that he was really hurrying her. Adrian was patience personified and would, Laura didn't doubt, have waited for her for ever without complaint. Her family said she led him a dance, and were probably right. When someone was unfailingly kind and considerate, never rising when she tried to needle them, it brought out the worst in her.

Her eyes refocused on her own reflection: small, oval face, creamily pale, framed by short, expertly cut hair, and enormous, long-lashed dark eyes – her father's eyes, her mother always said, and as a child, Laura had never known if that was a good or a bad thing. Now, she couldn't bear to think of her father.

She straightened abruptly, smoothing the silk dress over her almost non-existent breasts. It was a long-standing source of grievance that her younger sisters were all better endowed in that area than she was. In fact, with her slight frame and close-fitting cap of dark hair, she cut an almost boyish figure, redeemed, however, by a wide, sensual mouth that was totally feminine.

Adrian stood up as she came towards him, and took her hands. 'Will you marry me, lovely Laura?' he asked smilingly. It was a question which, variously couched, he posed every three or four weeks, and she gave him the usual reply.

'We have the best of both worlds – sex, our own space, independence – so why bother?'

'I don't want my own space, I want yours,' he answered, dropping a kiss on her dark head. Though not tall himself, he topped her by several inches. 'Tell me why we need two expensive flats, two phone bills – both extortionate, since we're always ringing each other – two council taxes, and God knows what besides.'

'You speak as though we were on the brink of penury,' she said lightly.

'Must be my Scottish ancestry!'

The truth, she thought as she preceded him into the lift, was that she was not at all sure she wanted to marry him. Their present arrangement suited her admirably, but in the long term his continual compliance might end by boring her. She had always been the dominant partner in their relationship, and that, also, might pall.

She studied him as he stood opposite her – not exactly a Prince Charming, she conceded; rather a typical boffin, with his round glasses and small beard – and wondered how it would be, to be married to him. His family was wealthy and owned a grouse moor in Scotland – facts of only academic interest. She'd met his parents a couple of times, and knew, from her own observations and Adrian's veiled comments, that they would welcome a match. Her own family, from her mother down, thought he was 'sweet'. Well, time would tell.

They reached the ground floor, and Adrian took her arm as they went outside to find a taxi. They were going to a drinks party hosted by the firm he worked for – a fund-raising event to generate backing for their research. 'Everyone' would be there, she'd been assured, including minor royalty; she might even make some useful contacts herself.

While she had known Adrian was fairly bright, Laura was unprepared for the esteem in which everyone at the reception seemed to hold him. Time and again one of the partners would bring across some distinguished-looking personage, saying, 'I'd like you to meet Adrian Crawford, our chief

23

chemist', and in the ensuing technical talk – on this social occasion necessarily brief – her attention would wander.

It was during one of these interludes that she became aware that she herself was the object of scrutiny. Across the room, an attractive woman had been staring fixedly at her, and turned quickly away as their eyes met. Laura's brow creased as she tried to place her. In her mid-forties, she had vibrant, red-gold hair that flamed amid the browns and greys of the other women and was set off to perfection by the green velvet of her trouser suit.

Perhaps she'd been present at some function Laura had catered for; she now had a wide list, corporate and private, whose offices or homes she visited; and though she made a point of memorising faces as well as names, the odd guest at some of the larger gatherings might have escaped her notice. Nevertheless, she was unlikely to have forgotten that hair.

Ten minutes later, she again found herself under observation and, when she was able to reclaim Adrian's attention, asked him who the woman was.

'Sorry, darling, can't help. Let's go and sample some of those canapés before I have to meet another stuffed shirt!'

But as they made their way to the buffet table, Laura felt a touch on her arm and turned to find the red-haired woman beside her.

'Forgive me,' she began with a nervous smile. 'I do apologise for subjecting you to such a prolonged examination, but you remind me so much of someone I used to know.'

She fingered the neckline of her blouse, as though it were suddenly too tight. Then, moistening her lips, she said rapidly, 'I suppose you're not ... could you by any chance be related to Jeremy Page?'

Laura's hand reached blindly for Adrian's, which grasped it reassuringly. 'Yes,' she acknowledged after a minute, 'he ... was my father.'

The woman released her breath in a long sigh. 'I *thought* he must have been – you're so like him. I suppose you're used to hearing that?'

'My mother says I have his eyes,' Laura admitted.

'Yes.' There was a pause while the woman scanned her face almost hungrily, before making a charming gesture of apology. 'I'm so sorry, I haven't introduced myself. I was a friend of Jeremy's; my name is Georgia Prentiss.'

Laura's eyes widened and her nails dug suddenly into Adrian's hand. '*No!*' she whispered, shaking her head violently. 'Oh, *no!* I'm sorry,' she added rapidly, not meeting their eyes, 'I don't feel ... excuse me!' and, turning away, she pushed her way frantically through the crowded room, making for the door.

With an apologetic glance at Ms Prentiss, Adrian set off after her.

Part 1 – 1973–74

One

Wrapped in their own thoughts, they hadn't spoken since leaving home, but as they approached Rushyford, Rita Marlow glanced apprehensively at her husband. 'I'm sorry to say this, love, but I dread going to see your mother these days.'

He merely grunted, his eyes on the road.

'It's not just that it's painful to watch her going downhill,' she continued; 'it's all this business about the house.'

'I know.'

'I don't want to upset her when she's so ill, but she's that set on our moving there, and I tell you straight, Gordon, I'm not going to. We'll have to tell her, *make* her understand. I *know* it's a lovely house, and that Rushyford is prettier than Beckhurst, but I'm happy where I am. We've spent years getting it the way we want it, we know everybody, and—'

'All right, all right, we've been through all this.'

'Well, it's different for you. Since you're out of the house all day, it doesn't mean as

29

much to you.'

'The garden does,' he retorted with grim humour. 'I've spent most of my free time in it over the last twenty odd years!'

They were now driving down the main street, with the river keeping pace with them on their left. On its grassy banks, children and dogs were playing, while to their right the pavement was thronged with Saturday shoppers.

As they turned right at the traffic lights, they could see Sandford Lodge up the hill ahead of them, its pink walls and white-framed windows gleaming in the sunshine. Most people would give their eye-teeth for such a house in such a position, Rita acknowledged, but not her.

Gordon said, 'She hates the thought of strangers moving in; no one but the family has ever lived there.'

'Well, that can't go on indefinitely, can it? Tell me honestly,' she challenged him, 'do *you* want to?'

What was the use? he thought wearily. He'd grown up at Sandford, and loved it with a deep, possessive love. Moreover, like his daughters, he'd automatically assumed they'd move there after his mother's death, as she and his father had when his grandparents died. It was only recently, when Ma had become ill and started talking of the future, that Rita had astounded him by remarking that she'd no intention of living at Sandford, and hadn't realised it would be expected of her.

Over the last few weeks they'd had increasingly acrimonious discussions, though he had argued solely from his mother's viewpoint. He accepted that his wife had no inkling of how deeply he himself felt about it – which was his own fault; he'd never been able to discuss things that mattered to him. One fact was abundantly clear, though: if he insisted on moving, his life wouldn't be worth living.

They had reached the open gateway and he turned into it, coming to a halt outside the porticoed front door. As he switched off the engine, they could hear a bird singing in the cherry tree.

Rita was still waiting for his answer. 'Gordon?'

He sat for a moment in silence, staring out of the window at the green lawns and colourful flower beds he had known all his life. 'I'm easy either way,' he said at last. 'But if you're so dead set against it, fair enough. All I ask is that you don't say anything to Ma. She's not got long, and if it makes her happy to think of us living here after she's gone, why rock the boat?'

'But it seems deceitful, somehow, pretending—'

'Better a bit of deceit at this stage than a

downright row,' he said firmly, getting out of the car.

They were met in the hall by Hettie Freeman, Mrs Marlow's nurse-companion, brisk and cheerful as always.

'How is she today?' Gordon asked in a low voice.

'Much the same, sir. She had a restless night but we're managing to control the pain. If you'd like to go through...' She opened the door on the left and stood aside for them to enter. Together they crossed the sitting room to the conservatory extension, where the invalid was seated in her wheelchair, a rug over her knees, though the temperature, with the sun streaming through the glass, was well into the eighties.

At sixty-nine, Phyllis Marlow looked twenty years older. The flesh of her face had fallen away, making nose, chin and cheekbones unnaturally prominent, and her once luxuriant hair barely covered her scalp. The hands lying idle on her lap were like the claws of a small bird.

They bent, one after the other, to kiss her withered cheek.

Rita laid a bunch of blossoms on the low table for Hettie to deal with later. 'I brought you some mock-orange from the garden,' she said. 'It won't last long, but I know you like the scent.'

The old woman glanced at the creamy

petals and nodded. Behind her, through the windows of the conservatory, the garden sloped away up the hill. At the far end a frayed rope still hung from the apple tree, reminding Rita, with a rare stab of nostalgia, of how her daughters had enjoyed swinging from it when they were young.

'Well, sit down, sit down,' Phyllis Marlow said testily, breaking into her reminiscences. 'I presume you *are* staying for a few minutes?'

'Of course.' Hastily they pulled up basket chairs, and Rita braced herself for yet another allusion to their occupancy of the house. Gordon, avoiding her eyes, was sitting forward, hands between his knees, staring at the tiled floor.

Mrs Marlow looked at them sharply. Her eyes, bright and blue, were the only parts of her body not to have let her down over the years and, had either of her relatives glanced at her, they would have seen a flash of spirit in them.

'About the house,' she began, and raised a hand as her daughter-in-law instinctively stiffened. 'I have the feeling, Rita, that you're not particularly enamoured with the idea of living here. Am I right?'

Rita flushed hotly, the crimson of her face at odds with her ginger hair. 'Oh, I ... I can't think why...'

Again the raised hand. 'All right, all right.

Perhaps that was unfair, and I hope I'm mistaken. Obviously I can't force you, least of all after my death; but I want you to promise me something, Gordon.'

He looked at her miserably. God, don't let her ask him something he couldn't do.

There was a pause while she coughed painfully, her thin body wracked by the paroxysm. After a moment she went on, her voice sounding fainter than before. 'You know how I feel about strangers owning it – I've made that plain enough. Perhaps it's foolish to mind so much, but there it is. So I want you to promise me that even if you don't come here yourselves, you won't sell the house. Let it, rent it, whatever; but keep it in the family for one more generation. Then, if either of the girls wants it when the time comes – and they've both loved it since they were tots – it would still be there for them.'

She looked at her son, who was once more examining the terracotta tiles. 'Well?' she prompted. 'Surely that's not too much to ask?'

He looked up then, his eyes suspiciously bright. 'Of course it isn't, Ma,' he said, 'and of course I promise. I give you my word I won't sell Sandford.'

Phyllis Marlow closed her eyes briefly, and wiped her lips with a lacy scrap of handkerchief. 'Thank you,' she said after a minute.

'It's not as though you'll be in need of the capital; as you know, your father invested wisely and there will be a nice little nest egg.'

Rita glanced from her husband to her mother-in-law, aware of raw emotions just beneath the surface. It was up to her to lighten the atmosphere.

'Now, that's enough talk of dying,' she said rallyingly. 'Let's turn to something more cheerful. As you know, Ma, it's Ellie's birthday next week, and she's counting on your coming over for it. I do hope you will; it'll do you good to have a change of scene.'

Phyllis Marlow opened her eyes and smiled ruefully. 'A week may be a long time in politics, but it's even longer in my state of health. Ask me again nearer the time. And dearest love to both her and Fay.'

It was, they realised, their dismissal. After the strain of making her wishes known, she was exhausted and needed to rest. Promising to phone in a few days, they kissed her and took their leave.

'Thank God she's given up on us living there,' Rita said, as soon as they were in the car. 'And without our having to spell it out, too. As for the girls, they might love the house, but whether or not they'll want to stay in the area when they're married is another question. For one thing, their husbands might be working in London, or even abroad. Rushyford isn't the centre of the universe.'

'There's nothing to stop them selling it, if that's the case,' Gordon said. 'But at least Ma's tied it up as best she can, so she can rest happy on that score.' He just wished, futilely, that she hadn't sensed Rita's reluctance, and been robbed of the certainty that they'd be living there themselves.

That same afternoon, Ellie and Fay, having opted out of visiting their grandmother, were sunbathing at home.

'I'm sick of having to pretend we'll be living there,' Ellie commented, rubbing cream on her arms. 'Do you think Gamma knows Mum doesn't want to?'

'She soon will, if Mum gets that set look on her face,' Fay retorted. 'She bit my head off when I asked about it the other day, but we've *always* been told we'd live there when Gamma died.'

'Only by Gamma,' Ellie reminded her.

'Suppose we tell them how much we want to?'

'Wouldn't make any difference; it's Mum who's holding out, and you know what she's like once her mind's made up.'

'But *why?* That's what I don't understand. It's a wonderful house – much nicer than this dump!'

'Don't let her hear you say that!'

'Well, it doesn't compare with Sandford, does it? If you look out of these windows, all you see is other houses and garages, instead of a view down the hill to the river.'

They were silent for a while, soaking up the hot sunshine. Then Fay said idly, 'Are you doing anything this evening?'

Ellie strove to sound casual. 'Yes, actually. I'm ... seeing Patrick.'

Fay's eyes flew open as she turned her head towards her. 'Are you, indeed? You've kept very quiet about it! When was all this arranged?'

'At the last film evening. He mentioned wanting to see a Spanish film that's on at the Regal – it'll be years before we get it at the Society. And when I said I did too, he suggested we go together. It's no big deal.'

'Who are you kidding?' Fay scoffed. 'You have been mooning over Patrick for months!'

Ellie flushed. 'I have *not!*'

'Every time you go to the Film Society, it's Patrick this and Patrick that! What's he like, anyway?'

'Nice.'

'Very helpful! What does he *look* like? Tall or short, dark or fair, good-looking or just interesting?'

'Honestly, he's nothing special,' protested Ellie treacherously. 'Tallish, light-brown hair, a nice smile.'

'What does he do?'

'He's a dentist – in Rushyford, as it happens.'

'Ugh! Fancy spending your time peering into people's mouths!' Fay shot her a sly glance. 'Where are you meeting? I've a good mind to come along and take a look at him.'

Ellie sat up. 'Fay, you wouldn't!'

'No, you idiot, of course I wouldn't; I've better things to do. We're going to the tennis club dance.'

Ellie lay down again, her heartbeats returning to normal. She'd thought she had disguised her interest in Patrick, but it seemed not. Fay could afford to be offhand about her admirers, but Ellie herself was less in demand, and each Monday had to fend off questions in the staff room about how she'd spent the weekend, while the other girls related their amorous adventures. It was the ultimate failure, to stay in on Saturday evenings.

Beside her, Fay stretched, running her fingers through her damp hair. 'I think I've had enough sun,' she announced. 'I'm going to have a bath and wash my hair.'

Ellie squinted up at her. Clad in the briefest of bikinis, Fay's body was a uniform golden brown, her hair bleached by the sun to silver-gilt. No wonder the boys came running, Ellie thought enviously.

'You shouldn't stay much longer, either,'

Fay commented, glancing down at her. 'You're starting to go pink, and you don't want to look like a lobster for Patrick, now do you?' And, trailing her towel behind her, she strolled, hips swaying, back to the house.

Though all the doors and windows were open, it was oppressively hot in the pavilion, and Steve's hand in hers felt damp and sticky. Fleetingly, Fay thought of her sister, wondering if the unknown Patrick would be holding *her* hand in the stuffy dark of the cinema, and if so, whether it would be as sweaty as Steve's. Truth to tell, she was not enjoying herself as much as she'd expected. The disco was samey and the noise level as voices shouted above the music did not help the headache she'd developed after lying in the sun.

She was about to use it as an excuse to leave when Steve suddenly gave a whistle. 'Well, we *are* honoured! Look who's just arrived!'

Fay turned her head. 'Who is it? I can't see.'

'Jeremy Page, no less. He doesn't often come slumming these days.'

'Jeremy Page?' Fay repeated, her voice rising. 'Here?'

'As large as life. And he's had a few on the way, by the look of him.'

Jeremy was the local hero, and had been the pin-up of all the girls at Fay's school. Apart from his good looks, he played cricket for the county, had captained the tennis club and – crowning glory – been a member of the British team at the fateful Munich Olympics. Like everyone else in the neighbourhood, Fay had avidly followed his career – until last summer, when, after a complicated shoulder injury, it had been cut tragically short – but she'd never met him, nor ever expected to.

She stood on tiptoe, eagerly craning across the bobbing heads, and, as the dancers slowly gyrated, caught sight of the group by the door and the unmistakable figure in its midst. Almost unconsciously, she began to move in his direction, Steve still clinging to her hand.

'Hey, hang on!' he protested. 'Where are you going?'

'To get some air,' she replied, moving purposefully towards the door. By this time, news of Jeremy's arrival had spread, and excited whispers were going round the room as the dancers slowed, straining to see the figure in the doorway.

Steve was right, Fay thought as she drew nearer: Jeremy did seem a little tipsy. Face flushed, shirt unbuttoned, he was swaying slightly, a benign smile on his face as he gazed at the scene in front of him. Beside

40

him, the two men he'd arrived with were chatting to the club secretary. Fay's only intention was to have a closer look at him, but as she reached her vantage point she was suddenly jolted from behind, and went stumbling forward almost into his arms.

'Oh, I'm sorry!' she gasped, flushing, as he put out a hand to steady her.

'Are you?' said Jeremy Page, his hand still on her arm. 'I can't say I am. Come and dance with me, golden girl.' And, putting an arm round her, he drew her into the throng of dancers.

There was a burst of laughter from his companions and a cry of, 'Good old Jay! Never misses a trick!'

Fay was briefly aware of Steve's startled, indignant face; then as Jeremy pulled her closer, she gave him her full attention, not least because he was leaning on her in order to keep upright. He wasn't as tall as she'd expected – about her own height – and his breath, warm in her ear, smelt strongly of beer.

'My lucky night,' he said, slightly slurring his words. 'Most beautiful girl in the room throws herself into my arms. Unbelievable! What's your name, gorgeous?'

'Fay,' she said breathlessly. She was acutely aware of the amused glances that followed them, of his stumbling feet which more than once came down heavily on hers. She'd be covered in bruises tomorrow, but what did she care? She was dancing with Jeremy Page.

Fay had always prided herself on her ability to handle men, allowing them as much licence as she felt was warranted, and no more. At nineteen she was still a virgin, a fact that might have surprised her friends. Up to now, kissing and light petting had satisfied her and she'd had no desire to go further; but as Jeremy nuzzled her neck, she felt suddenly and alarmingly out of her depth. She tried to push him upright, but instead of cooperating he gave a low laugh, pulled her behind a convenient pillar, and started to kiss her. Used as she was to keeping the upper hand, she was totally unprepared for the rush of sensations that engulfed her, sweeping her away on a tide of passion.

Their total absorption with each other was finally interrupted by a tap on Jeremy's shoulder and a voice said resignedly, 'Come on, Jay. Time to pack it in. We're due at the Green Parrot at ten.'

Jeremy raised his head, and Fay saw a couple looking smilingly back at them as they danced past. What must they think of her? she thought in confusion.

'Whass your name?' Jeremy asked again, and again she replied, 'Fay.'

He fumbled in his trouser pocket and

produced an old train ticket. 'Write it down,' he instructed.

'I haven't got a pen.'

He raised his voice and called after the couple. 'Danny, got a pen on you?'

The man appealed to came back, proffering a topless ballpoint, which Jeremy handed to Fay. 'Write it down,' he repeated, 'and your phone number.'

With shaking hands she rested the crumpled ticket against the pillar and did so. He'll have lost it by the morning, she thought despairingly, as he tucked it into his shirt pocket.

'Fay!'

She spun round to see Steve glaring at her. 'Where were you? I've been looking for you.'

She hesitated, glancing back, but Jeremy had draped his arm round the shoulders of Danny's partner and was whispering in her ear.

Holding back tears of uncertainty and humiliation, she smiled brightly at Steve. 'Just coming,' she said.

Phyllis Marlow did not attend her granddaughter's birthday. By the following week she was unable to leave her bed, and instead the whole family paid her a brief visit to enable her to give Ellie the gift which Hettie had been delegated to buy. She died peacefully in her sleep a few days later.

43

After the funeral, everyone had gone back to Sandford, where Rita had been grateful for Hettie's help. Now, she was busy washing glasses while the dishwasher, still a novelty, dealt quickly and efficiently with plates, cups and cutlery. Rita covered the uneaten sandwiches and small cakes with an upturned plate. 'You might like to have these for supper,' she said. Hettie would be leaving at the end of the week: the closing of another chapter. She had been with Mrs Marlow for years, as had Gladys, the woman who came in daily to clean. She, too, would be looking for another job.

Rita longed to go home and change out of her suit and high heels. The girls had disappeared, the first time she could remember their voluntarily leaving Sandford. Gordon was running a few of the more elderly guests back to their retirement home at the other side of Rushyford. He shouldn't be long now. He'd shown little sign of distress at his mother's death, shaking off Rita's awkward attempts at comfort; but then he'd always been undemonstrative.

Since Hettie seemed as disinclined for conversation as herself, she went out of the kitchen and stood for a minute in the hall. Thirteen feet square, it was a room in its own right, and its pale cinnamon walls and white woodwork made for a warm and welcoming entrance. The chimney breast on her right gave rise to two alcoves, the far one containing two small windows at right angles to each other, and beneath them a built-in padded bench. A bookcase filled the nearer alcove, and an easy chair in front of it invited one to sit down and read.

Rita moved to the dining-room doorway, surveying the mahogany suite and silver candelabra. They'd have to go through the house before it was offered for rent, either removing everything of value, or locking it all in one room. At least they wouldn't have to redecorate; all the rooms, though true to their Edwardian origins, looked fresh and bright.

Glancing into the sitting room, she could see the conservatory beyond, seeming more spacious without the accustomed wheelchair and, with the comforting, familiar atmosphere of the place enfolding her, Rita appreciated for the first time her mother-in-law's wish to keep the house in the family. Though still not wanting to live here herself, she realised to her surprise that she was actually glad there was a chance one of her daughters might do so one day, and her grandchildren play here in the hall as her own girls had.

Turning away, she caught a glimpse of herself in the hall mirror, a small, square figure in her black linen suit, and for a startled moment it was as if her mother looked back at her. Mabel Blackledge had had the same large bust and trim waist, the same pale sandy hair as now confronted her daughter across the hallway.

That was the trouble with funerals, Rita thought: they set you remembering others you'd attended, and people once close to you about whom you seldom thought any more – her parents, for instance, solid, no-nonsense northerners. 'I'm a self-made man and proud of it, lass,' her father would say. 'You might be better educated than your mother and me, but never be ashamed of your roots.'

She recalled how apprehensive they'd been when she'd met and married Gordon Marlow, a southerner. It was not what they'd either expected or hoped for, having a poor opinion of those who lived south of Birmingham. Nor were they happy about the rushed wedding, but Gordon was doing his National Service at the time, and had been posted overseas. 'Marry in haste and repent at leisure,' her father had warned, with typical lack of originality. But she hadn't repented – not really. All right, Gordon could be irritable and taciturn, and admittedly they argued a lot, but he was a good husband and she'd never, even at the start, been a romantic. They'd been happy enough, and had two healthy children to show for it, Ellie now teaching at Beckhurst Primary and Fay at secretarial college.

Rita settled herself on the hall chair, letting the memories come. Ellie had been a honeymoon baby; by the time Gordon was demobbed she was two, and had screamed every time he went near her. It was natural enough in so young a child, but he'd taken it badly and, making no attempt to win her round, had simply ignored her. When, after another two years, Fay had come along, smiling, enchanting baby that she was, the contrast in his behaviour was marked. Rita had pleaded with him to be even-handed, but when he'd made no attempt to disguise his favouritism, she had tried to compensate by being stricter with Fay than with Ellie. Now, she wondered if that had created more problems than it had solved.

The sound of a car drawing up outside broke into her musings, and she rose as her husband came into the house.

'All tidied up?' he asked briskly.

'Yes; Hettie's just finishing the glasses.'

'Ready to go home, then?'

'More than ready. I'll just let her know we're leaving.'

When she returned, he was standing in the hall looking about him, as she had done. 'Already it feels different,' he said.

'It's bound to.'

'Yes.' He turned abruptly to the door, but

not before she'd seen tears in his eyes. Not as hard as he made out, she thought affectionately. Knowing better than to offer sympathy, she said merely, 'It'll be good to be home.'

He nodded, opening the car door for her.

'I'm glad we're not selling the house,' she added, as they started off down the drive. It was by way of a peace offering, and he took it as such.

'Me too,' he said gruffly.

It was all that needed to be said.

Fay had said nothing at home about her meeting with Jeremy. The encounter had left her shaken and unsure of herself, and during the long hot nights the memory of his embrace returned to torment her. For a day or two she'd half-wondered if he'd phone, and when he did not, she dispiritedly continued her lack-lustre relationship with Steve.

Ellie was faring no better. She, too, had prayed for a phone call following Saturday evening, but none was forthcoming and her hope quickly withered. Looked at realistically, Patrick's invitation, which in her darkest moments she admitted she herself had prompted, was unlikely to be repeated. No doubt at the next film evening he'd sit beside her as usual and later join her for coffee, and she was forced to accept that in his eyes their evening out, on which she'd built so many dreams, had been no more than an extension of that. The only blessing was that Fay, going through one of her prickly phases, had not enquired about it.

Rita noticed that both her daughters were subdued, but put it down to sulks. There had been a brief scene after the funeral when she and Gordon arrived home. Fay had met them in the hall and, blocking their way, had immediately demanded: 'Are we or are we not going to live at Sandford, like Gamma always said?'

Rita and Gordon had exchanged a glance. 'No,' Rita began carefully, 'we didn't think—'

'*You* didn't, you mean!' Fay exploded. 'We've always been told we would! You know Gamma didn't want anyone else living there! How *can* you go against her wishes, the minute she's out of the way? It's—'

'That's enough, Fay,' Gordon broke in. 'You don't know the facts. We—'

'I know the only fact that matters!' she cried, and ran upstairs without giving them a chance to explain.

'Don't worry,' Gordon had said quietly. 'When she calms down a bit, we can tell her the arrangement.'

They had still not done so. Since probate had not yet been granted, the question of renting the house hadn't arisen, and Rita

49

had no intention of raising the matter until she had to. The girls could sulk all they liked, she told herself; it wouldn't alter anything. It was the way she had always dealt with what she thought of as their 'moods'. Her concern for her daughters had always been practical rather than emotional, nursing them through childish ailments, making sure they did their homework, and taking them to the seaside for two weeks every August. It had never occurred to her to ask their opinion on anything, from the clothes they wore or the food they ate, to the current issues of the day. She did not invite, and therefore did not receive, confidences, but remained totally unaware of anything lacking in the relationship.

Steve, meanwhile, puzzled by the change in Fay but used to her moods, had waited patiently for her to snap out of it. She wouldn't even let him kiss her, for God's sake, turning her head away and saying she didn't feel like it. What the hell was that supposed to mean?

His patience finally snapped one evening a fortnight after the dance, as they were sitting in his car outside her house. 'What's got into you all of a sudden?' he demanded in frustration. 'I'm used to you blowing hot and cold, but this has gone on long enough.'

She spun to face him. 'Is this what you want, then?' she demanded, and, seizing his face between her hands, she started to kiss him as she'd kissed Jeremy. After an instant of total shock he began to respond, but almost immediately she pushed him away.

'Fay!' he gasped. 'My God, Fay!'

She stared at him for a moment, her eyes enormous in the half-dark; then, as he reached for her again, she fumbled the door open and ran up the path to the house, leaving him staring after her.

Ignoring her mother's call from the sitting room, she rushed upstairs to her room and flung herself across the bed. She'd needed to know if kissing Steve that way would have the same effect. It did not. It seemed only Jeremy Page could light that particular fire, which was her bad luck.

It was on the following Monday that the phone rang, and Rita, coming out of the kitchen, lifted it and gave the number. To her surprise, a male voice said, 'I'm sorry to trouble you, but does someone called Fay live there?'

Rita frowned. 'Who's that speaking?'

'Jeremy Page.'

Had he said 'The Prince of Wales', she could not have been more startled.

'I ... beg your pardon?'

'It's Jeremy Page – we met at the tennis club.'

Fay had met Jeremy Page? Why hadn't she said? A dozen questions flooded Rita's mind, but she managed to say merely, 'I'll get her for you.'

She put the phone down and stared disbelievingly at it. Then, conscious of the impact her announcement would make, she pushed open the sitting-room door, where her husband and daughters were watching the nine o'clock news.

'Jeremy Page on the phone for you, Fay.'

'*Who?*' demanded Gordon and Ellie together, but Fay turned towards her a face blank with shock. After a minute she got to her feet and walked past her mother out of the room, closing the door behind her.

In the hall she stood motionless, staring at the phone. Did she, after all, want this call? Why had he kept her waiting so long? What might happen if they met again? She drew a breath, moved forward, and lifted the receiver.

'Hello?'

'Is that Fay?'

'Yes.'

'This is going to sound barmy, but I've just found your name and phone number. I ... believe we met at the tennis club?'

'You don't seem too sure about it.'

'I admit it's all a bit blurred.' He sounded apologetic; then a smile came into his voice. 'But you must be beautiful, or I wouldn't have asked for it!'

'I'm surprised you still have it. You made

me write it on an old ticket.'

'I know; I've been in Greece for the last couple of weeks, and when I got back, it was on my dresser. My cleaner found it in my shirt pocket when she was doing the laundry.'

It sounded feasible, Fay conceded to herself, and would explain the long silence.

He waited for a minute, and when she made no comment, added, 'It sounds as though I owe you some sort of apology.'

'Not really,' she said coolly.

'Could I at least buy you a drink to ease my conscience? Please?'

Decision time. If she said no, she would never see him again, and gradually the painful memory of him would fade. But he sounded so contrite, so eager to make amends. And – heavens above! – this was *Jeremy Page* pleading with her! She said slowly, 'All right, then. Thank you.'

'Tomorrow? If it's a nice evening, we could drive out to a country pub.'

'That would be fine.'

'I'll call for you, then. About eight o'clock? Where do you live?'

She told him.

'You'll be relieved to hear,' he said, 'that I'm *not* writing this down on a train ticket! See you tomorrow, then.'

'Yes. Goodbye.' She carefully replaced the phone and wiped her hand on her skirt. She

53

wanted, desperately, to be alone in her room, to play back their conversation word for word and consider the prospect that had suddenly opened up before her; but her family, she knew, would be impatiently awaiting an explanation. As she opened the sitting-room door, they all turned to face her and her mother switched off the television.

'Well?' she demanded.

'I'm going for a drink with him tomorrow.'

'He told me you met at the tennis club. You never said.'

'It was very brief,' she defended herself, and added, less truthfully, 'There was nothing to tell.'

'Well,' Rita declared roundly, 'I don't mind telling you *I'd* have mentioned it if I'd bumped into Jeremy Page, no matter how briefly. He's the nearest thing we have to a celebrity.'

'I'd be glad to meet him myself,' Gordon remarked. 'He won us that match against Wiltshire last year – a hundred and four, not out. Absolutely tragic, his career ending like that.'

Ellie was the only one who hadn't spoken, and Fay glanced at her, then quickly away. It struck her uncomfortably that her sister might well have a suspicion of why she hadn't boasted of her meeting with the famous Jeremy Page.

54

Two

'Well?' Danny asked, coming into the room as Jeremy put down the phone. 'What did she say?'

'She didn't exactly fall over herself, but she agreed to see me. I hope I'm not going to regret this. Are you sure she seemed OK?'

'You weren't having any doubts when I saw you, and she was right in there with you.'

Jeremy flung himself into an armchair. 'I do recall snogging some girl at the tennis club, but that's about it. I wish to God I could remember what she looked like.'

'No worries on that score; she's stunning.'

'Well, on your head be it; it was you who said she was worth following up.'

'All I did,' Danny corrected, 'was jog your memory when you gazed in total bafflement at that ticket. Having said which, if I'd seen her first, you wouldn't have had a look-in!'

Jeremy smiled. 'Was she with anyone?'

'There was a guy lurking in the background, but since it hasn't stopped her seeing you, it can't be big-time. Like to

55

make it a foursome?'

'No way – you've got designs on her yourself! Anyway, I need to suss her out first.'

'You mean see if she's up for it.'

'Read me like a book, don't you?'

Danny picked up the evening paper. 'When is it Mel gets back?' he asked idly.

'Next weekend.'

'Cutting it a bit fine, aren't you?'

'That's what makes life interesting,' Jeremy replied.

By the next evening, Fay was regretting her decision. No doubt he thought she was a pushover, after her embarrassing behaviour at the dance. Well, he would find differently; she'd no intention of repeating that humiliating performance – the memory of it still made her cheeks burn – and since she didn't underestimate his attraction, she must take care that a similar situation didn't arise.

The family gathered in the sitting room as the time for his arrival approached. Fay noted sardonically that her mother had put a vase of flowers on the table. You'd think they were expecting royalty.

'He's here,' Ellie said suddenly, as a red sports car drew up outside. Rita and Gordon hastily stood up and, shielded by the net curtains, watched as Jeremy climbed out and came up the path. With icy hands and thundering heart, Fay went to answer the doorbell.

He was standing on the step, looking considerably smarter than the last time she'd seen him. 'Wow!' he said softly. 'How could I not remember you?'

To her annoyance, she felt her colour rise. 'Will you come in for a minute?' she said stiffly. 'My father's a fan of yours – he'd like to meet you.' Without waiting for an answer, she turned and led the way into the sitting room. Introductions were performed, and her father, his usually impassive face lighting up, immediately embarked on a discussion of last year's county match.

Rita hovered anxiously, feeling something was required of her; but since they were going out for drinks, it was pointless to offer any, and in any case she didn't want Jeremy over-imbibing when he had to drive.

'Jeremy', she repeated to herself; it was the first time she'd thought of him by anything other than his full name, but she supposed he could now be regarded as a friend – a friend of Fay's, anyway. What would they say at Meals on Wheels, when she told them who'd been in their sitting room?

She perched nervously on the arm of a chair, taking stock of her famous visitor and liking what she saw. That he was good-looking she'd already known, but she was impressed by his easy, natural manner, and the way he seemed genuinely interested in the points Gordon was making.

Fay was still standing by the door. She looked a picture, Rita thought fondly, but there was a tenseness about her which, as usual, her mother misinterpreted.

'We mustn't hold them up, Gordon,' she broke in. 'They'll be wanting to get off.'

'Yes, of course.' Gordon looked crestfallen. Obviously he'd have liked the conversation to continue, but he stood up and shook Jeremy's hand. 'It's a pleasure to have met you, my boy.'

'You too, sir.'

Then they were outside, walking down the path, and he was opening the car door for her. They had not exchanged a word since he'd followed her into the house.

It was a warm, sultry evening, and the open top provided a welcome draught of air as they moved off. 'Where are we going?' she asked.

'I thought we'd try the Mallard. Do you know it?' She shook her head. 'It's on the river, not far from Rushyford. The gardens go right down to the water.'

'My grandmother lived at Rushyford.'

He glanced at her. 'Past tense?'

'Just.'

'Oh. I'm sorry.'

'I miss her.' There was a catch in her voice, and she took a breath before continuing. 'She had the most fabulous house, up on the hill with a view down to the river. My sister and I adored it. When I was little, I cried every time I had to go home. Mum used to get quite cross with me.'

He smiled. 'I was a lot closer to my grand-mother than to my parents.'

'Were you?' The idea surprised her, the more so since she wondered if it were true of her, too.

'She brought me up,' he continued. 'My parents were out in Kenya, and I only saw them in the school holidays.'

'Are they still there?'

'No,' he said shortly, and did not elaborate. His face, when she glanced at it, was set, and she did not probe further.

They drove in silence for a while, through the outskirts of Beckhurst and into the lush green countryside. This man beside her was a total stranger, Fay thought with a touch of disquiet; they'd exchanged barely half a dozen words before their passionate embrace, and even now, all she knew about him was that his parents had lived abroad. Her own parents had been charmed by him, as, no doubt, he had intended, but was the charm genuine or assumed?

Whether or not he divined the direction of her thoughts, he broke into them by saying, 'You've not forgiven me, have you?'

Startled, she turned to look at him. 'For what?'

'For whatever happened at our last meeting. I really must have blotted my copybook.'

She felt the colour flood her face. 'I blotted mine, too,' she admitted quietly.

'Really? Then if I forgive you, will you forgive me?'

Sensing his amusement, she smiled in spite of herself.

'There!' he exclaimed in triumph. 'I knew you could do it, if you tried hard enough!'

'I'm sorry,' she said awkwardly, meaning it. 'Shall we start again?'

'With pleasure. And we might begin by introducing ourselves. I still don't know your surname.'

'Marlow.'

'Delighted to meet you, Miss Marlow. And here we are at our destination.'

The charming old pub, thatch-roofed and white-walled, nestled comfortably on the river bank, and its creaking sign was duplicated by a live duck that strutted on the grass in front of them. The car park was crowded on this warm summer evening, and it took a minute or two to find a space. Then, his hand lightly under her elbow, Jeremy led her inside. Immediately a wave of heat and noise engulfed them as they made their way through the throng to the bar.

'What would you like to drink?' he asked

her. 'Long or short?'

'Oh, long in this heat. Shandy, please.'

'Anything to eat?'

'No, thanks.'

She waited while he gave the order, aware that he was attracting notice, though no one approached him. It must be difficult, she thought, to be recognised everywhere you went.

Jeremy turned from the bar and took her arm again. 'They'll bring it outside; let's see if we can find a table.'

It was a relief to emerge from the smoky heat to the lesser warmth of the garden. Tables were set up all over the grass and most still had their umbrellas up, but the sun was going down now and shadows were lengthening on the grass. Several of the tables had lighted candles on them. A couple were just vacating one down by the water and Jeremy moved swiftly to claim it.

'Perfect!' he said, pulling out a chair for her. She sat down and he seated himself opposite her.

'Now,' he began, stretching out his legs, 'I want to know all about you.'

'There's not much to know,' she hedged, embarrassed to find his eyes steadily on her.

'You have just the one sister?' he prompted.

'Yes, Eleanor. She teaches at Beckhurst Primary.'

'And what do you do?'

'Nothing very interesting at the moment. Until I settle on something, I'm filling in time with a secretarial course.'

'That sounds delightfully old-fashioned – almost like being a governess!'

She flushed. 'Hardly. We're learning to use computers, which everyone says will be the things of the future.'

He leaned forward to put a hand briefly over hers. 'Sorry – I didn't mean to criticise. It's refreshing these days to meet a girl who isn't set on a Career, with a capital "C".'

'Now *you* sound old-fashioned,' she retorted with asperity. 'I didn't say I don't want a career, only that I haven't decided on one.'

Their drinks came and were set down on the table in front of them.

'Anyway,' she challenged him, 'what about you? What do you do, now that you—' She broke off, appalled. 'I'm so sorry,' she said in a low voice, not looking at him. 'That sounded dreadful. I didn't mean...' She took a quick sip of her drink and put her glass carefully down on the table. 'It must have been terrible, having everything snatched away from you like that, at the height of your career.'

He shrugged. 'There are no guarantees in this life; you make the most of what you're dealt. I'd had six terrific years, which is more than most people can say. But to answer your question, I'm PE and games master at Caverstock Grammar, for my sins.'

'You live in Caverstock?' She was remembering the absent parents.

'Yep, I share a house with two mates. It works very well.'

The two who were with him at the tennis club, she thought. He took out his cigarette lighter and held it to the candle on their table. As the flame leapt, she studied his face, intent and withdrawn, his eyes in shadow. Still a stranger, though she was learning more. She knew she was being spiky with him, but better that than what had happened last time. What should she do when he kissed her goodnight? Although she badly wanted him to, she was afraid of losing control again.

He looked up, meeting her eyes across the flame, and she said quickly, 'Have you any brothers or sisters?'

'No, I was an only one. That's why I value my friends.'

He started to tell her about Danny and Bruce, how they had known each other from schooldays and shared the same interests. She only half-listened. The ducks had come out of the water now, and she could just make out the dark humps they formed with their heads tucked under their wings. Overhead the sky was full of stars and a sickle moon hung, golden and new. Music drifted down from the pub, and the darkness of the garden was studded with candle flames. *On such a night as this...*

Fay couldn't remember, afterwards, what they had talked about, leaning towards each other over the table. She was acutely aware of him, of the shape of his hand holding the tankard, his quick smile, the deep, almost soporific sound of his voice. She sensed that the garden was gradually emptying, but was loath to break the spell they'd woven round their table by the water. At last, though, Jeremy stretched and looked at his watch.

'Well, young lady, I'd better be getting you home, or your father will be pacing the floor.'

Reluctantly she stood, and again the touch of his hand guided her up the garden and round the side of the lighted building into the shadows. She half-hoped that here, where no one could see them, he might kiss her, but he didn't slacken his pace, and they emerged into the floodlit parking area, where he opened the car door for her and helped her inside. He switched on the radio and she leant her head back, closing her eyes as dreamy music filled the car. They drove home in almost total silence, not feeling the need to talk, and all too soon they were drawing up at her gate. She tensed expectantly, half-turning towards him, but he was already climbing out of the car, saying, 'I'll see you to the door.'

Slowly, uncertainly, she went with him up the path. He took the key from her, fitted it into the lock, and swung the door open. Then he lifted her hand and gently kissed her fingers.

'Good night, Fay.'

'Thank you for a lovely evening,' she said numbly.

He smiled. 'We must do it again.'

There was nothing for it but to go inside, and as she turned to close the door behind her, he was already walking back down the path. Fay went slowly up the stairs to her room, closed the door and burst into tears.

Ellie had inadvertently witnessed the home-coming. Up in her room she had turned out the light and was about to open the window when the sports car, its brilliant red dulled to orange by the street lamps, drew up at the gate. Not wanting to spy on her sister, she was turning away when, to her surprise, she saw Jeremy get out and open the door for Fay. They came up the path together, and below her Ellie heard the door open, a murmur of voices, then the door close again. A minute later came the sound of Fay's slow footsteps on the stairs.

Ellie frowned, pushed the window open,

and climbed into bed. This was not the manner in which Fay's escorts usually left her. Had they quarrelled? She, too, had been aware of her sister's tension during those few minutes in the sitting room, but, unlike their mother, had recognised its cause as sexual. There was something between those two, but she was not sure what. It was most unlike Fay not to have blurted out at once that she'd met Jeremy Page – as Mum said, anybody would have. So what had happened at the tennis club that night? Whatever it was, it explained why Fay had never enquired about her evening with Patrick: she was afraid of reciprocal questioning.

Ellie lay down and pulled the sheet up to her chin. It would be interesting to see what developed. Watch this space, she thought, and, turning over, settled down to sleep.

'So how did it go?' Bruce enquired, looking round from the television. 'Lust in the dust as per usual?'

'Not at all,' Jeremy replied, tossing his car keys into the bowl. 'I kissed her hand chastely as we said goodnight, and that was all.'

Danny stared at him. 'You're not serious?'

'Never more so.'

'Well, you amaze me. Then I apologise for raising your hopes. I take it you won't be seeing *her* again?'

'On the contrary. I intend to phone her tomorrow.'

'For God's sake, Jay, are you turning into a masochist?'

Jeremy laughed. 'Relax. She really is something, Danny. The vibrations between us positively hummed, but she's playing it cool. Fair enough; I'm not going to spoil things by rushing her. She'll be worth the wait.'

'And Mel?' queried Bruce with raised eyebrows.

'Can take it or leave it.'

'I can't be hearing this! You're going to risk what you've got going with Mel for a girl you don't even know will come across?'

'Trust me,' Jeremy said enigmatically. 'I know what I'm doing.'

The next week played havoc with Fay's emotions. Jeremy took her out every evening – to the theatre, the cinema, for drinks, for meals – but when he saw her home, the routine was always the same: the accompaniment up the path, the kiss on the hand.

Not usually one to share confidences, she finally blurted out her bewilderment to Ellie. 'What am I doing wrong?' she wailed. 'If he doesn't fancy me, why does he keep asking me out?'

'Oh, I think it's safe to assume he fancies you,' Ellie returned dryly. She eyed her sister's distraught face. 'What happened, exactly, when you first met?'

Fay flushed. 'He was tight,' she said.

'At the tennis club dance?'

Fay nodded, then, as Ellie waited, reluctantly went on: 'He asked me to dance – I practically had to hold him up – and then he ... took me behind a pillar and kissed me.'

'And that's all? Hardly a new experience, surely?'

'You don't have to be sarcastic,' Fay snapped. 'And as it happens, you're wrong. It *was* a new experience – totally new.' She shuddered and put her face in her hands. 'It was mind-blowing, Ellie. If someone hadn't come up, I don't know what would have happened. I only know what I *wanted* to happen – more than I've ever wanted anything in my life.'

'Sex rears its ugly head.'

'Have you ever felt that? That you're dissolving inside, that you can hardly stand?'

Ellie stared down into the street. 'Something on those lines.' But without the kisses, she thought ruefully.

'I know he wanted it as much as I did,' Fay went on. 'So why is he being so withdrawn?'

Ellie turned back to face her, half-sitting on the sill. 'Because he overstepped the mark last time?'

Fay looked up.

'Could that be it? Did you give him the

I'm not that sort of girl treatment? You were pretty distant when he came to the house.'

'He did say he must have blotted his copybook,' Fay admitted.

'Perhaps he's being careful not to blot it again.'

'But surely he could manage a goodnight kiss?'

'He mightn't trust himself.'

Fay drew in her breath. 'Oh Ellie, do you think that's what it is?'

Ellie looked at her reflectively. 'You've got it pretty bad, haven't you? I've never seen you like this before.'

'I've never *felt* like this before.'

'Well, go easy, love. He's a good-looking guy; he must have had dozens of girlfriends. Perhaps he's after you because you *haven't* leapt into bed with him. The thrill of the chase, and all that.'

'You make it sound so ... calculated.'

'I'm only warning you. Don't go falling for him till you know he's serious.'

Wise words; if only she had followed them herself.

On the last Tuesday of the month, it was with mixed feelings that Ellie took the bus into Caverstock to the Film Society. As she'd anticipated, Patrick's attitude had not changed, and though he sat with her as usual, he made no reference to their evening together. It was as if they'd not met since the previous month. The film that evening was a German one, about an athlete training for the Olympics, and afterwards, during their usual discussion over coffee, Ellie commented, 'I found it specially interesting, because my sister's going out with Jeremy Page.'

She was gratified by Patrick's immediate interest. 'Is she? Good God! I heard he'd joined the games staff at the Grammar School. Bit of a comedown, poor devil. What a tragedy, things ending like that. I'd followed his career right from the beginning, while he was still at school. What's he like, as a person?'

Ellie's heart began a slow, muffled beat. 'Would you like to meet him?'

His eyes lit up. 'Are you serious? Would that be possible?'

'Perhaps we could all have a meal together.'

There she went again, taking the initiative; but Patrick was saying, 'God, Ellie, that would be great! Do you think you could arrange it?'

'I don't see why not. They see each other all the time, so what evening would be best for you?'

'Any time at all. If there was anything on, I could cancel it.'

'I'll see what I can do,' she said. 'Let me

have your phone number, so I can let you know.'

'Well, I suppose it would be all right,' Fay said ungraciously.

'You did say you'd like to meet Patrick,' Ellie reminded her, 'and he's a great fan of Jeremy's.'

Fay hesitated, but the temptation to flaunt Jeremy as her partner proved too strong. 'OK, I'll see what he says.'

Jeremy was amenable, and a date was fixed for the following week. In the meantime, that Saturday things came to a head.

Looking back afterwards, the entire day held a dreamlike quality: the drive out into the country, holding hands as they walked over the long grass carrying the picnic hamper; the pebbly stream – a tributary of the Rush – and its surprisingly cold water on their bare feet. Then the picnic itself – French bread, cheese and wine – and Jeremy, propped up on one elbow, indolently popping grapes into her mouth.

And, at last, the moment she'd been anticipating with such conflicting emotions, when he tilted her chin back and began, systematically, to kiss her. The sensations that had so alarmed her before returned in full measure, but this time she welcomed them and, as his hands continued to caress her, they spiralled totally out of control, so

71

that, half-crying and half-laughing, she could only cling to him, her passion equalling his as, finally and triumphantly, he entered her.

When it was over, they lay side by side, staring up at the blue sky, gripping each other's hands. 'Oh, Fay,' he said softly, 'I knew you'd be worth waiting for. It was your first time, wasn't it?'

'Yes.' The stupid tears were still trickling down her cheeks. She turned her head to look at him. 'But – shouldn't we have taken precautions of some kind?'

He met her gaze blankly. 'Surely you're on the pill?'

'No,' she whispered. 'I told you: this was the first time.'

'Yes, but you must have been expecting ... Hell, I wish you'd said.'

'I kept thinking you'd do something, and then suddenly it was ... too late.'

'Well, at least I'll know next time. But in the long term, sweetie, the pill's the best bet. I suggest you go and see the doctor.'

Fleetingly she thought of Dr Carpenter, who'd known her all her life, and what his reaction would be to a request for contraception; but there was a Family Planning clinic in the same road as the secretarial college. *In the long term*, he had said. She thought her heart would burst with happiness, but a niggling worry persisted.

'It'll be all right, though, won't it?' she asked anxiously. 'Just this once?'

'Of course it will,' he assured her, kissing her gently. 'Nothing ever happens the first time.'

It had been arranged that Patrick should call for Ellie, and they would meet the other two at a Chinese restaurant in Beckhurst. As she watched out for his car, Ellie remembered her parents' excitement preceding Jeremy's first visit. On this occasion, her mother had merely said, 'The dentist from the Film Society? That'll be nice, dear.' There was no request to bring him in to meet them, so Ellie went out to the car as soon as he arrived.

'You look nice,' Patrick commented, not noticing her flush of pleasure. 'I'm afraid you'll have to direct me,' he added as she fastened her seat belt. 'I don't know my way round Beckhurst.'

'It's quite straightforward. We can park in the multi-storey, and from there it's only a short walk to the restaurant.'

The other two were there before them, and Jeremy stood as they approached the table. Ellie introduced Patrick, and they all sat down. She hadn't seen the two of them together since that first evening, and was immediately conscious of the electrical charge between them. Love shone in Fay's eyes and she glowed with happiness, while Jeremy, though not so transparent, frequently touched her hand or her arm as they discussed the menu.

It was also the first time Ellie had spent more than five minutes in Jeremy's company, and she could quite see the attraction he held for Fay. He had charm, good looks, and a tragedy in his background – a potent mix indeed. It was obvious to Ellie that they were lovers, and she could only hope that, having attained that goal, his interest in her sister would not wane. Though succumbing in some measure to his charisma, she wasn't sure she could trust him.

It was Jeremy who was holding the floor, telling one amusing anecdote after another, which kept them all laughing. Their order was brought, a series of dishes laid out on hotplates, and they began to eat, Jeremy – typically, Ellie thought – with chopsticks.

'Ellie and Patrick belong to the Caverstock Film Society,' Fay told him, nibbling her prawn cracker.

'Ah yes, you meet in the art gallery, don't you? What kind of stuff do they show? Not porn, I trust!'

'Hardly,' Patrick replied. 'It's mainly foreign films and old classics. We meet fortnightly during the winter, but we also have a short summer season, which we're now in the middle of. Last week's offering was in

German, about someone training for the Olympics.' Remembering this was a sensitive subject, he went on quickly, 'Before that, we saw *Perfidie*, in which an artist murders his wife's lover and feeds him bit by bit to the fishes.'

Fay shivered. 'Sounds gruesome.' She looked at Jeremy from beneath her lashes. 'Would you kill for love, darling?'

'Without hesitation,' he replied, spearing a king prawn.

'What about you, Patrick?'

Patrick hesitated. 'To be honest, I've never thought about it; but possibly, under certain circumstances.'

Fay laughed. 'How cautious! A very British answer! I've often wondered what it must have felt like to have duels fought over you. Rather exciting, I should think.'

'Provided no one was killed,' Ellie put in.

'A very British proviso!' Jeremy teased her. 'Don't forget it used to be quite the thing, to die for love.'

'A somewhat pointless exercise,' Patrick observed, and they all laughed. The evening wore on; eventually the subject of Jeremy's past career came up, and Patrick was able to discuss with him various of his triumphs.

'It doesn't worry you, to talk about them?' Patrick asked diffidently.

'Not at all. Let's face it, I haven't much to talk about now, have I? Except my beautiful

Fay, of course!' And he raised her hand to his lips.

'Well,' Ellie asked Patrick as he drove her home, 'what did you think of him?'

'He's good company, isn't he?' He paused. 'How does he strike you?'

'I'm not sure. This is the first time I've spent any time with him. Fay's quite besotted, of course.'

'Yes. I hope he doesn't let her down.'

So that had occurred to him, too. They were drawing up at her gate – no sign, yet, of the other two. No doubt they'd stopped off somewhere. She felt a sharp stab of envy, glancing at Patrick's rather set profile. As he opened the car door for her, she thought bleakly that even a kiss on the hand would be welcome, but it seemed he wasn't going to see her to the door.

'Thanks so much for arranging the evening,' he said. 'Perhaps we could do it again some time.'

Hope surged. 'Yes, that would be lovely,' she said eagerly.

'Good night then, Ellie.'

'Good night.' She waited while he started up the car, and stood watching until its tail lights disappeared round the corner. Then she slowly walked up the path to the house.

Had she known Patrick's thoughts as he drove home, Ellie would not have gone to bed as happy as she did.

He had not previously given much thought to this sister of Ellie's, about whom she'd occasionally spoken; the sole object of the evening, as far as he was concerned, was to meet Jeremy Page, the local hero. Well, he'd met him. He had also met Fay Marlow, and his senses were still reeling.

It wasn't only that she was so lovely, he thought, trying to rationalise his dry mouth and quickened heartbeat; there was a spark, a magnetism about her that he'd never come across before. God, she was gorgeous! She was also, he told himself uncompromisingly, 'besotted' with Jeremy Page – Ellie's word, but an apt one. It was obvious from the way she looked at him; and Jeremy, the smug bastard, sat back and lapped it up. If she ever looked at him like that, there'd be nothing he wouldn't do for her – including murder, as she'd laughingly enquired.

Leaving Beckhurst and its street lamps behind, Patrick turned up his headlights and attempted to rein in his emotions. After all, there was no such thing as love at first sight. Physical attraction, yes, and that he was experiencing in spades. He felt the sweat start in his armpits. Though he'd had quite a few girlfriends over the years, part of him had always remained detached and in control. He had never, even at the height of passion, considered himself in love; in fact, he'd been coming round to the idea of settling for some nice girl he was fond of – someone, perhaps, like Ellie. She was intelligent, pretty, good company, and they had several shared interests. She didn't light any fires in him, but they could probably have been happy enough.

Now, in the space of one evening, that had gone totally by the board. He'd been shown what he was capable of feeling, and from now on, he could settle for nothing less.

God, he thought in near panic, what could he *do?* The answer was clear enough: for the moment, absolutely nothing. His only option was to sit back and wait until, as might well happen, Jeremy moved on, and then try to pick up the pieces.

His mind still in turmoil, Patrick parked the car and let himself into the flat above the surgery that he shared with Andrew Bly. Andrew, who owned the practice, was several years older than himself and had moved into the flat after his divorce the previous year.

Hearing Patrick's key in the door, he appeared at the bathroom door, brushing his teeth.

'Well?' he asked indistinctly, 'how did it go? How was the great man?'

'Pleasant enough,' Patrick answered shortly.

Andrew's eyes narrowed. 'You're looking a

bit flushed, old son. Haven't driven home over the limit, I trust?'

'No.'

'OK, OK, I only asked. You're not very communicative, I must say. Come on, spill the beans. Did you have a good evening?'

Patrick drew a deep breath. 'It was the most momentous of my life,' he said.

Three

It was easy to underestimate Patrick Nelson, and many people did. As Ellie had admitted, there was nothing outstanding about his appearance. He was pleasant-looking without being handsome: tall, grey-eyed, with light-brown hair and a diffident smile. It was the smile that caused the mis-conception, making him appear vulnerable and unsure of himself. He was neither.

He and his elder brother had been born in Australia, returning to the UK with their parents when they were six and eight respectively. At school, their accents had been mercilessly mocked, leading to almost daily fights in the playground, and Patrick of necessity had learned how to defend himself. Those early skirmishes had also revealed a quick temper, about which his teachers had discreet words with his parents.

As he grew older, however, he progressed well, displaying an unwavering single-mindedness in pursuit of whatever goal he set himself, and almost always achieving it. A rather solitary boy, he did not, like his brother, make friends easily, but those he did make he tended to keep. Girls, deceived by that smile, invariably tried to mother him and, to his amusement, he was seduced by the school flirt – who supposed him to be a virgin – and quite enjoyed the experience.

His parents, meanwhile, were increasingly unsure what to make of him. He didn't, like his brother Guy, regale them with his amorous adventures, inveigle them into attending rugby matches in the rain, or play his radio at full volume. By the time he started at dental college, his natural reserve had created a barrier which, though they tried, they were unable to penetrate. Quite simply, he had grown away from them, and his visits home became less and less frequent. Throughout this time, his great friend and companion was Roger Hastings, and the friendship continued after they qualified. Roger had recently married, and had invited Patrick to be his best man.

'Your turn next, matie!' he'd said jovially on his stag night. 'You can't escape indefinitely, you know! They'll pierce your defences in the end!'

Patrick remembered that phrase as he peered into an elderly woman's mouth the morning after his meeting with Fay. Roger was right, damn him; his defences had been well and truly breached, and to his frustration he could do nothing about it.

The next few weeks passed for Fay in a cloud of happiness. She spent all her free time with Jeremy, and they continued to make love regularly. Rita and Gordon noted the bloom on her and implicitly gave the couple their blessing, never dreaming how far the relationship had progressed. Ellie kept her own counsel, and Fay volunteered nothing.

It was towards the end of July that Fay realised, with a clutch of fear, that the date marked in her diary had passed unnoticed. She'd been late before, she told herself; it must be the unaccustomed sexual activity that had set it back. Anyway, Jeremy had assured her there was nothing to worry about. It would come any day now – it was sure to.

To Ellie's delighted surprise, Patrick phoned to suggest that Fay and Jeremy might like to join them at the Film Society the following Tuesday. 'It's *Singing in the Rain*, which they might enjoy. And I was thinking that perhaps we could have supper first? There's that little Italian restaurant just round the corner.'

'That's a lovely idea – I'll ask them.' She hesitated. 'Suppose they can't make it?'

'We'd have to try another time.'

So it was all of them, or nothing. Still, at least he'd used the words 'join us', as though it were accepted that they'd be together.

'I'll come back to you,' she said.

Fay, who had seemed somewhat subdued for the last few days, agreed to ask Jeremy, who was again happy to fit in with the suggestion. 'He's rather sweet, your Patrick,' Fay observed, and Ellie flushed with pride, even while demurring, 'I keep telling you, Fay, he's not mine.'

Fay merely smiled and switched on the television.

So the four of them met again, and again Jeremy kept them entertained throughout the meal, though it seemed to Patrick that Fay didn't sparkle quite as much as before. There were shadows under her eyes, and to his shame he wondered with a surge of hope if the relationship was in difficulties. However, during the film the two of them sat close together, Jeremy's arm across Fay's shoulders, so it might have been wishful thinking on his part.

As before, Ellie arrived home ahead of Fay and, also as before, Patrick left her at the gate. She told herself that in the beginning Jeremy, too, had bided his time, and hoped passionately that the end result might be the same.

She was reading in bed when she heard Fay return, and to her surprise her sister tapped on her door and came in.

Ellie looked at her expectantly. 'Enjoy the evening?'

'Yes, thanks. It was very pleasant and ... undemanding.'

Ellie waited. Fay seated herself on the end of the bed, took off her earrings and dropped them into her bag. Then she said without looking up, 'I'm two weeks late.'

Ellie gasped. 'Are you sure? You haven't mixed up your dates?'

'Of course I'm sure.' Fay sounded close to tears.

'But you ... have been taking precautions, haven't you?'

'Except for the first time,' Fay said in a low voice. 'And Jeremy said nothing ever happens then.'

'Oh, Fay!' Ellie said softly.

Fay looked at her with frightened eyes. 'Isn't that true?'

Ellie shook her head, and Fay burst into tears. Ellie scrambled out of bed and sat down beside her. 'Have you told him?'

She shook her head. 'I wanted to be sure. I kept thinking it would come any day, but

83

I've never been as late as this. How can I find out?'

'I think you have to take a sample to the doctor.'

'Or Family Planning?'

'Yes, if that would be easier. Go tomorrow; then at least you'll know, one way or the other.'

'Will you come with me, in your lunch hour?'

'Oh, I'm sorry, Fay, I can't. I'm on playground duty this week.'

Fay nodded, took out a handkerchief and blew her nose. 'OK, I'll go. As you say, it's worse not knowing.'

It surprised neither of them that the test proved positive, and since there was nothing to be gained by further delay, Fay steeled herself to tell Jeremy that evening. She'd not admitted to Ellie how much she dreaded the prospect, uncertain what his reaction would be or if he'd hold her to blame, and decided to tell him when there were plenty of people about, in the hope that he'd be less likely simply to storm off and leave her.

As it happened, he took her to the Mallard, where they had spent their first magical evening together, and again they were sitting at a candle-lit table near the river. Fay hoped it was a good omen. As soon as they were settled, she reached across and gripped his hand tightly.

'Hey,' he protested, 'relax, honey! I'm not going anywhere!'

'I've something to tell you,' she said. With her other hand she drained the glass of sherry that she had requested instead of shandy, to give her Dutch courage.

'And what might that be?' he asked lazily, stroking her fingers with his free hand.

'I'm ... going to have a baby.' The words came out in a rush. His hand stilled on hers. Then he said, still lightly, 'No problem, my love. All you have to do is go home, sit in a very hot bath, and drink half a bottle of gin.'

'I'm serious,' she pleaded.

'And so am I, darling. It works every time.'

But that was what he'd told her about their first coming together, and she no longer believed him. 'Please help me,' she whispered. 'Would it be so awful to have it?'

He shrugged, disengaging his hand and sitting back in his chair. 'It's up to you, love. I've given you my advice, but let it be a lesson to you. This is what can happen after unprotected sex.'

'But you said the first time would be all right, and ever since then we've—'

'Oh come on, Fay. By that time it was too late to do anything about it, and it was what you wanted to hear, wasn't it? No point in worrying yourself senseless; it might never have happened.'

'But it has,' she said in a low voice.

'So it would appear.' He paused. 'I presume it is mine?'

Seeing the shock in her eyes, he leant forward to pat her hand. 'All right, sorry; I just wanted to be sure.'

'So what happens now?'

'I told you, you take a hot bath and—'

'*Seriously*, Jeremy!'

'I'm being serious.'

'Are you saying you don't want a baby?'

'Me?' He looked surprised. 'I can't say the patter of tiny feet is part of my agenda. Not yet, anyway. But don't worry, there are other ways, if the gin doesn't work.' He put a finger under her chin and raised her head until her swimming eyes met his. 'Come on now, golden girl; it's not the end of the world. Plenty of other people have found themselves in this position, and survived unscathed. I'll see you right.'

She didn't know what he meant, but was incapable of pressing the point any further, and after a minute, almost to her relief, he changed the subject and it wasn't referred to again. They stopped as usual to make love on the way home, and Fay wondered if perhaps he was hoping to dislodge the baby in some way; but that hadn't happened in the weeks since that first time, and she had little hope of it happening now.

For the second evening in succession, she

went to Ellie's room. Ellie's heart sank at her distraught face, but she asked brightly, 'How did he take it?'

'He wants me to get rid of it.'

'*What?*'

'Oh, not an abortion. At least, he didn't actually suggest that. Just a hot bath and some gin.'

'You really do love him, don't you, Fay?'

'Of course I do. I'll never love anyone else this way.' Her eyes filled again.

'Then there's only one thing for it. You'll have to tell the parents.'

'Ellie, I can't! They'll kill me!' She watched as Ellie got out of bed and reached for her dressing gown. 'What are you doing?'

'I'm coming with you, for moral support.'

'You mean *now?*'

'You won't get any sleep if you leave it. They'll be awake; they never put their light out till midnight and it's only eleven thirty. Come on.'

She took hold of Fay's arm and led her across the landing to their parents' room. Sure enough, there was a light under the door. Ellie knocked, and after a minute her mother's surprised voice said, 'Yes?' and they went in.

Gordon and Rita were sitting side by side reading – he the evening paper, she a women's magazine. Rita, resplendent in a blue hairnet, regarded them blankly.

87

'What on earth do you two want at this time of night?'

Ellie moistened her lips. 'Fay has something to tell you,' she said.

Two pairs of eyes swivelled to Fay, who took a deep breath. 'I'm very sorry – really I am, but ... I'm pregnant.'

There was a long silence. Then Rita said flatly, 'I don't believe you. You can't be.'

'Mum, please...'

There were bright spots of colour on Rita's cheeks. 'That's not the way I brought you up. You were taught self-control, to have some dignity, and now you're telling me you gave in to him, like a common little tart?'

Gordon laid a restraining hand on her arm as her voice rose. 'Easy, love,' he said.

'Easy nothing!' Rita snapped. 'If you hadn't always spoiled her, let her have her own way in everything, this would never have happened.'

'Hold on now, you can hardly blame me! Let's get to the bottom of this.' He looked at his younger daughter. 'You are sure about this?'

She nodded.

'I presume it's Jeremy's?'

Another nod.

'What does he say about it?'

Fay swallowed and hung her head.

'He wants her to get rid of it,' Ellie said. Gordon flushed darkly. 'Does he indeed?

All the pleasure and none of the responsibility, eh? My God, I'll skin the hide off him!'

Fay began to cry again and, as Gordon reached out a hand, went to him. Rita sniffed contemptuously. 'All very well crying now, my girl; you should have thought of this before. Never entered your head, did it, the disgrace you'd bring on us all?'

'Oh, Mum,' Ellie protested, 'it's not like that now.'

'Now everyone's gone permissive, you mean? There's been no permissiveness in this house, my girl, and there never will be; but that won't stop your father and me getting the blame for not bringing you up right. I'll never be able to hold my head up again.'

Gordon said quietly, 'Do you love him, Fay? Enough to marry him?'

'Of course I do, Dad; it's what I want most in the world.' She gazed at him piteously, tears glinting on her lashes, and Ellie, even while she sympathised, wondered how their father would have reacted if she rather than Fay had been in this position.

Gordon patted Fay's hand. 'Then go to bed and try not to worry,' he said. 'I'll sort it out.'

A glimmer of hope shone in her face. 'But how, Dad?'

'Never you mind how. Now off you go, the

89

pair of you. We've heard quite enough for one night.'

Out on the landing, the sisters regarded each other. 'What did he mean, do you think?' Fay whispered.

Ellie shrugged. 'At least it's out of your hands now. Dad will see to it.'

Behind their closed bedroom door, Gordon let out his breath in a low whistle.

'What did you mean, telling her you'd sort it?' Rita demanded. 'Going to get your shotgun out, are you? I doubt if it works these *permissive* days.' She gave the word a full measure of scorn.

'I don't think it'll be necessary to go that far,' Gordon said slowly.

She turned to face him. 'Meaning?'

'The girl's set her heart on him, Rita. All right, they shouldn't have gone this far – we know that – but it's my bet he's pretty fond of her, too. They've been seeing each other nearly every evening.'

'Of course they have, with him getting what he wanted and no strings attached. You surely don't expect him to come to you and say, "Sir, I wronged your daughter. I will do the honourable thing." I bet he's planning to go on playing the field without a thought of marriage in his head. Probably can't even afford it. He might have made some money before his accident, but he won't be getting much at Caverstock Grammar, and getting married's an expensive business, what with finding somewhere to live and furnishing it and everything.'

'Have you forgotten we hold a trump card?'

Rita frowned. 'What are you talking about?'

'Sandford Lodge,' he said simply.

'Sandford? What do you mean?'

'There's a house all ready and waiting, isn't there? Fully furnished and ready to move into immediately.'

Rita gazed at him. 'You're never thinking of giving them the house?'

'Not giving, no. That wouldn't be fair on Ellie. But we were going to rent it out, weren't we? Well, we'll rent it to Fay and Jeremy. Looks as though Ma will get her wish after all.'

Rita said slowly, 'You've still got to get him to agree to marry her.'

'But this should make it a lot easier. At the very least, he's fond of her – who wouldn't be, a lovely girl like that? And if she comes with a first-class house for which he won't have to lift a finger – well, I reckon that might just sway the balance. What's more, Fay can pay her share of the rent out of the legacy Ma left her, which should make the proposition even more attractive.'

Rita said sullenly, 'It doesn't seem right, somehow, that they should be rewarded for the way they've carried on.'

'I'm being realistic, that's all. Don't forget there's a baby on the way. They'll need a roof over their heads, and it might as well be a family one.' He patted her hand. 'Things could be worse, love. You're always swanking to your pals about your daughter going out with Jeremy Page. How about saying he's your son-in-law?'

'Do you think he'll go along with it?' Rita asked after a moment.

'We'll soon find out, but I reckon it'll be pretty tempting.'

Rita sighed and laid aside her magazine. 'Let's hope you're right, because otherwise Lord knows what we can do.'

It had occurred to Gordon that, having learned of Fay's condition, Jeremy might think twice about coming round that next evening, and it was with considerable relief that he saw the sports car draw up as usual outside. After the initial date, it had become the practice for Fay to watch for him and run out to the car without his having to come to the door. This evening, Gordon had instructed her to wait inside, a calculated risk, since Jeremy might sense trouble when she didn't appear, and drive off.

Fortunately, his strategy worked. After an impatient toot on the horn, Jeremy climbed out of the car and came up the path. It was

Gordon who opened the door.

'Good evening, Jeremy,' he said pleasantly, noting the younger man's startled expression. 'I was hoping to have a word with you. Come in; Fay's not quite ready.' And before Jeremy could collect himself, he had been firmly guided into the sitting room and the door closed behind him.

In the kitchen, Rita and the two girls waited nervously. Fay had been all for going to listen at the door, but Rita would have none of it. 'We don't go in for tactics like that,' she said firmly, and Fay and Ellie, who did, avoided each other's eye. It seemed a long time, but was in fact only fifteen minutes, before the sitting-room door opened and Gordon called to them.

Jeremy was standing by the fireplace, looking flushed and less sure of himself than Ellie had previously seen him. However, he smiled as they went in, and held out his hand to Fay, who hurried to his side.

'We have some rather exciting news,' Gordon said steadily. 'Jeremy has just asked my permission to marry Fay.'

Rita and Ellie exclaimed together as Fay, her face radiant, turned almost fearfully to Jeremy. Before any of them could comment, Gordon continued, 'And that's not all.' He glanced at his younger daughter. 'If I remember, you didn't give your mother and me a chance to tell you our plans for

Sandford, so I'll outline them now. We'd decided not to sell it, but to rent it out in case, at some future date, we should reconsider moving there. So what I propose is that you and Jeremy become our tenants and pay rent for your accommodation. As the owner of the property, I should, of course, be responsible for all the repairs and general maintenance.' He paused. 'How does that sound?'

Fay, bewildered by the enormity of what was on offer, said hesitantly, 'Jeremy and I would live at *Sandford*?'

'Exactly. Would that be acceptable?'

For answer, she ran to her father and flung her arms round his neck. 'I can't think of anything more wonderful!' she said.

Jeremy said smilingly, 'You told me about it the first time we went out, remember?' He turned to Gordon. 'I can't thank you enough, sir. It's extremely generous of you – not only Fay, but a house to go with her!'

They all laughed, and the nervous tension eased.

'I think champagne is called for,' Gordon said, and Rita and Ellie scurried in search of glasses.

'What do you make of that, then?' Rita asked her elder daughter as they set them out on a tray.

'I'm glad Sandford's staying in the family,' Ellie replied.

94

'He's not making them a present of it, you know,' Rita told her, noting the girl's over-bright eyes. 'It's just a case of needs must for the time being, that's all.'

Ellie met her mother's anxious gaze and realised that, for once, Rita did have some idea of how she was feeling. She forced a smile.

'Thanks, Mum,' she said.

'You're *what?*'

Danny and Bruce were staring at him disbelievingly.

'I said, I'm getting married,' Jeremy repeated with a smile. 'Fay's in the club – did I tell you?'

'No, you bloody didn't! Is that the reason? Surely you've both heard of the pill, or was this intentional on her part?'

'No, as it happens I was her first, and we each thought the other would be doing the necessary. By the time we discovered our mistake, the damage was done.'

'And you're telling us that simply because she's in the club, you're going to marry her?'

Jeremy flopped into a chair and draped one leg over the arm. 'It doesn't seem to have occurred to either of you cynics that I might love the girl. If you remember, Danny, you fancied her yourself. She's a stunner, she fancies me rotten, and...' he paused deliberately, surveying them over his

95

glass, '...we're being provided with a handsome, fully furnished house at a very fair rent. We drove over to look at it this evening, and it's great. Super position on a hill above Rushyford, large, airy rooms, nice garden. What do you think of that?'

'You seem to have landed on your feet,' Bruce said, 'provided you really do want to marry her. So when's this wedding of the year to take place?'

'As soon as it can be arranged. It'll be a quiet one, but naturally you're both invited.'

'What about your parents?'

Jeremy snorted. 'Give me a break.'

'But you'll have to tell them, surely?'

'If I can find their addresses. Dad was drinking his way round Africa, the last I heard, and Mum's unlikely to fly back from the States. She's rather lost interest now I no longer make the headlines.'

'But you're sure this is really what you want?' Bruce asked after a moment.

'Of course I am. I couldn't be happier.'

Neither of them dared probe any further.

Patrick said, 'I was wondering if we might have another foursome? Perhaps on a Saturday this time. We could take a picnic lunch out into the country somewhere.'

Ellie's hand tightened on the phone. 'I'd love to, Patrick, but I don't think Fay and Jeremy could make it. They're getting married in two weeks, and there's a lot to see to.'

There was total silence, and Ellie wondered briefly if they'd been cut off. 'Patrick? Are you there? We could still go, couldn't we?'

He did not appear to have heard her. 'This is all very sudden, isn't it?' His voice sounded strained.

'Yes, but they'll be living in my grandmother's house, so once they'd decided, there was no point in waiting.'

'She's not...?' He broke off and cleared his throat. 'What date are we talking about?'

'Friday the thirty-first. They couldn't get a Saturday, at such short notice.' She hesitated. 'It'll be a very small wedding, at the registry office in Caverstock.'

'Please give them my congratulations and best wishes.' He sounded very formal, and Ellie wondered despairingly if he was insulted at not being invited. She had begged that he be included, but her parents were adamant. 'We've no time to organise a big do,' her mother said firmly. 'Anyway, it wouldn't be seemly, in the circumstances. And if we invite just one or two friends, it'll cause trouble with the others, so it's safer to stick to family.' The sole exceptions were to be two friends of Jeremy's, since his parents were apparently unable to attend.

'Thanks, I will,' she said, and waited, but

97

he remained silent. 'We could still go for a picnic, if you like?' she suggested, with desperately crossed fingers.

'Better leave it for the moment. I'm sure that in the circumstances you'll be busy, too. Goodbye, Ellie.'

'Goodbye,' she said bleakly. It seemed that without Jeremy's reflected glory, the prospect of seeing her had lost its charm.

Ellie had never attended a registry-office wedding and was unsure what to expect. Fay was radiant in an ankle-length dress of cream organza, with a circlet of blue flowers in her hair. To her mother's relief, her waistline still gave no indication of what it was concealing. Jeremy, in a grey suit with a rose in his buttonhole, looked, Ellie thought, impossibly debonair and handsome as he stood chatting with his friends in the anteroom. He gave no indication whatsoever of being an unwilling bridegroom.

Since both Gordon and Rita were only children, they were a very small gathering, the only people present apart from immediate family being Rita's cousin and her husband from Blackburn and Jeremy's friends. It was not, Ellie knew, the kind of wedding Fay had dreamed about, but at least she was marrying the man she loved.

The ceremony, though shorter than the accustomed church service, was dignified and impressive, and when they emerged, it was to face a battery of cameras from a crowd of waiting reporters and television crews. News of the wedding had somehow leaked out, and Jeremy Page was still a big enough name for his wedding to be recorded by the nationals. The bride and groom made a handsome couple as they stood laughing on the steps outside the building and Rita, looking on with a mixture of pride and embarrassment, murmured to her husband, 'And to think we decided not to bother with a photographer!'

'Just as well,' Gordon replied. 'All we need do is buy tomorrow's papers.'

They had booked a table for lunch at the White Hart, Caverstock's best hotel, and found they'd been placed in a small alcove off the dining room, which gave an illusion of privacy. Wine flowed freely, both Gordon and Jeremy made short speeches, and after the dessert plates were removed, a waiter brought in a wedding cake decorated with silver horseshoes and sprigs of white heather. Ellie, who had brought her camera, took a photograph of the bride and groom cutting it.

When the meal was finally over, they went out to the hotel car park to wave the couple off on honeymoon. Jeremy's car had been decorated with tin cans and streamers and a large placard reading 'JUST MARRIED' was tied on the back.

'Thanks, guys!' he called to his grinning friends. Fay kissed her parents and sister, Jeremy shook hands all round, and then they were off, horn tooting and cans rattling, and the rest of the party, feeling rather flat, disbanded.

'Well,' Gordon commented as they drove back to Beckhurst, 'I reckon it all went off as well as it could, in the circumstances.'

'You did her proud, love,' Rita said with satisfaction.

Ellie, looking out of the car window, wondered if her parents shared her doubts about the long-term prospects for the marriage. She could only hope they were unfounded.

The honeymoon was spent in Scotland and lasted only a week, since Jeremy had to be back for the start of the new term. He would now have the forty-minute drive to Caverstock each day, but Fay's secretarial course had ended in July.

During their absence Rita and Hettie Freeman, with the help of Gladys the cleaner, had been through the house removing the last of Phyllis's personal belongings, making up the bed in the main bedroom with new sheets and blankets, and buying basic necessities for the larder and fridge.

Probate had still not been granted, but since Gordon was both executor of his mother's will and owner of the property, formalities were waived to allow the young people to move in straight away.

Fay telephoned as soon as they returned, to thank her mother for making the house ready and to report that they'd had a fabulous time. Rita invited them over for Sunday lunch, but Fay hedged, asking if she could postpone it for a week or two, to give them time to settle in.

'Sounds reasonable,' Gordon commented, when, feeling slightly rebuffed, she relayed the message. 'They've only just got home, after all, and he's back to work on Monday. Of course they want a bit of time to themselves.'

'They've had a week,' Rita retorted, tight-lipped. 'I just wanted to satisfy myself that all that driving hasn't tired her or caused any problems.'

'She'll be fine,' Gordon said, and returned to the evening paper.

For the first time that Ellie could remember, Patrick did not attend the next meeting of the Film Society. It was the last showing of the summer season; suppose he didn't renew his subscription in the autumn? What would she do without the monthly meetings to look forward to, especially since she'd become used to seeing him more frequently? She sat through the film – *L' Enfant*

Sauvage – in a cloud of misery, her eyes too blurred to make out the subtitles. Had he taken offence at not being invited to the wedding? Surely not, when he'd met Fay and Jeremy only twice.

Halfway through the film, it occurred to her that he might be ill, and she spent the rest of the time wondering what excuse she could give for phoning to find out. Salvation came in the form of a pile of newsletters on the table in the coffee room, and she took an extra copy when she left. Though she had Patrick's phone number, she didn't know his address; she'd phone and ask for it, so that she could post the newsletter on to him.

The next evening, it was an older voice that answered the phone.

'Is Patrick there?' she asked fearfully, only to be instantly reassured as the voice called, 'Patrick! A young lady on the line for you.'

'Patrick Nelson,' he said in her ear.

'Hello, Patrick, it's Ellie. How are you? I … was surprised you weren't at the Film Society; I hope you're not ill?'

'No, nothing like that. Rather a lot on at the moment, that's all.' He paused. 'Was it any good?'

Ellie, who could remember nothing of the film, told him that it had been. 'I took a copy of the newsletter for you,' she continued, 'and then realised I haven't got your

102

address.'

'Oh ... thanks. It's 4b Stable Road.'

She scribbled it down, wondering how she could prolong the conversation, and was relieved when he asked diffidently, 'How did the wedding go? I saw all the pictures in the paper.'

'Yes, that bit took us by surprise. It was fine, and we had a very pleasant lunch afterwards.'

'Have you seen Fay since she got back?'

'Yes, they came to lunch last Sunday. Married life seems to be suiting them.'

'Well, we're not allowed to advertise, but now that they're living in Rushyford, could you suggest they sign on at the excellent dental practice in Stable Road?'

Ellie laughed. 'I'll do that, and I'll put the newsletter in the post. Will you be at the next meeting?'

'Oh, I expect so,' he said.

And with that, she had to be content.

Four

After the traumas of the summer, life during the autumn settled for the Marlows into a new routine. It still seemed strange to see Fay's empty chair at the breakfast and supper table, but the arrival of a new member of staff proved a great help to Ellie in filling the gap left by her sister's departure. Jess Ridley was a tall, serious-faced girl with a singularly sweet smile, and she and Ellie struck up an immediate friendship which, had they known it, was to last all their lives.

Jess lived with her mother and elder brother on one of the new estates north of Beckhurst, and lost no time in inviting Ellie to supper one evening to meet them. Mrs Ridley was an attractive woman in her early fifties, who managed both her life and her home with cheerful efficiency. Ellie learned that she was a director of a wholesale clothing firm.

'Does your mother have a job?' she enquired, on Ellie's first visit.

'Not a full-time one,' Ellie replied. 'She does a lot of voluntary work – Meals on

104

Wheels, charity shops, and so on. My father's a chartered accountant,' she added, feeling that her parents should lay claim to some paid employment.

'My ex was in the Merchant Navy,' Alice Ridley told her. 'He was seldom here, so I hardly noticed when he left for good.'

Ellie, unsure how to respond to this, saw to her relief that all three Ridleys were smiling at her, so she smiled, too.

'Mother's always coming out with statements like that,' Mark Ridley remarked. 'It can be disconcerting at first, but you'll soon get used to it.'

There was something spontaneous about them all that appealed immensely to Ellie, who, at home, was used to having to think before she spoke. To her surprise, Alice Ridley seemed genuinely interested in her children's opinions, and over supper they had an animated discussion on education, which Ellie could never imagine having at home. By the end of that evening, she realised to her discomfort that she found Mrs Ridley much easier to talk to than her own mother.

In due course she prevailed upon Rita to invite Jess back, though not without some initial reluctance. Rita hadn't entertained her daughters' friends since they'd stopped having birthday parties at the age of twelve, and since she made no effort with her own girls, had no idea how to talk to a young woman of twenty-four. Conversation was at best stilted, but at least honour had been satisfied, and although Ellie visited the Ridleys fairly often, the invitation to Jess was not repeated.

The two girls fell into the habit of going to the cinema once a week, and frequently spent Saturdays in each other's company. Ellie agonised over whether or not to invite Jess to the Film Society, but decided against it. Her presence might inhibit Patrick from coming to sit with her, and she couldn't risk that.

As the date for the film evening drew closer, Ellie became more apprehensive. Was he still annoyed with her, as he'd sounded on the phone? More important still, would he even be there? Suppose he still 'had a lot on'?

The wave of thankfulness that swamped her as he came and sat beside her momentarily took her breath away. She made herself say lightly, 'Hello, stranger!'

'Hi. How are things?'

'Fine – and you?'

'OK. How's Fay settling down? Do you see much of her?'

'Not a great deal. They've been for a couple of Sunday lunches, and she sometimes spends the day with Mum, but of course I'm at school then, so I don't see her.' Ellie paused, then added casually, 'She's expecting a baby – isn't that lovely?'

So he was right! Patrick thought, taking little pleasure in the fact. 'That's great. When is it due?'

'In the spring sometime.' She was deliberately vague, and was saved from any further questioning as the lights went out and the screening began.

Over coffee, though, Patrick mentioned Fay again. 'Did you tell her about the dental practice?' he asked.

'I can't remember,' Ellie confessed. 'I might have done.'

'Well, if she's pregnant, it's all the more reason to have her teeth checked regularly. Tell her that from me.'

'Yes, sir.'

She threw him an amused glance, and after a minute he smiled sheepishly. 'Sorry, I didn't mean to preach.'

'Oh, I'm sure you're right, but I should think they'll already have briefed her at the antenatal clinic.'

In which case, she'd probably signed on elsewhere, Patrick thought in frustration. He'd *asked* Ellie to mention it; now, he'd probably missed the boat. Even though Fay was married and technically out of reach, he still ached to be near her.

'I'm sorry,' Ellie said, sensing his irritation. 'I'll ask her next time I see her, I promise.'

He forced down his annoyance. 'Have you been to visit them yet?'

'No, they've invited us this weekend.' She paused. 'To be honest, I don't really want to go. I have mixed feelings about them living there.'

'Why's that?'

'Oh, I'm just being silly, but I love the place so much, and when we were little, Fay and I always thought we'd live there after our grandmother died. Now, I feel rather as though it's been ... snatched away from me.'

Patrick frowned. 'That's not fair – surely you've an equal right to it?'

Though warmed by his indignation on her behalf – directed, had she known it, against Jeremy – she hastened to clarify the position. 'It doesn't belong to them,' she said quickly. 'They're just renting it from Dad.'

'Until they find somewhere else?'

'I suppose so. I hadn't thought that far ahead.' Nor, she was sure, had Fay. Having once established a claim to Sandford, however tenuous, she was unlikely to relinquish it willingly.

It was a couple of days later that, to his astonished delight, Patrick caught sight of Fay herself in Rushyford, and hurried after her.

'Fay! Wait!'

She turned in surprise, her face clearing as she saw him. 'Hello, Patrick! Of course, you work here, don't you? I'd forgotten.'

His eyes went hungrily over her, noting with a pang the soft swelling of her body, the rounding of her face. 'You look well,' he said.

'I'm fine.' She patted her stomach. 'I suppose Ellie told you about the baby?'

'Yes.' He forced himself to add, 'Congratulations. Look ... have you time for a coffee?'

She seemed surprised, as well she might, but he couldn't let her go so soon. He added with a smile, 'Do you good to sit down for a minute or two.'

She laughed. 'All right, then.'

They walked together along the pavement, his hand lightly under her elbow, and turned into the Regency Tearooms. It smelled deliciously of cakes, new bread and spicy buns, but there was also a counter further along doing a brisk trade in salads and various hot dishes. He remembered that it was his lunch hour, and turned to Fay.

'Shall we make it lunch, since we're here?'

'Oh, I ... I don't know, I was really on my way home.'

'There's nothing spoiling, is there?'

'No, I was going to make myself a large helping of pasta.' She smiled apologetically. 'I get ravenously hungry.'

'Then let's see what's on offer, and afterwards I'll run you home. I've been doing the week's shopping, so I have the car with me.'

The next hour was pure enchantment for Patrick. They talked about houses and gardens and any number of inconsequential things, but he paid little attention, content simply to sit and watch her as she tucked robustly into her shepherd's pie.

'Would you like anything to follow?' the waitress asked as she removed his plate.

'No, thanks,' he answered absently.

'What about your wife?'

Patrick's heart jerked, but Fay, though she smiled, did not correct the girl. 'Could I possibly have a piece of gateau?' she asked Patrick, who would willingly have given her the world.

'Of course you can. I've changed my mind – make that two,' he added.

Fay laughed. 'I'm leading you astray. I bet you don't usually have gateau for lunch. I shouldn't either, but it looked so good as we came in. It's been fun, thank you so much,' she went on. 'It's a real treat, not to have to cook a meal. I'm afraid cooking doesn't come naturally to me, as Jeremy doesn't fail to point out! The family's coming to lunch on Sunday, and frankly I'm terrified! I'll probably poison them or something. How do you manage? You live alone, don't you?'

'No, actually, my colleague moved in

when he split with his wife. We share the cooking, though. I quite enjoy it. I find it relaxing after a day in the surgery.'

'I'll have to employ you as my secret weapon!' Fay said. 'Bribe you to come to the back door with the meal ready cooked!'

'You'll be fine,' he told her, thinking how young she looked. How old would she be? Nineteen, twenty?

'I'll have to get Ellie to give me lessons. How is she, by the way?'

'Fine,' he answered, slightly taken aback. 'I saw her on Tuesday at the Film Society.'

'Ah yes, the last Tuesday in the month. Can you believe we're into November already?'

'When's the baby due?' he asked.

'The end of March.' Her dancing eyes held his. 'Just the teensiest bit early – premature, perhaps!'

'Perhaps.' He couldn't help smiling back.

'I shall call it a honeymoon baby. That's what Mum says Ellie was, and I'm sure no one ever questioned it.'

'Perhaps,' Patrick suggested dryly, 'because she *was* a honeymoon baby.'

Fay laughed. 'Don't disapprove of me, Patrick!'

'As if I could!' But would Jeremy have married her, he wondered, if it hadn't been for the baby? And, came the disloyal thought, had Fay realised that?

He said quickly, 'If you've finished, we'd better be going, or I'll be late for my next appointment.'

She glanced at her watch. 'Don't bother running me home. After that lunch, the exercise will do me good.'

'Nonsense, it's no bother. Anyway, it's started to rain.'

He took her arm and hurried her along the wet pavement to the meter where he'd left the car. His time had run out but, as he'd known it would, his luck was holding on this wonderful day and there was no ticket tucked behind his wipers.

Following Fay's directions, he turned up the hill and drove through the gates of the house that stood at the top.

'What a magnificent position,' he commented, drawing up at the door.

'It's a magnificent house,' she replied. 'I have to keep pinching myself that I'm really living here, and with Jeremy.'

It was a timely reminder. He got out with her and as she put the key in the door, she said, 'Would you like to come in and look round? I love showing it off!'

'I'd love to, Fay, but I really must get back. Another time, perhaps?' Better, in any case, to have something else to look forward to.

'Of course – you and Ellie must come over one evening.' She turned in the doorway to face him, shaking the raindrops off her hair.

'Thanks again for lunch, Patrick. It was very kind of you.'

'A pleasure,' he said.

The family lunch passed off reasonably enough, and if the beef was overdone and the potatoes hard, nobody commented on the fact. It seemed odd, Ellie thought, to be sitting round the dining table as they had with Gamma, but with Jeremy and Fay at either end.

Afterwards, Fay took them upstairs to the little room they were decorating as the nursery. Ellie couldn't help glancing through the open door of the main bedroom as she passed, and noting that the bed coverings were new. Otherwise, the house seemed exactly as it always had, and she ached with a renewed sense of loss.

The walls of the nursery, as Fay already called it, were covered in primrose emulsion, and on the uncarpeted floor a low chair and a trolley awaited a second coat of paint.

'No sexist colour scheme, you'll note!' Fay told them, as they admired the animal frieze round the walls.

'What would you like it to be?' Ellie asked.

'Oh, a girl,' Fay answered decidedly. 'It has to be a girl – I wouldn't know what to do with a boy!'

'What nonsense, darling!' Jeremy said,

slipping an arm round her waist. 'You've always known *exactly* what to do with them!'

Rita flushed and turned away and as Ellie caught her brother-in-law's eye, he closed it in a conspiratorial wink.

'Did Patrick tell you we had lunch together?' Fay asked as they followed their parents downstairs.

Ellie looked at her quickly. 'No, when was that?'

'On Thursday. We bumped into each other on Riverside Walk, so we went to the Tearooms.'

Ellie was aware of intense jealousy. It was so unfair; why couldn't she bump into Patrick in her lunch hour? The obvious answer – that she was in Beckhurst and he in Rushyford – proved no consolation.

'Did he ask you to sign on with him?' she asked after a moment.

'Sign on?'

They'd reached the bottom of the stairs and were turning into the sitting room.

'At his dental practice.'

'Oh ... no, he didn't mention it.'

'I was supposed to have asked you before, but I forgot.'

'Well, it wouldn't have made any difference; we're registered with someone else.'

Rita was standing in the conservatory looking out at the winter garden. 'Those rose bushes could do with pruning,' she commented. 'Come to that, the windows need cleaning, and all.'

Gordon, noting the mutinous expression on his son-in law's face, addressed himself hastily to Fay. 'You must be finding the house too much, love, in your condition. Should we get Gladys to come in, at least for a while? You'll need some help after the baby's born.'

Fay, close to tears at her mother's criticism, nodded gratefully.

'As for the garden,' Gordon continued, 'I dare say it's in the landlord's interest to keep it in shape. For a limited time, anyway, till you're both more in the swing of things. I'll get in touch with some contract gardeners.'

'Thank you,' Jeremy said, his charm resurfacing. 'That would be a great help. Never having had a garden, I'm pretty clueless, I'm afraid.'

'As I've said before,' Rita commented acidly, 'some people have the knack of always landing on their feet.'

There was a brief, uncomfortable pause, which Ellie finally broke by asking brightly, 'Have you thought of any names for the baby?' and the tension dissolved into laughter as more and more outrageous suggestions were made.

The weeks passed, and Patrick did not receive an invitation to Sandford Lodge.

Nor, though he patrolled Riverside Walk at every opportunity, did he see Fay again.

Since the Film Society didn't meet in December, after the November showing the Committee served cheese and wine instead of coffee, and as he and Ellie stood together with their glasses, he couldn't resist asking after her.

'I hear you had lunch together,' Ellie said.

To his annoyance, Patrick found himself making excuses. 'Yes; we actually went in for coffee, but they were serving lunch, so...' His voice tailed off and he hesitated, considering the wisdom of his next comment but too desperate not to make it. 'Afterwards, I ran Fay back to the house and she invited me in to look round. Unfortunately, I hadn't time, but she said she'd ask us again.' The 'us' stuck in his throat, but it seemed to be the only way he'd manage to see Fay.

Ellie's reaction was not dissimilar; she'd have preferred to be alone with Patrick, but if Fay and Jeremy offered her only chance of seeing him away from the Film Society, so be it.

'I'll remind her,' she said.

Christmas came and went, and the dank, cold days of January. One evening towards the end of the month, Patrick had arranged to meet Roger and Pammy Hastings at a pub midway between Rushyford and Caver-

116

stock, where they were then living. As he waited for them to arrive, a laughing, noisy group of six men and women came in and seated themselves at the far side of the room. One of the men, who had his back to Patrick, turned to shout something to the barman, and he saw with a shock of disbelief that it was Jeremy. Moreover, he had an arm possessively round the shoulders of a girl with long hair, who was very definitely not Fay.

Patrick felt slightly sick. What the hell was he playing at, and where had he told Fay he would be this evening? A wave of intense anger washed over him, and it was all he could do to stop himself from going over.

'Hi! Sorry we're late.'

Roger and Pammy were sliding on to the chairs beside him. 'What's the matter, Patrick?' Roger enquired, studying his face. 'You look as if you've seen a ghost.'

Patrick forced his gaze away from the group. 'Not a ghost,' he said grimly, 'just the husband of a friend, out with another woman.'

'Oh dear. Would you rather go somewhere else?'

'No, I'm damned if I'm going to let him drive me away. I don't care if he does see me; in fact, I was thinking of going over there.'

'Just as well we came when we did,'

117

Pammy said sensibly and, after holding her eyes for a moment, Patrick gave a shamefaced grin.

'You're quite right; it's none of my business. What can I get you to drink?'

But his eyes kept returning to the noisy table, and at one point he saw Jeremy turn his companion's head towards him and kiss her lingeringly on the mouth. Oh God, Fay! he thought sickly. He hadn't expected the marriage to last, but he'd have given it more than five months. After an hour or so, the group left without Jeremy glancing their way, and Patrick was at last able to give his full attention to his friends.

That night, though, he lay awake for hours wondering what he could do. Should he let Jeremy know he'd been seen? Frankly, he doubted if that would do much good. He could confide in Ellie, but the Film Society had already met this month, so it would mean arranging a meeting. It wasn't something they could discuss over the phone. Eventually, he decided to wait for a few days before deciding what, if any, steps to take.

It was at the beginning of February that, most unusually, Ellie received a phone call at school and, having hurried to take it, was surprised to find her sister on the line.

'Fay, what is it? Are you all right?'

'Yes, I'm ... fine,' Fay said, not very

118

convincingly. 'I was wondering, could you possibly come over for supper this evening? Jeremy's going to be out again, and I'm feeling a bit down. Do you think Dad would lend you the car?'

Ellie had passed her driving test a few months previously.

'Well, I don't know; I'm not used to driving in the dark.'

'Please, sis. I really would like to see you.'

Ellie frowned. It was unlike Fay to beg; something must be wrong. 'All right, provided I can have the car, I'll come.'

'Shall I ask Dad for you?'

Ellie flushed. The unthinking offer underlined Fay's unspoken assumption that their father was more likely to be won round by her than by Ellie.

'No, thanks,' she said crisply, 'I'll do it. He doesn't get in till six, so if you don't hear from me, I should be with you about a quarter to seven.'

It was Rita rather than Gordon who raised objections. 'But I've got your lamb chop here. What am I supposed to do with it?'

'I'm sorry, Mum, but I think she's lonely. I really feel I should go.' Ellie, better at dealing with her mother than her father, added smilingly, 'I'm sure the chop would be the better choice, though!'

And Rita, relenting, said with a sniff, 'I wouldn't argue with you there.'

119

Having negotiated the long, unlit country road, Ellie was more than thankful to arrive safely at Sandford Lodge, but concerned when her sister opened the door. Fay, whom she hadn't seen for a week or two, looked pale, and her eyes were puffy as if she'd been crying. Probably antenatal depression, Ellie thought, if there was such a thing. Fay led the way into the sitting room. With the conservatory closed off behind thick curtains and the lamps lit, the room seemed warm and welcoming. Its layout was unchanged since their grandmother's day, and Ellie's eyes went lovingly over it: the blue-and-cream brocade sofa, the delicate, spindly-legged chairs, the deep, soft rug before the fire. Even the ornaments on the mantel were the same, the Dresden shepherd and shepherdess she had loved as a child, the melodiously ticking clock.

'I thought we'd eat in here, if that's all right,' Fay said. 'And you'll be glad to hear I bought a tin of steak-and-kidney pie. Even I can't go wrong with that.'

'You're doing very well,' Ellie said, encouragingly rather than truthfully.

'I told Patrick you should give me lessons.'

Ellie's heart jerked. 'You've seen him again?'

Fay shook her head. 'No, over lunch that time.'

'He did say you were going to ask us over.'

'I know, but to be honest I just can't be bothered. I'm getting very tired at the moment.'

'Isn't Jeremy any help?'

To Ellie's alarm, Fay's eyes filled with tears. 'I didn't realise he'd be out so much. I thought we'd have cosy evenings in together, watching TV and playing tapes.'

'So why don't you?'

'It's with him being in Caverstock all day. If he wants to meet his friends in the evening, it's simpler for him to stay there, than come home and have to go all the way back.'

'But why can't you meet them too?'

'I told you, I'm too tired. Quite honestly, Ellie, it's all I can do to keep my eyes open after nine o'clock, and as you can imagine, Jeremy's not too impressed with that. It wouldn't be fair to try to make him stay in, when I spend half the evening asleep. I just wish he wanted to, that's all.'

'Well, you've not long to go now,' Ellie said rallyingly. 'Only another six weeks or so.' Though Fay was likely to be just as tired once the baby was born, she thought worriedly.

Fay levered herself to her feet. 'I'm off the booze, but there's a bottle of wine, if you'd like some.'

'No, thanks. It took me all my time to drive here stone-cold sober! Let me help you bring the meal through.'

Ellie followed Fay into the kitchen, where, as children, their grandmother's cook had let them scrape round the bowl when she was baking. 'How are you getting on with Gladys?' she asked, opening the oven door to check on the pie.

'All right. She still insists on calling me Miss Fay. She comes two mornings a week, but I can't settle when she's in the house. I feel I should be doing the cleaning myself, or at least helping her.'

'Well, you very definitely shouldn't, just at the moment. Sit down, Fay; you make me nervous, hovering about like that. I'll drain the potatoes. Would you like them mashed?'

Fay lowered herself on to one of the kitchen chairs. 'What would I do without you?'

'What time does Jeremy get back?' Ellie asked, taking the butter and milk out of the fridge.

'I don't know. I'm always asleep.'

'He doesn't go out *every* night, does he?'

'I suppose not, but sometimes it seems like it. I'm terrified of sounding like a nagging wife and driving him away completely.'

'Oh, Fay!' said Ellie helplessly.

That weekend, Patrick finally steeled himself to phone Ellie. 'I wondered if you'd like to come out for a drink this evening,' he said.

Ellie's heart lifted. 'I'd love to. Thanks.'

'I'll call for you about eight, then, if that's OK?'

'Fine, I'll look forward to it.'

When they were seated at a corner table in the wine bar with their drinks in front of them, Patrick said abruptly, 'Have you seen Fay lately? She must be almost due, surely?'

'No, actually, not till the end of March.' Ellie could hear the tart note in her voice as she added, 'Honestly, anyone would think you were a doctor, not a dentist.' Then, seeing his surprise, she sighed. 'I'm sorry, but I didn't come out to talk about Fay.'

'Well, I'm sorry too,' Patrick said quietly, 'because I did.'

She stared at him. 'What do you mean?'

His eyes dropped and he began fingering his tankard. 'Perhaps I shouldn't be telling you this, but I don't know what the hell else to do.'

'Patrick, what is it? What's wrong?'

He looked up, and she was disturbed by the distress in his eyes. 'I saw Jeremy out with another girl,' he said.

Ellie said softly, 'Oh God!'

'He didn't see me, but they obviously had something going. He actually kissed her.' He paused, glancing at her downcast face. 'You don't seem too surprised.'

'I saw Fay on Wednesday. She said Jeremy's often out, but she doesn't blame him because she's feeling so tired at the moment.'

'Is there anything we can do?' Patrick asked anxiously.

'Even if he *is* out a lot, it needn't necessarily be with that girl,' Ellie pointed out reasonably. 'That could have been a one-off.'

'It didn't look like it.'

'Well, if we interfere, it might make matters worse. The main thing is to keep it from Fay, particularly for the time being.'

'Of course.'

Ellie straightened her shoulders. 'Then since we've decided there's nothing we can do, let's not spoil the evening by talking about it any more.'

He made an effort, she had to admit, but though they kept the conversation going without further reference to Fay, the evening was not a success. Quite obviously, Patrick's purpose in arranging it had not been to see her, but to pass on his concerns about Jeremy. She had made no progress at all.

Five

Fay's baby daughter was born at five o'clock in the evening on Thursday the twenty-eighth of March. The first pains had begun at six in the morning, and at seven Jeremy had taken her into the hospital. Having been told the birth would not be for several hours, he phoned the Marlows and then went to school as usual.

Ellie also had to go to school, but begged her mother to phone her as soon as they had any news. When she'd heard nothing by lunchtime, she rang home, only to be told Fay had been given a sedative, since the birth was still not imminent.

'I had ten hours' labour with you,' Rita said, 'so you might as well put it out of your mind till you get home. There won't be any news before then.'

'Anything wrong, Ellie?' Jess asked, coming into the staff room as Ellie put down the phone. Their paths hadn't crossed that day.

'My sister's having her baby, and it seems to be taking a very long time to me.'

'Oh, poor thing. Rather her than me. Is

her husband with her?'

'No, he's doing the manly thing and carrying on as usual.'

Jess laughed. 'Just as well I know what you mean by "carrying on"!'

But you don't, Ellie thought bleakly, adding a silent prayer that Jeremy would stop playing around and be there for Fay.

The call, as Rita had predicted, came soon after Ellie arrived home.

'It's a girl,' Jeremy told them jubilantly. 'She's an absolute poppet!'

'Are they both all right?' Rita demanded.

'Fine, and before you ask, the baby weighed six and a half pounds.'

'What are you calling her?'

'We're making the final decision now. We'll tell you when you get here.'

Rita immediately phoned Gordon at his office, and he left at once, stopping only to collect the two of them before setting off for Rushyford General. Fay was still in a small room off the delivery room, sitting up in bed looking strained but happy, the baby in her arms and an enormous vase of red roses on the table beside her.

'Oh, *look* at her!' Ellie whispered, leaning over to peer into the tiny face. The baby's skin was creamily pale, and a black, silky down covered her head. Her eyes were closed, the long black lashes lying on her cheek, but as Ellie and Rita bent over her, she suddenly opened them and stared back up at them.

'Hello, little one!' Ellie said. 'What's her name, Fay?'

'Laura Louise,' Fay answered, reaching up for Jeremy's hand.

'Laura Page,' Rita said consideringly. 'Yes, I like that. Hello, young Laura; I'm your grandma! She's got your eyes, Jeremy.'

Jeremy grinned. 'Dark and inscrutable, eh?'

'Well, congratulations, both of you,' Gordon said heartily. 'She's a fine baby.' He put a hand on his wife's shoulder. 'Our first grandchild, Rita. How does that make you feel?'

'Old,' said Rita, who was forty-six.

'How long will you be in hospital?' Ellie asked.

It was Jeremy who replied. 'She's coming home tomorrow.'

'Tomorrow? Isn't that rather soon?'

'They say that as the baby's already feeding well, there's nothing to keep her.'

'Well, you'll be breaking up next week, won't you?' Ellie said. 'It's worked out pretty well, all things considered.'

Jeremy glanced at Fay's sullen face. 'Unfortunately not. I've been roped in to give the First Eleven extra coaching – there's an important match at the beginning of next term. I'll be home earlier than usual, but I'll still have to go over there each morning.'

'Surely, in the circumstances—' Rita began, but Jeremy said briskly, 'Not negotiable, I'm afraid.'

'Well,' Ellie said after a moment, 'we break up too, remember, so I'll be free for three weeks. If it would help, I could come over during the daytime to lend a hand.'

'Oh, Ellie!' Fay exclaimed. 'Could you really? That would be great.'

'If I stay till Jeremy gets back, you'll always have someone with you,' Ellie continued, daring her brother-in-law not to comply. 'By the time school starts again, you'll be an old hand!'

In the car going home, Gordon said a little gruffly, 'It's good of you to give up your holiday to help Fay, Ellie.'

'Nevertheless,' Rita put in, 'it's Jeremy's place to be there. I don't understand why he took on this coaching – he knew the baby would be here.'

'Oh, it doesn't matter,' Ellie said quickly. 'I'll enjoy helping, and it will give me a chance to be with Laura. She's gorgeous, isn't she?'

'You'll be spending a fair amount of time on the bus,' Rita commented. 'Have you thought about that? It must take a good hour each way, and you won't be able to borrow Dad's car, because he needs it to get to work.'

'You could afford a little run-around of your own, you know,' Gordon said after a moment. 'No harm in dipping into the money your grandmother left you – there's enough of it. If we can find something cheap second-hand, I'll lend you what's required until Probate comes through. Would you like me to have a look round?'

'Oh, Dad, that would be wonderful! I'd feel much more independent, with my own transport.'

Gordon was as good as his word, and by the following Saturday, Ellie was the proud owner of a three-year-old Ford Prefect. She spent the whole of Sunday morning washing and polishing it, and in the afternoon drove to Jess's house and took her out for a spin.

'It's great,' Jess said, looking round the car admiringly. 'Perhaps during the holidays we could drive down to Devon or somewhere?'

'Oh, Jess, I'm sorry, but I'm going to be tied up the whole three weeks. I promised Fay I'd go over every day to help with the baby. That's the main reason for getting the car.'

'Never mind,' Jess said philosophically, 'we can go another time.'

The more Ellie thought about it, the more unlikely it seemed that a team of school-boys, however keen, would be expected to attend for coaching every day of the school holidays – or, for that matter, that a games master would be required to forfeit his own holiday to instruct them. She could, perhaps, accept a couple of mornings a week, which might have provided Jeremy with the excuse he needed. The family, after all, were unlikely to check. What was indisputable was that he had no intention of spending the next three weeks waiting on his wife and daughter. What was it he'd said? *Not negotiable.*

Ellie kept her suspicions to herself, and on the Thursday of the following week her new schedule came into effect. It was as well that she was there; Fay, still emotional, was given to easy tears, and panicked every time Laura vomited or cried for any length of time. Although Ellie knew no more about babies than she did, she was able, at one remove, to remain calm and restore her to an even balance.

Unfortunately, the evenings were Laura's most unsettled time, and Fay, abandoning the meal Ellie had left for them, spent most of the time up in the nursery trying to soothe her to sleep. Jeremy's patience was notably wearing thin, the more so since their nights were also disturbed, with Fay having to get up two or three times to feed the baby.

'For God's sake, can't you give her something to make her sleep?' he burst out one night, as Fay again climbed wearily out of bed.

'What do you suggest?' she asked, her voice dangerously calm. 'Chloroform? Anyway, I don't know why you're complaining. You're asleep again before I get out of the room.'

'It's still a disturbed night,' he retorted. 'At least you can sleep in until she wakes; I have to leave the house at eight, remember, to be at school for nine. I feel like a limp rag.'

'Join the club,' Fay said briefly, and left the room to attend to her daughter.

It was Fay's twentieth birthday on the eleventh of April, and since it wasn't practical to look for babysitters with Laura so unsettled in the evenings, Ellie offered to cook a special meal at Sandford, to which their parents were invited. By the time she arrived that morning, Jeremy had, as always, already left. Fay, still in her dressing gown and with her hair dull and straggly, looked exhausted, but she opened the parcel Ellie had brought, and exclaimed with delight at the lacy nightdress.

'It will make you feel glamorous again,' Ellie said.

'It'll help, certainly,' Fay agreed. 'I know I look a fright, but Laura excelled herself last night. Believe it or not, I was with her from two until four thirty. She kept falling asleep while she was feeding, but as soon as I tried to put her down, she woke and started screaming. In the end, I gave up and took her back to bed with me. She snuffled a bit and disturbed Jeremy and he stormed off into the spare room. Then she dropped off and I did too. She's still asleep, and I only woke ten minutes ago. Jeremy left this on the bedside table. Isn't it pretty?'

Ellie admired the thin gold chain. 'It's lovely, Fay. Now, go and have your bath and wash your hair. The health visitor will be here at ten, remember. If Laura wakes, I'll see to her.'

The day passed much as usual. The health visitor came and Laura was weighed and measured. Fay asked anxiously about the disturbed nights, but it appeared this was normal, which was little help.

'She'll grow out of it,' the woman said comfortingly. 'Sleep when she does – that's the best advice I can give you.'

'Did Jeremy say when he'll be back?' Ellie asked over lunch.

'No, but it'll be the same as usual, I expect, between four and five.'

'Well, the parents are coming at seven and I was aiming to eat at half past. If Laura starts to cry, we could try bringing her cot down. She might settle if she's in the room with us.'

Fay slipped an arm round her waist. 'You are a brick, Ellie. Thanks so much for everything.'

Most afternoons, Fay went to bed for an hour or so and Ellie wheeled the baby down to the shops to buy ingredients for the evening meal and the next day's lunch. Today, however, with the birthday dinner to prepare, she had brought her provisions with her, and as Fay retired upstairs, went into the kitchen and began to unpack them. Jeremy's cavalier behaviour was to her advantage, she reflected; it was wonderful to spend her days here at Sandford, and her little niece was a bonus.

However, Jeremy did not return between four and five, and at six o'clock there was still no sign of him. Fay rang the school, but there was no reply.

'There wouldn't be; they're closed for the holidays,' Ellie pointed out.

'Surely he'd have phoned if he was going to be late?' Fay said worriedly.

'He'll be using the cricket pavilion, and there's not likely to be a phone there.' If, she thought privately, he was there at all.

By seven, Fay was convinced he'd had an accident. Her parents attempted to calm her down. 'You'd have heard if anything had happened,' Gordon assured her. 'He's sure to be back soon.'

Ellie, concerned now about her meal,

looked anxiously at the clock, wondering how long she could delay without ruining it. Really, she thought with exasperation, he could have made the effort to be back on time, today of all days. It was Fay who came to her rescue. With her parents' reassurances, her anxiety had turned to a cold anger.

'We won't wait,' she said. 'I'll leave Jeremy's in the oven, and it's his own fault if it dries up.'

Ironically, that was the first evening Laura slept through, allowing them to enjoy the meal undisturbed. Ellie served crab mornay, followed by chicken marengo with rice and spring vegetables, and a lemon cheesecake. Two spots of colour burned on Fay's pale face, but she joined in the general conversation and ate everything in front of her, as did the rest of them.

Ellie excused herself to go and make coffee and took the opportunity to slip upstairs to look at the baby, scarcely able to believe she'd slept for so long; but Laura still lay fast asleep, her breath soft and regular in the quiet room, and Ellie tiptoed out again.

She couldn't remember, afterwards, what prompted her to go into the guest room; as Jeremy had spent part of the night there, perhaps she'd hoped for something that would explain his absence. She found it, but it was not what she expected. As she switched on the light, her eyes fell on a note propped on the dressing table which read simply: *Sorry, love, I'm not cut out for this. No hard feelings. J.*

For a long time, Ellie stood with the note in her hand, staring down at it. What did it mean? Not, surely, what it seemed to mean?

With leaden footsteps she went back to the dining room. The three of them looked up, expecting her to bring in the coffee.

'I found this,' she said, and handed the note to Fay.

Fay read it, lifting anguished eyes to hers. 'No!' she whispered. 'Oh Ellie, no!'

Gordon reached across the table and took the note from Fay's hand. Then he looked up, meeting his wife's startled, questioning eyes.

'He's gone,' he said baldly. 'God damn him, he's gone.'

Rita's hand went to her mouth as Fay began to cry quietly. Gordon came round the table and drew her up into his arms. 'Come on, love; he'll be back. Did you have a row?'

Fay shook her head. 'It was just too much for him,' she sobbed. 'Never having any time to ourselves, and the baby crying, and being woken up all the time.'

'It's the same for every other father,' Gordon said grimly. 'He's no sense of responsibility, that's his trouble. Well, go and pack a

135

case, love; you're coming back with us.'

'I can't, Dad,' Fay wailed. 'Suppose he comes home?'

'He'll know where to find you.'

'But all Laura's things are here! There's her cot and her pram and bath and all her clothes and nappies. I can't pack everything up at a moment's notice!'

'Suppose I stay here tonight,' Ellie suggested, 'and bring them home with me tomorrow? That'll give us more time, and if Jeremy does come back later, we'll be here.'

'I shouldn't hold your breath,' Rita said. 'In the meantime, how about that coffee, Ellie? We could all do with some.'

By the time Ellie returned with the coffee, Fay's tears had dried. She seemed stunned, sitting huddled in the chair in the sitting room where her father had led her. Fay put a cup of coffee into her hand and she obediently sipped at it. She was obviously exhausted, and at ten o'clock Gordon got to his feet.

'If you're sure you want to spend the night here, we'll be making a move; but your room's ready waiting for you. We can push the bed over a bit – there'll be plenty of room for the cot.'

'Thanks, Dad,' Fay said dully.

'Have you any pills you can take to help you sleep?'

'Not while I'm breast-feeding. Anyway, I

mightn't hear Laura.'

'Don't worry, Dad,' Ellie assured him. 'I'll look after her.'

As Fay kissed her parents and went with them to the door, the first wail sounded from upstairs.

'Perfect timing!' Ellie said. 'I'll bring her down.'

'She'll need changing.'

'OK.'

Ellie lifted the baby from her cot and the crying stopped. She laid her on the trolley, changed her, and wrapped her up again in her shawl. *Bye, Baby Bunting*, she thought, *Daddy's gone a-hunting*.

It was the longest night Ellie could remember. While Fay fed the baby at ten o'clock, she cleared the dining-room table, loaded the dishwasher and washed the glasses. They both went upstairs at eleven.

'Take clean sheets out of the airing cupboard,' Fay said expressionlessly. 'I'll find you a nightdress.'

Ellie stripped the bed that Jeremy had left unmade, putting on fresh sheets and pillowslips. He must have been lying here when he decided to leave, she thought. Or maybe he'd reached the decision earlier. But how could he have done it on Fay's birthday? Because, she wondered, playing devil's advocate, he knew she'd have her family with her that evening, for support? Or was that being too charitable?

Having slept all evening, Laura was awake most of the night. Several times, wrapped in Fay's old dressing gown, Ellie went through to sit with her in the nursery, not wanting her to be alone in the night watches with what must be very disturbing thoughts. But Fay gave no further sign of tears. She sat in silence, gazing down at her baby's head, leaving Ellie to wonder if after all she'd prefer to be alone. Twice, she went down to the kitchen and made hot drinks. At last, at about four, Fay stood up with the wakeful baby in her arms.

'I'm taking her back to bed,' she said. 'No one to disturb tonight.'

Ellie stood too, aching with weariness. At the bedroom door, Fay turned. 'Thanks for being here, Ellie,' she said.

And Ellie, her own eyes full of tears, felt that the long hours of wakefulness had been worthwhile.

The following day was Good Friday, a fact borne in on Ellie as a sombre tolling of church bells dragged her from a deep, dreamless sleep. She slipped out of bed and went to peep into Fay's room. She and the baby lay curled together in the big bed. Jeremy had not come back, then.

Ellie had a shower and spread toothpaste on her finger to rub on her teeth. She was about to go downstairs when Fay's low voice reached her from the bedroom, and she glanced in to find her feeding the baby. She looked up as Ellie appeared in the doorway.

'It wasn't a dream, then.'

' 'Fraid not. Would you like some coffee?'

'Please.'

The phone rang while she was making it, momentarily raising their hopes, but it was only Gordon, asking if they'd had a reasonable night.

'Not really,' Ellie said. 'Laura was awake for most of it, and so were we.'

'No sign of Jeremy, I suppose?'

'No.'

She heard him sigh. 'Well, get her over here as soon as you can. She needs to be out of that house.'

By the time Laura had been bathed and dressed and Fay and Ellie had gathered her things together and loaded as much as possible into the car, it was nearly eleven.

'Do you think he'll come back?' Fay asked tonelessly, as she locked the front door of Sandford behind them.

'I don't know, honey. Try not to worry. In the meantime, it'll be good to have you home again.'

In fact, she did not stay long. Used by now to being mistress in her own home, Fay found it hard to submit once more to Rita's authority. Added to that, there were constant differences of opinion about the care of the baby. Rita decreed that if it was not time for her feed and there was patently nothing wrong with her, Laura should be left to cry, a course Fay refused to countenance, causing Rita to comment – repeatedly – that she was making a rod for her own back and spoiling the child into the bargain.

Nappies were another bone of contention, her mother having been horrified to come upon Fay loading them into the washing machine.

'I do the serviettes and tablecloths in there!' she'd exclaimed.

'But you're *supposed* to put dirty things in it!' Fay protested, bewildered. 'It's a *washing* machine, for God's sake!'

'Quite apart from the question of hygiene,' Rita continued, as if she hadn't spoken, 'nappies need boiling to keep them white. I used a galvanised container for yours, and it's still in the washhouse. I'll go and get it.'

'Don't bother!' Fay flared. 'If you think in this day and age I'm going to slave over a panful of steaming nappies every day, and rinse them all out by hand, you're very much mistaken. I've quite enough to do without that!'

'Like what?' Rita snapped. 'Seems to me you have me and your sister running round after you all day.'

Fay said no more, but she continued to

use the washing machine.

Gordon, meanwhile, had been round to Jeremy's previous address, to which, as they'd guessed, he had returned.

'He apologised!' Gordon reported to his wife and daughters on his return. 'Quite casually, mind you; you'd think he'd broken a plate, or forgotten an errand or something. He's "sorry it didn't work out".'

'Did you insist that he comes back?' Rita demanded.

Gordon avoided their eyes. 'I'm afraid there's no question of that,' he said. 'He's prepared to let Fay divorce him, and agreed to pay for their upkeep. Has it all worked out, apparently.'

'But I don't *want* to divorce him!' Fay sobbed. 'I want him back!' To which there was nothing they could say.

By the end of a week, Fay had decided to return to Sandford Lodge, and nothing any of them said could dissuade her.

'You do realise term starts next Thursday?' Ellie said. 'I shan't be free to help any more.'

Fay hesitated. 'I was wondering if you could possibly ... reverse the process, just for a while. Instead of being there during the day, come in the evening and stay overnight. I know it means a drive to and from school, but it's only about the same distance as Jeremy did each day, and we'd have the weekends together.'

'Well, I must say you have a nerve!' Rita exclaimed. 'Ellie gave up the whole of her Easter holidays for you, and now you expect her to move in. If you need company that much, you should stay here.'

'Ellie?' Fay beseeched her.

She hesitated. It would add almost two hours to the school day, but the prospect of living, even temporarily, at Sandford overrode other considerations.

'Just for a while, then,' she conceded.

It was not an easy time for Ellie. Although it was she who had to be up early and face the forty-minute drive to school, it was also she who went to Laura in the night, rocking her in her arms when, after her feed, she refused to settle, and Fay, opting out, lay sobbing in her bed; but during those night watches, with the small body resting on her shoulder and the baby's wet cheek against hers, a bond developed between the two of them which was to last a lifetime.

On the first Saturday of this arrangement, while Ellie was wheeling Laura in the town, she came face to face with Patrick.

'Ellie!' he exclaimed. 'What are you doing here? Is this Fay's baby?' He peered into the pram and was met by a pair of black eyes that stared unblinkingly up at him. 'Her father's colouring, I see. Where's Fay?'

'At home, resting.' Ellie paused, but there

was no point in prevaricating. 'I might as well tell you, Patrick,' she said steadily, 'that Jeremy's left her.'

He turned and stared at her, the expression in his eyes unreadable. 'When?'

'Just before Easter. She came back home for a while but couldn't settle, so for the moment I'm staying over here with her.'

'Is it the girl I saw him with?' Patrick asked in a low voice.

'I don't know that it's any girl.' Which was not strictly true; Ellie had overheard Dad telling her mother that Jeremy, 'as bold as brass', had offered to provide evidence of adultery. 'It was all I could do to keep my hands off him,' Gordon had added.

'He said he wasn't cut out for being a father,' she said.

'Or a husband, apparently. Well, I'm only a few minutes away, remember. Needless to say, I'll do anything I can.'

Ellie looked at him in surprise. 'How do you mean?'

'Well, things that he saw to – cutting wood for the fire, bringing in the coal, that kind of thing. Or changing a light bulb, come to that,' he added smilingly.

'I think we can manage a light bulb, and we haven't bothered with an open fire, but it's kind of you to offer.'

She hesitated. For as long as she was at Sandford, she'd not be able to attend the

143

Film Society, virtually her only contact with Patrick. Here was a chance to seize at least one opportunity of seeing him.

'Would you like to come and have supper with us?' she asked. 'You still haven't seen round the house.'

His face lit up. 'That would be great. Thanks very much.'

'This evening then, about seven? It'll do Fay good to see someone different.'

'I'll bring a bottle of wine,' he said.

'I warn you,' Ellie added dryly, 'it might not be the civilised meal you're imagining. In all likelihood, Fay will spend most of it upstairs in the nursery.' And, leaving him wondering whether or not she was serious, she continued on her way.

Patrick was shocked at the change in Fay, no longer the lovely, vivacious girl he'd first met. Even at their lunch together, though tired by her pregnancy, she'd retained that spark which had so attracted him. Now, she looked pale and thin, with violet shadows under her eyes and a general air of listless-ness, and his heart ached for her.

Sandford Lodge, on the other hand, was all that she had said: a charming Edwardian house, full of character, which had obvi-ously been lovingly tended all its life. There was a warmth, an air of restfulness about it that immensely appealed to him, and the fittings and furnishings were so much a part of the whole, it was impossible to imagine them anywhere else. No wonder both the girls loved it so much.

To Ellie's relief, the meal passed off without any signs of embarrassment or strain on anyone's part, and she was glad that Jeremy's departure did not seem to have lessened Patrick's willingness to spend time in her company. Laura woke only as they finished eating, and Fay immediately excused herself and went upstairs, leaving Ellie and Patrick to have coffee without her.

'She looks exhausted,' he commented. 'Does she have any help in the house?'

'Yes, two mornings a week. I'm pretty exhausted myself,' Ellie added a trifle tartly. 'I'm up in the night almost as much as Fay is, and the drive to and from school is pretty wearing, with a busy day in between.'

'I'm sure,' he answered absently. He drained his cup and looked at his watch. 'I mustn't keep you from your bed,' he added. 'I'm sure you need all the sleep you can get.'

'Oh, no,' Ellie protested, seeing the longed-for time alone rapidly dwindling, 'I didn't mean...'

'Really, I must be going. It's been a super evening. Thank you.'

'We must do it again,' she said flatly, out of her disappointment.

'I'd love to.'

There was nothing to do but rise with him and see him to the door.

'Say goodnight to Fay for me.'

She nodded, and stood watching as he got into his car. Why, she wondered despondently, did every evening she spent with Patrick end with a feeling of anticlimax? With a sigh, she closed the door and went to clear the table.

Having satisfied himself that Jeremy had no intention of returning, Gordon lost no time in taking Fay to see his solicitor. Wading through all the legal phrases, it appeared that, with Jeremy admitting adultery, there was nothing to prevent the process going through fairly quickly. In fact, Gordon grudgingly admitted, he was being very obliging about the whole affair; no hard feelings, as he'd said in his note. Matters were further simplified by the fact that there were no assets to divide, since all they had was contained in Sandford, which was Gordon's property. The divorce would be 'in full settlement' to rule out the possibility of claims later, and the maintenance agreed was more than sufficient to cover Jeremy's share of the rent. Fay should have no financial problems.

On the evening after the visit to the solicitor, Patrick again came for supper. It was obvious that Fay was still on edge, and

Ellie regretted not having postponed the invitation – the more so when she returned to the dining room with the coffee tray, to find her sobbing on Patrick's shoulder. She came to an abrupt halt, spilling the liquid as her heart began a slow, uncomfortable beating.

'She'll be all right in a minute,' Patrick said, patting Fay's shoulder. 'Today's been a bit too much for her, that's all.'

That scene, with the two of them standing close together in the softly lit room, continued to haunt Ellie. There was worse to come. Patrick, unable to return their hospitality in the evening because of the baby, instead started taking both Fay and Laura out to lunch, during which the baby was guaranteed to sleep. Fay, noticeably beginning to recover her spirits, prattled artlessly to Ellie about the various restaurants they visited, and how the other diners had admired Laura, seeming not to notice her lack of response. The next time Patrick came to supper, it was at Fay's rather than Ellie's invitation.

In a haze of misery, Ellie felt the ground shifting beneath her feet. She was increasingly aware of the way Patrick's eyes rested on Fay, his tenderness in speaking to her, and realised with a sense of shock that for the first time since he'd met her, Fay was available – and a previously unrecognised threat to herself.

What was more, she thought despairingly, it was she who had given him the entrée to Sandford by inviting him that first time. It would not have occurred to Fay, and whatever his feelings for her, Patrick would never have initiated it. The stark truth dawned on Ellie that it was in order to see her sister, not Jeremy, that he had kept contacting her. What a blind fool she'd been.

The turmoil of her feelings made her reluctant to spend time in Fay's company. While she was at school all day, there was no particular problem. They had their meal – usually prepared by Ellie, though Fay had been home all day – and afterwards either Fay retired early to bed or they watched television, which cut out the need for conversation; but during half-term week, with both of them together all day, they were thrown into each other's company, and Fay's innate selfishness began to grate.

Matters came to a head halfway through the week. Fay had clearly had something on her mind all morning, and it was at lunchtime that she said with studied casualness, 'Ellie, would you mind very much if I went out this evening?'

Ellie stared at her. 'What about Laura?'

'She's had a bottle once or twice; I could leave one ready and it would only need warming up. And often she settles better for you than she does for me. I shouldn't be late back.'

'Where are you thinking of going?' Ellie asked woodenly.

'Actually, Patrick's invited me out for dinner.'

Ellie put her fork down. 'You're asking me to babysit for *you and Patrick?*'

Fay flashed her a nervous smile. 'You wouldn't mind, would you?'

'Aren't you forgetting he's supposed to be my friend?'

'No, but you always insisted you weren't serious.'

Ellie closed her eyes. So she had.

'And Patrick assured me there wasn't anything between you. I did ask, to make sure.'

'That's all right then.' Ellie's voice sounded ominous, even to herself.

'Look, Ellie, can I tell you a secret? He says he's in love with me, has been ever since we first met, at the Chinese. I'd no idea!'

Ellie sat unmoving.

'I don't love *him* of course,' Fay rushed on. 'I'll never love anyone but Jeremy.' Her voice wobbled, though if she was looking for sympathy, it was from the wrong quarter. 'But I do desperately need someone, to look after Laura and me. You won't tell anyone, will you – not even the parents? We have to be very careful till the divorce goes through,

149

because it might complicate things; but once I'm free, he wants to marry me.'

'Does he indeed?'

Fay leant forward and put a hand over Ellie's rigid fist on the table. 'You're not cross, are you? Don't grudge me a second chance, Ellie.'

Ellie snatched her hand away and stood up. Her flesh was burning and there was a buzzing in her ears.

'Yes, Fay, I *am* "cross", as you put it. In fact, I feel extremely hurt and ... and betrayed. I've put myself out for you, flogging to school and back each day, cooking your meals, nursing your baby at night. But I draw the line at babysitting for you and your lover. I'm sorry if you think that's unreasonable.'

Fay gasped, genuine surprise on her face, and out of the torrent of complaint, seized on the last item. 'He's not my lover!' she said.

'It's only a matter of time, isn't it? And whether or not there was anything between Patrick and me, you knew quite well, despite my denials, that I was interested in him. I can't believe you're doing this to me.'

'But Ellie, I didn't do anything! It was Patrick! And if he's felt like that about me all along, there'd never have been a chance of anything between you, would there?'

Ellie drew a deep breath. 'Well, at least one

good thing has come out of all this. As you now have someone else to look after you, I can go home and start living my own life again. I'll go up and pack now. The dishwasher needs emptying, by the way, and you're out of bread. I was going to buy some this afternoon.'

Fay burst into tears and, as Ellie continued inexorably up the stairs, trailed up behind her. 'Ellie, I can't manage without you – you know I can't! I'm hopeless – I can't even cook!'

'Then you'd better learn.' Ellie lifted her suitcase on to the bed and opened it.

'*Please*, Ellie! All right, I shouldn't have asked you to babysit – I'll phone Patrick and tell him I can't go – but please, please stay!'

'Sorry, Fay, you've blown it this time. Anyway, it was only supposed to be for a week or two, while you got into a routine. I've been here six weeks, and was coming every day for a month before that. I've not had any life of my own since Laura was born.'

She turned to face her weeping sister. 'One thing more: if you *ever* tell Patrick that this row was over him, I'll ... I'll kill you! Do you understand?'

Fay, looking frightened, nodded dumbly.

'You can make up anything you like – just never drop so much as a hint that it had anything to do with him.'

151

There was a wail from the pram in the back garden, and Fay instinctively turned, then hesitated.

'Go to her,' Ellie instructed. 'I'll see myself out.'

Intermission – The Present Day

Adrian said mildly, 'Are you going to tell me what that was all about?'

They were sitting side by side in a black cab, snarled up in the evening traffic. Reaching for Laura's hand, he was surprised by its coldness.

'Darling, what is it?' he asked more urgently. 'What was it about that woman – or, more particularly, her name – that put the fear of God into you? Had you heard it before?'

Laura was staring straight ahead of her. 'I don't want to talk about it,' she said.

'But she seemed pleasant enough. Not ... threatening in any way?'

Just when he'd decided she wasn't going to reply, she said jerkily, 'You know I don't like talking about my father.'

'But sweetheart, he was well known. His name is bound to come up every now and then, and you can't just scuttle away every time like a frightened rabbit.'

'I don't want to talk about it,' she repeated

153

stubbornly, and with a sigh, curiosity unsatisfied, he let the matter drop.

Christa Nelson stood at the window of the flat her grandfather had had made at the top of Sandford Lodge. Originally the servants' quarters, the largest of the rooms had been their playroom when they were all growing up. Now, the flat comprised a bathroom, a sitting room and a bedroom, even a rudimentary kitchen behind a screen, where the old man had heated up soup or coffee when not inclined to join the family downstairs.

She could, of course, have used her old bedroom, which still held some of her books and other possessions; but somehow, in the present circumstances, that would have seemed a retrograde step. Better by far the semi-independence of the flat, where, though under the family roof, she was afforded a measure of privacy.

She turned and surveyed the pleasant room that was now doubling as an office, with computer, printer and fax set up incongruously amid the easy chairs. She'd been living here for three months now, since she had fled London. Fortunately, being self-employed, she had always worked from home, translating books, journals and, occasionally, correspondence, from French and Italian originals – which was how she'd met Neville Henderson.

She drew a sharp breath, deliberately pursuing the memory as one might prod an aching tooth. Smooth, sophisticated Neville, nearly twenty years her senior, successful businessman, bon viveur, and married to an equally high-profile wife, the television presenter, Marcella Henderson. She had called at his offices to deliver the transcript of a quotation from a French company, and Neville came into the room as she was explaining a somewhat ambiguous turn of phrase to the senior partner.

'You understand French?' he'd demanded. 'Then you're just the girl I'm looking for! I'm in the process of buying a house in Provence, and I can't make head nor tail of the advocate's letter. Come and have lunch with me, and I'll tell you about it. If you're free, that is?' he'd added, raising an enquiring eyebrow.

Christa, who had been envisaging a solitary sandwich at home, admitted that she was, and he'd taken her to a small Greek restaurant, where they sat in an open courtyard with a fountain playing, surrounded by pots of vines and olive trees. They ate dolmades and moussaka, shared a bottle of retsina, and finished with fresh figs and strong black coffee, and throughout the meal he had leaned towards her across the table, talking about politics and art and travelling, with a passionate intensity that left her breathless. She'd never met anyone like him, never been so aware of a man's inherent virility underlying all that charm. He made her feel vital, alive, fizzing with excitement, and tinglingly aware of him in every inch of her body.

When they'd parted, it was arranged that they'd meet the following evening, for Neville to hand over the lawyer's letter. 'Let me know the rate you charge,' he'd said. 'This is a business arrangement.'

A business arrangement. As well to remember that, she'd told herself that night, lying awake in the dark; but the excitement of him remained with her, and she was counting the hours to their meeting.

This time he'd taken her to a tapas bar, and after he'd produced the file of correspondence for her to take home, they'd settled down to talk and nibble the tempting morsels that were set before them in seemingly endless succession. He encouraged her to talk about herself and her ambitions, and sought her opinion on current topics, listening intently to her answers as though they really mattered to him; and all the time she was acutely aware of him, of the mole beside his mouth, the strong black hairs on the back of his hand, the white flecks in the hair above his ears. But after an hour, to her intense disappointment, he'd glanced at his watch and announced that he was sorry, but he had to leave as he was going to a concert.

'No need for you to rush, though,' he'd added as he rose to his feet. 'Have as much as you like – I've squared it with the waiter. Enjoy your evening, and phone me when the translation's ready.' And he'd dropped his card on the table and was gone, leaving her bitterly aware of how far short of her dreams the evening had fallen.

She'd been a fool, she told herself; he had done nothing to indicate that he thought of her as other than a pleasant, intelligent girl who was going to do some work for him. As a man about town, it wouldn't have occurred to him that she would read more into his casual hospitality than he had intended.

A few days later, she'd phoned him and, in her best executive voice, informed him that the translations were ready and suggested dropping them in at his office. If she'd adopted that procedure before, she thought bitterly, she'd have spared herself all those futile dreams.

'Oh, fine,' he'd said, and her bones melted at the sound of his voice. 'But no need to come all this way; meet me at twelve at the Grapes Wine Bar in Leghorn Street.'

So once more she'd set out to meet him, her heart in her mouth, and was surprised to see him waiting for her on the pavement. Despite herself, her heart sank. Not even a drink this time, then. But, having taken possession of the transcript and handed over her cheque, he utterly confounded her by saying abruptly, 'I should like to take you to bed. Would you mind?' – and smiled his crooked smile at her confusion. 'Only trouble is,' he'd added outrageously, 'I have a meeting in an hour, so there's no time to waste. Fortunately, my flat is just round the corner.'

Which was how it had begun. In those early days, their comings together had consisted of hastily arranged meetings and hurried love-making, but she hadn't minded, caught up in the thrill of what was truly a whirlwind romance. After a month or two of snatched kisses and clock-watching, Neville had suggested moving in with her. 'Only during the week, of course, angel. At weekends I trot off up to Cheshire like a dutiful husband, but at least it will give us the maximum time together, and might ward off the ulcer which I'm sure is imminent!'

So, for the last four years he had shared her flat during the week and returned home at weekends, and life had been blissful. Several times, they had paid fleeting visits to France, where he stood by benignly as, translating his instructions, she conducted negotiations with the horde of builders, plumbers and carpenters who were then occupying the house.

He made only a token effort at secrecy, taking Christa quite openly to dinners and receptions, where he brazenly introduced her as his translator. 'Which, my darling, you are in more ways than one,' he told her, 'since you continually translate me from this mortal plane to untold ecstasy!'

Despite herself, she smiled at the memory, seeing in her mind his smiling face with its crinkled forehead, astute blue eyes and the cleft in his chin which she told him made him look like Michael Douglas.

Once, she'd asked him if his wife knew about her.

'Not you specifically,' he'd replied, 'but she's aware I have the odd fling.'

'Fling? That's how you think of me?'

'That's how I *portray* you. It makes you sound harmless.'

'And I'm not?'

'Beloved, you're lethal!'

How, she asked herself rhetorically, could she have resisted him?

The telephone rang behind her. It was her aunt.

'Chrissie, could you be an angel and look up Roger's phone number for me? I've been meaning to ring him about the dinner all week, and keep forgetting to bring it with me. It's in my address book in my room, but I can't phone from home, since your mother's not supposed to know about it. I did try Directory Enquiries, but he's ex-directory. Must be worried about people ringing him in the night, wanting a filling!'

'OK, I'll get it.' And, discarding her memories, Christa ran down the flight of stairs to her aunt's bedroom.

'Do you think Aunt Ellie's sleeping with Mark?' Jenny asked her husband idly, as he helped her clear the table.

Oliver Drake gave a bark of laughter. 'You do come out with the most extraordinary things, darling! How the hell should I know?'

'But what do you *think?*'

'The esteemed headmistress of Rushyford High School?' he teased. 'The very idea!' Then, seeing she was determined to get an answer, he went on, 'If you want a completely off-the-cuff opinion, then I'd say yes, in all probability.'

'I often wondered,' Jenny said. 'He's been around for yonks. I wonder why they never married.'

'Perhaps they're happy as they are.' He kissed the back of her neck. 'You're turning into a veritable matchmaker, Mrs Drake. Not everyone wants to trip down the aisle, you know. Look at your sisters.'

'Oh, they'll get there in the end,' Jenny said placidly. 'Adrian will wear Laura down, and Claire *is* only twenty-one. Christa had better change her tune, though; there's not much future in going round with married men.'

'What happened there, do you know?'

'I asked Mum, and she says he was seeing someone else.'

'Apart from his wife, you mean?' Oliver asked dryly.

'Quite. What did she expect? All the same, I gather she's pretty cut up about it.'

Jenny thought for a minute about her bright, ambitious sister. Not everyone, she told herself, was as lucky as she was. She'd loved Oliver since she was fourteen, when he was a school prefect and hadn't even known of her existence. She slipped a hand in his.

'Do you think it would be stealing Mum's thunder if we told them our news at the dinner?'

'Not if we wait till the end of the meal.'

Jenny smiled. 'I wonder how she'll react to the thought of being a grandmother.'

'She'll love it,' Oliver said positively. 'The family has been your mother's whole life. She thinks the world of you all.'

'We're all she's got really, aren't we? Poor Mum, she's had a pretty raw deal, losing two husbands like that.'

'Losing' being a euphemism in both cases, Oliver thought. He remembered the gossip six years ago, which had threatened to

161

overwhelm the Nelson family. It was a wonder, really, that they'd emerged as unscathed as they had, and for that Fay deserved full credit.

'On the plus side, though,' he said, seeing his wife's momentarily downcast face, 'she has four beautiful daughters, a supportive sister and a lovely house to live in. It could be a lot worse.'

'I wonder if she'll marry Roger,' Jenny mused.

'There you go again! I tell you, you're incorrigible!'

'I just want everyone to be as happy as we are,' Jenny said simply, and gasped as her husband's arms came tightly round her, squeezing the breath out of her.

'And so do I, my love. So do I.'

'Happy birthday, Fay!'

Ellie was standing in the bedroom doorway bearing a cup of tea.

'Oh God!' Fay struggled into a sitting position, dragging a pillow behind her back. 'Ellie, I'm forty-seven! Isn't that *frightful?* Why do people persist in celebrating birthdays? They ought to go into mourning!'

'You certainly don't look it,' Ellie commented, setting the cup on the bedside table. 'And I'm still four years ahead of you, if that's any comfort.'

'You've arranged another blasted dinner,

haven't you?'

'I don't know what you're talking about.'

'Much! Is Roger coming?'

'No, unfortunately he couldn't make it. I was late contacting him, and he said that as he knew you spent your birthday with the family, he'd made other arrangements.'

'Thank God for that, at least,' Fay said devoutly, sipping her tea. 'So it's just the family?'

'Plus hangers-on, in the persons of Adrian and Roy. Fay, you will *pretend* to be surprised, won't you? Christa's gone to so much trouble.'

'Don't I always give an Oscar performance?'

There was a tap on the door, and Christa's voice called, 'May I come in?'

'Of course, darling.'

She appeared with a beautifully wrapped parcel, which she dropped on the bed as she bent to kiss her mother. 'Happy birthday, Mamita!'

'Thank you. This looks very exciting.' Fay pulled off the ribbon and tore the paper aside to reveal a gossamer nightdress nestling inside.

'For my glamorous mother!' Christa said.

Fay caught her breath, her eyes meeting Ellie's in a shared moment of flashback. The colour had drained from her face, and Christa said sharply, 'What is it, Mum?

163

Aren't you well?'

'Just a twinge of indigestion,' Fay replied with an effort. 'It's absolutely lovely, darling. Thank you.' And she reached up to kiss her daughter.

Ellie turned blindly and went out of the room. In her ignorance, she had assumed that twenty years of marriage to Patrick had diluted the shock of Jeremy's desertion. She'd been wrong; and that, she told herself in an agony of self-reproach, was why Fay never wanted to celebrate her birthday. How could she have been so crass as not to realise?

The Watermill restaurant had been sympathetically renovated, and a glass window in the foyer gave a view of the old wheel and the river Rush flowing swiftly beneath them. There were also, Claire saw, tanks of live crabs and lobsters, which she carefully avoided looking at. It might well be she would choose such a dish later, but she couldn't look her intended victim in the eye. From the humorous quirk of Roy's mouth, she knew he'd seen her evading action.

'Hypocrite!' he whispered in her ear.

They had been given a window table overlooking the river. Mrs Nelson, Roy noted, looked as attractive as ever, but there was a brittle air about her, as though at any moment she might shatter into a hundred

164

pieces. He studied her surreptitiously as they settled into their places, the soft, fly-away hair piled on top of her head, the grey, dark-lashed eyes with their faraway expression. There had, he knew, been traumas in her life, and they'd left her with a vulnerable air that was immensely appealing. Claire said she was seeing someone, and the idea of her still having a man friend at her age was strangely exciting. He could almost fancy her himself, he thought, startled.

He looked quickly away. As an only child, he was fascinated by families, the similarities and differences between the various members. This was the first time he'd met all of Claire's, and he amused himself by slotting what he knew about them into the living people across from him. Her aunt, for instance, was headmistress of the local girls' high school, and he didn't doubt that, gentle though she looked, she could exercise authority when needed. Her face was smooth and unlined, and her hair, which had probably been auburn when she was young, had leached into the pepper-and-salt of middle age. There were no rings on her fingers. How different her life had been from that of her sister.

There were a lot of sisters round this table and, of them all, only Claire and Jenny bore any real resemblance to each other. Laura, who, he remembered, ran some sort of cookery business in London, was small and dark, and he could find nothing at all in her appearance to link her with the rest of them. Christa, next to her, was the one who'd had an affair with a married man and come home to get over it. Her face had a closed, intense look, and although her eyes were the same grey as those of the younger two, her hair was several shades darker, more golden-brown than blonde. Jenny and her husband he'd met once before, and they'd got on well together. He wondered how they'd all react if they knew he and Claire were planning to move in together.

'Adrian! Fancy seeing you here!'

Roy looked up, as they all did, as a tall, florid man stopped at their table. Laura's partner pushed his chair back and took his proffered hand. 'Hello, Pete. I didn't know you were from this neck of the woods.'

'Caverstock, actually, but we've come to suss out this new joint. It's had a great write-up. How are things? I see in the press you're still making waves with your research.'

Adrian, embarrassed, turned to the rest of them. 'This is Peter Hardy; we were at school together. I can't introduce you all, but it's Mrs Nelson's birthday' – he indicated Fay, who nodded and smiled – 'and she's the mother of my girlfriend, Laura.'

166

Laura was close enough to take the hand Hardy offered her.

'Well, have a good time, all of you,' he said, and moved on to join the rest of his party, who were seating themselves at a table further down the room.

'What does Adrian do?' Roy asked Claire in an undertone as conversation resumed.

'He's a boffin of some sort, up there among the big boys. Oliver thinks he'll get the Nobel Prize one day. He adores Laura, but she's keeping him dangling.'

The menus came, and talk became general as they discussed what they would choose. Ellie kept an anxious eye on Fay. She'd felt subdued all day, consumed with guilt over having subjected her sister all these years to an annual reminder of Jeremy's perfidy. Fay was flushed already, and Ellie noted her wine glass was empty.

Orders were taken and, when it came, the food was as good as had been reported. 'I shall adapt some of the recipes myself,' Laura said. 'I'd never have thought of using those particular herbs with lamb.'

Ellie relaxed. Fay was chatting animatedly to Oliver, and everyone seemed to be enjoying themselves. As the dessert plates were removed, she excused herself and made her way to the ladies' room.

She was in one of the stalls when she heard two women come in chatting. 'Who was that man Pete stopped to talk to?' one was asking.

'Adrian Someone he was at school with. Terribly bright, it seems, but Pete always had doubts about his orientation, if you know what I mean. He must have been wrong, though; he's with his girlfriend this evening.'

'The small, dark one? Um.'

'What do you mean, "um"?'

'Well, she is rather boyish, isn't she?'

'God, you're right!' There was a short laugh; then they moved into stalls on either side of Ellie. Cold and sick, she emerged from her own, rinsed her hands, and made her escape. How *dare* they? she thought with impotent rage. How *dare* people go round spreading poisonous rumours like that, not caring who might hear them?

Her pleasure in the celebration totally gone, she returned to the table and her blissfully ignorant family; but for the rest of the evening she found it difficult to meet Adrian's eye.

Part 2 – 1994

Six

Gordon Marlow climbed the stairs to his flat on the top floor of Sandford Lodge and dropped wearily into his chair, confident there was no one to witness his breathlessness. He had firmly vetoed all Fay's attempts to install a chair-lift; he wasn't that decrepit, he'd told her, and it would ruin the appearance of the house.

He smiled to himself a little grimly, acknowledging another example of what Rita had called his fixation with Sandford – a fixation inherited by both their daughters. When, after Rita's death, Fay had suggested he came to live in what was, after all, his own house, the conversion of the top floor into a flat had been supervised with almost paranoid conformity to the original architecture; and a good job they'd made of it, he thought approvingly, looking about him. It had always felt like home. The few things from Beckhurst that he'd wanted to keep had been comfortably accommodated, and Ellie and Fay had had their pick of the rest before it went to auction. It pleased him to see glasses and dinner services still in use, both at Sandford and in Ellie's little house, which she'd bought when he came here.

It had been a good move. He'd kept his independence, but the voices of his grand-daughters drifting upstairs made him feel part of the family and prevented the loneliness he'd been dreading; and here he had been for the last nine years. Incredible to think it was so long since Rita died. When he thought of her these days, it was with a gruff tenderness that had perhaps been lacking when she was alive. They'd fought like cat and dog at times and, though basically fond of each other, could never have been called close. In particular, he'd resented her stubborn refusal to move here when his mother died, though from Fay's angle it had worked out for the best.

Fay. Frowningly he considered his favourite daughter. It had been a rum business, that. One minute she was heartbroken over that scoundrel Jeremy's defection, the next she was happily informing them she was marrying her sister's boyfriend. They'd never got to the bottom of it. Ellie had returned home unexpectedly, white-faced and uncommunicative, and even Rita, who was quite close to the girl, couldn't fathom out what had happened. It wasn't till some six months later, when the divorce had gone through, that the major shock came with the announcement of wedding plans, and they'd realised to their distress that Fay and Patrick must have come together soon after Jeremy left.

By that time, however, Ellie had recovered her equilibrium, and nothing he or Rita could say would have made any difference. Basically, too, they both liked Patrick, so after Rita's initial outburst they had held their peace, hoping that Fay's second marriage would give her much-needed stability. He had even, by default, let them go on renting the house. No point in turfing them out and having to look for new tenants, who might be dishonest, or not take care of it.

Well, he thought now, it had turned out all right and they all seemed happy enough. Patrick was a decent man, obviously devoted to Fay, and Ellie had made a good life for herself, though it was a shame she'd never married. She was shortly to be appointed headmistress of the High School, a real feather in her cap, and he was proud of her.

And Fay? No career woman there. Her life was centred on her home and family, and she tended Sandford, house and garden, as lovingly as his mother had. She had even, Gordon reflected smilingly, turned into a reasonable cook.

After his death, Sandford would go jointly to her and Ellie. She could either buy Ellie out, if her sister was agreeable, or continue paying the rent to her instead of himself. In the meantime, his dearest wish had been realised, and he was once more living in his former home. Contentedly he settled back in his chair, closed his eyes, and prepared to take his post-prandial nap.

What was she going to do about Laura? Fay asked herself distractedly as she struggled with a persistent bindweed. It broke her heart to see the girl shutting herself away from them, joining less and less in family occasions. Though Fay was devoted to all her children, Laura was Jeremy's daughter, and grew daily more and more like him. Her smile, the turn of her head, could make her mother's heart stand still.

Yet it was because she was Jeremy's daughter that the problem arose. The other three were fair, grey-eyed and tall for their age. Laura's hair and eyes were almost black, and even Claire, at fourteen, now topped her in height. More worryingly, while the two youngest were amenable enough, there had always been rivalry between Laura and Christa, Patrick's eldest daughter. In particular, they vied with each other for Fay's attention, which she found increasingly wearing. When they were younger, their fights had been physical, rolling about on the floor pulling each other's hair. Now, at eighteen and twenty,

174

they resorted to snide comments and spiteful asides – temporarily suspended, thank God, since Christa had recently left home to attend university.

Though she refrained from taking sides, it was Laura who had Fay's sympathy. Christa, she felt, could fend for herself; she had no position to defend: she was one of three. It was Laura who stood alone. Fay's heart ached to see the small hunched figure in the corner of the room, bent over a cookery book while the others exchanged gossip or watched television; but any attempt to draw her into the fold only drew attention to her apartness.

Patrick couldn't see the problem, but Fay had an ally in Ellie, who'd always been close to Laura.

'She's as prickly as a hedgehog,' she'd confided the other day. 'Whatever I say seems to be wrong, yet those huge dark eyes follow me round the room like a puppy wanting to be loved. And she *is* loved, Ellie, God alone knows how much.'

'She's loved by us,' Ellie had said shrewdly, 'but not by her father. He couldn't get away from her quickly enough. How old was she? Two weeks?'

Fay gazed at her, stricken. 'But he sends her presents,' she stammered.

'Sometimes. More often than not he forgets. I've seen that child flying out to greet the postman on her birthday, riffling through the pile of cards and parcels, and coming back to the house like a dejected sparrow because one in particular wasn't there. She's never even *seen* him, Fay, from the day he left.'

'But she has Patrick,' Fay said weakly. 'He treats her exactly like the others.'

'It's not the same.'

'You think that's what's causing all this?'

'Partly, but it's not that simple, poor love. From what she's let slip over the years, what she feels for Jeremy is a love-hate thing. She desperately wants his love, but at the same time she can't forgive him for deserting her. What's more, I think she imagines you secretly blame her for losing him.'

Fay was appalled. 'But what can I do?' she burst out. 'I can't invite him here – Patrick would go spare! Even if we met him out somewhere, he'd be furious.'

'He'd have no right to be,' Ellie retorted crisply. 'She's entitled to see her own father.'

Fay straightened from her weeding, her mind still on the conversation. Was Ellie right? Had Jeremy done Laura irreparable harm by abandoning her when he did? She had wept, constantly, for herself, without considering the effect his departure might have on his infant daughter. For a long time now she'd schooled herself not to think of Jeremy, and his name was seldom

176

mentioned. Perhaps that, too, was wrong. Perhaps she should start introducing him into the conversation, rather than avoiding the subject of her first marriage, as though it were something shameful. But how would Patrick react? She felt torn between her daughter and her husband, incapable of helping one without hurting the other, for, as she'd hinted to Ellie, Patrick remained profoundly jealous of Jeremy.

'You need never think of him again, my love,' he had said in the early days, and she soon realised that what he meant was that she *must* not. Any time Jeremy's name came up, Patrick became tight-lipped, and as soon as possible changed the subject. Perhaps he sensed she could never love him as she had her first husband.

He had adopted Laura soon after they were married, Jeremy having raised no objection. Indeed, why should he? He had no interest in the child, and the reprieve from paying maintenance for the next eighteen years was in fact a bonus.

'If she has the same name as the rest of us, she won't feel any different,' Patrick had said at the time. Now, Fay wondered cynically whether it was his way of denying Jeremy any foothold in the family and home to which Patrick had succeeded him.

She had learned a lot about her husband in twenty years. When their association had begun she'd scarcely known him, and then only as Ellie's friend. She still felt twinges of discomfort, remembering Ellie's flare-up when she realised they were seeing each other; but she'd always strenuously denied anything between herself and Patrick, and he had confirmed it. Nevertheless, Fay acknowledged privately, she'd have grabbed at him, regardless of her sister's feelings. At the time she had been distraught, desperate, needing to know that a man loved her.

Gradually, though, she'd come to appreciate there was much more to Patrick than the dentist who attended the Film Society, and some of those traits made her uneasy. She'd been surprised, for instance, by his rift from his family, which seemed all of his own making. At her insistence, his parents and his brother and wife had been invited to their wedding. She'd thought them very pleasant, but Patrick barely exchanged the time of day with them. When she'd tried to tackle him on the subject later, he had said dismissively, 'I've nothing against them; we've just grown apart, that's all.'

It was the same at the christenings, and when Fay took the children to see their grandparents, Patrick rarely accompanied them. Each year the Nelsons sent birthday and Christmas presents to all four girls, and in the thank-you letters that Fay presided over, she made a point of enclosing up-to-date photographs. Tragically, they had been killed in a car crash just before Claire's tenth birthday. She and Patrick had attended the joint funeral, but he'd shown little emotion and it was she who had cried.

Though uncomfortable with it, she'd also become accustomed to his self-containment, which at times amounted almost to secrecy. As a result, he was still capable of surprising her, as when she discovered he'd submitted a short story to a magazine.

She had walked into the spare room, now doubling as his office, as he was slipping the rejected manuscript into his desk. 'I didn't know you were interested in writing,' she'd accused him, when, reluctantly, he had admitted what it was.

'No point in broadcasting it, when I'm no good,' he'd replied.

Another time, she had overheard him speaking fluent Spanish on the phone, and stood amazed in the doorway as the lilting phrases poured effortlessly out of him. If she'd not been watching him, she wouldn't have believed it was her husband who was speaking.

'A new patient,' he'd said briefly, by way of explanation. 'He's not been in the country long, and hasn't mastered the technical dental terms.'

'But I never knew you spoke Spanish!'

'Why do you think I enjoy all those foreign

films?' he'd replied.

She'd asked Ellie about that later, but she hadn't known of his ability. 'A dark horse, your husband,' she had said.

There were times when he irritated her to distraction, Fay reflected, pulling off her gardening gloves; particularly when he displayed that streak of stubbornness, or the unwavering single-mindedness which no amount of argument or pleading could sway. All in all, though, the marriage had worked well enough, and life had proceeded on an even keel without any of the highs and lows she'd experienced with Jeremy.

As to Laura, no doubt Ellie's advice was sound, but now was not the time to reintroduce Jeremy into family conversation. Patrick had invested heavily in some shares which had unaccountably slumped, and there were also problems at the practice. As a result, he'd become increasingly irritable of late, snapping at the girls and losing his temper over trifles, though he usually apologised afterwards.

Nor could she contact Jeremy, even if she wanted to, since she was unsure of his whereabouts. He'd left Caverstock Grammar soon after they'd split up, and gone to a school near Edinburgh as PE and games master; but a few years ago, in one of his infrequent birthday cards to Laura, he'd mentioned that he was now managing a sports and leisure complex in the Midlands.

She'd make some discreet enquiries, she decided, and in the meantime try to spend more time with Laura – which, in itself, would be difficult, since she was now travelling to Caverstock each day to attend a catering college. Even as a little girl she'd been passionately interested in cookery, and by the age of eight had been producing some very acceptable meals for family supper. She was talking of starting a catering service once she qualified, which, Fay thought with a tug of the heart, no doubt meant moving to London.

She sighed, and, with none of her problems resolved, put her gardening tools away in the shed and returned to the house.

It was a Sunday afternoon in October, and Jess was coming to tea. Ellie hadn't seen her for a few weeks, and was looking forward to hearing her news.

Thank goodness she'd never confided in her about Patrick, Ellie thought as she laid the tray, though in the early days she'd been tempted more than once. It would have been good to have someone to talk to, but she'd held to her resolve, and when her world fell apart, nursed her wounded heart in private. No one, with the possible exception of Fay, had any idea she'd been in love with him, and not even Fay suspected that,

God help her, she still was. Patrick's own attitude towards her was totally relaxed. To him, she was simply a sister-in-law of whom he was fond, and he frequently confided in her when he didn't want to worry Fay.

Jess, though, had deduced that something was wrong when Ellie returned from Sandford all those years ago, and when gentle probing proved unfruitful, had taken it on herself to arrange a whole series of outings 'to take your mind off whatever's worrying you'. These excursions frequently involved a foursome with her brother Mark and his partner at the veterinary clinic, Ed Marshall, and it soon became obvious that Jess and Ed were growing close. They had married a couple of years later, and Ellie was godmother to their elder son, Dominic, now almost eighteen.

Jess had given up teaching when Dominic was born, but became restless once Lucy, her youngest, started school, and had looked round for an outside interest. When the veterinary clinic had moved to larger premises in Rushyford ten years ago, she'd persuaded her husband and brother to build on a boarding cattery. Always a cat-lover, this was now her main occupation.

As for Ellie and Mark, they had continued to see each other, becoming over the years occasional lovers as well as good friends. It was a comfortable relationship, though Ellie knew Mark would have liked it to go further. He had asked her more than once to marry him, and it did not help that she was unable to give a reason for her refusal. In fact, she was deeply resentful of her continuing fixation with Patrick, acknowledging that it was ridiculous for an intelligent, well-balanced woman to nurse this secret passion all these years. It would have been easier if one or other of them had moved away and they weren't forced into such regular contact, but for all that she should have had the strength of will to put it behind her years ago. Until she could, it would be unfair to marry Mark. He deserved better than second place.

She indulged in these little self-homilies every so often, resolved, as she might have written on a school report, to 'do better', but so far, to her chagrin, without success.

Jess duly arrived, bearing a jar of home-made plum jam and a bunch of dahlias from the garden. Her hair had turned completely white at the age of forty, and looked oddly attractive with her still-youthful face. She joked it was her sons who'd turned her white, but in fact they had been and still were delightful boys, and Ellie enjoyed their company as a respite from the totally feminine environment of both school and her own family.

'I thought we might sit outside,' she said,

putting the flowers in a vase. 'We won't be able to for much longer.' She was very proud of her small garden, and found a bout of digging therapeutic at the end of a long and sometimes frustrating day at school.

'Lovely!' Jess agreed contentedly, seating herself in a chair on the terrace. 'So, what's been happening since we last met?'

They exchanged family news while they ate. 'How's your mother?' Ellie enquired. 'I really must go over and see her.'

'She'd love you to. She's fine. Still cycling to the shops every day.'

'And she's still all right, living alone?'

'Absolutely. We keep suggesting she comes and joins us, but she won't hear of it. As you know, she's always been independent, and all her friends are in Beckhurst – she plays bridge most afternoons.'

Mark had stayed on with his mother after Jess married, and, in fact, right up until the move to Rushyford, though he'd joked to Ellie about it.

'Marry me, for God's sake!' he'd implored. 'You know what they say about middle-aged bachelors still living with their mothers.'

'No?' Ellie had replied, interested. 'What?'

But he had simply rolled his eyes at her. While the Marshalls lived in the large house that contained the clinic, he took up residence in a small cottage nearby. 'Not worth

184

buying a proper house till we get married,' he'd said. And that, Ellie reflected with a twinge of guilt, was nearly ten years ago.

'Have you heard anything of Jeremy lately?' Jess asked suddenly.

Ellie looked up, startled. 'No. What makes you ask?'

'I just wondered what he's doing these days.' She paused, and flashed Ellie a glance. 'Actually, we heard in a roundabout way that he'd left that leisure centre under something of a cloud.'

Ellie frowned. 'What kind of cloud?'

'Oh, some rather unsavoury business with one of the members. I don't know how much truth there is in it.'

'Plenty, I should think,' Ellie said flatly.

'Does Fay ever mention him?'

'As it happens she did, the last time I saw her. She's worried about Laura, and wonders if she should let the two of them meet. But if he's in trouble—'

'I don't know that it's serious,' Jess said hurriedly.

'Who was it who told you?'

'A colleague of Ed's. He's been up in Worcester at a conference, and people were talking about it. Jack only passed it on because he knew Jeremy came from round here – "Caverstock's King of Sport" and all that.'

'Gosh, that's going back a bit!'

'It might only be a rumour. I shouldn't say anything to Fay.'

'I won't, but if she starts looking for him, she might find out.'

'He never married again, did he?' Jess asked idly.

'Not as far as we know. That was the trouble: he's not the marrying sort.' If Dad hadn't thrown in Sandford Lodge, Ellie thought privately, he might not have married the first time. Then what would have happened? Would Patrick and Fay still have ended up together? In all probability, she decided.

Jess had been watching her anxiously. 'I hope I didn't speak out of turn, Ellie. Perhaps I shouldn't have said anything.'

Ellie shrugged, refilling her cup. 'It doesn't make any difference. I just hope, though, that if he *is* in trouble, Laura doesn't find out. I have the feeling she's built him up into some kind of fantasy figure: famous sportsman, injured in his prime and forced to give up – that kind of thing.'

'Well, so he was,' Jess said reasonably. 'I haven't admitted it before, but when I was at school I had a picture of him on my wall.'

Ellie laughed. *Et tu, Brute?* Well, what do you know? Still, I don't think we need worry on his behalf. Being Jeremy, he'll have some woman or other on hand to soothe his brow and offer comfort.'

Jess looked at her thoughtfully and did not reply.

Patrick said, 'Isn't Laura back yet? Her car's not there.'

Fay glanced at the kitchen clock. 'No. She didn't say she was going to be late.'

He put down his glass and picked up an envelope from the table. It was becoming a habit, Fay thought uneasily, this stopping off to pour himself a drink before even coming through to see her.

'Letter from Pammy?' he asked.

'Invitation, actually. They're having an anniversary party.'

'God, it's not their twenty-fifth already?'

'No, twenty-second, but they're having a party anyway.'

'When is it?'

'You should know – you were their best man! Two weeks on Saturday, the twenty-ninth.'

'Have we anything on?'

'No, though we'd have to go anyway. They're our oldest friends, after all. Hasn't Roger mentioned it?'

Patrick's mouth tightened. 'There hasn't been much time lately for social chat.'

'Then it's time we made some,' Fay said firmly. 'Shall we invite them round one evening?'

'Leave it for now, love. The way the two of

us feel at the moment, we're seeing quite enough of each other during the day.'

'Ah, thought I heard your voice, Patrick.' Gordon stood in the doorway.

Patrick turned, consciously controlling his irritation. It was impossible these days to have a conversation with his wife without either her father or one of the girls butting in. 'Can I get you a drink?'

'A whisky would be nice, thanks, if that's what you're having.'

Patrick walked past him out of the room. The old man always said that, as though it made any difference what Patrick was drinking. Unless, of course, it was a veiled hint that he was hitting the bottle rather too often these days. Since he'd come downstairs, they'd presumably be having his company for dinner, and a considerable part of the evening afterwards.

Not, Patrick told himself, pouring the drink, that he'd any real problem with Gordon. He was lonely, poor sod. Also, he was their landlord, and it behoved them to keep on the right side of him.

He arrived back at the kitchen, glass in hand, at the same time as his two younger daughters. 'Hey, you two, you should be upstairs doing your homework.'

'I've just finished my maths, so it seemed a good place to stop,' Jenny answered, perching on a corner of the table. 'Anyway, it's nearly dinner time, isn't it?'

'Where's Laura?' Claire asked.

'I think that was her car now,' Fay said, somewhat distractedly. 'Can you get out of my way, all of you, while I dish up?'

No one took any notice. 'Sue Parsons says her sister's had a letter from Oliver Drake,' Claire remarked to no one in particular.

'So?' queried Jenny, with heightened colour.

'Just thought you'd like to know.'

'Who's Oliver Drake, when he's at home?' Gordon asked, enjoying the family banter as he sipped his drink.

'He was a prefect last year, but he's gone to Bristol Uni. Very dishy, isn't he, Jen?'

Jenny was saved from replying by the sound of the front door bursting open and running footsteps in the hall. Laura came catapulting into the room, her usually pale face rosy and her eyes aglow.

'You'll never guess who I've been speaking to!' she announced breathlessly.

'Then tell us,' suggested Patrick, without much interest.

Laura paused, so that they all turned expectantly to look at her. 'My father!' she said, with dramatic emphasis. 'My *real* father – the legendary Jeremy Page!'

Seven

Fay put a hand behind her, feeling for the rim of the sink for support. Patrick's colour had drained away, she noticed detachedly, and her father had sat down suddenly at the kitchen table.

'*Jeremy?*' she echoed disbelievingly, and her voice cracked on the word.

Laura met her incredulous eyes with a triumphant gaze. 'Yes, Jeremy. He's back in Caverstock, and he wants to meet us all.'

'Like hell he will,' Patrick said in a low voice.

Gordon held up a hand that shook slightly. 'Hold on a minute. How did you come to meet him, Laurie? Not by chance, surely?'

'He was waiting for me when I came out of college. He knew where I was, because I'd mentioned it on my Christmas card.'

It would have been easy enough for Jeremy to pick her out, Fay thought numbly, and once he approached her, she'd have known him from photographs.

'He asked if we could go for a coffee, so we did. Mum, he's lost his job and I think he's

190

a bit hard up, though he didn't say so.'

'So he's hoping for a hand-out, is he?' Patrick demanded harshly, and immediately, seeing the astonished hurt in Laura's eyes, wished the words unsaid. 'Sorry, poppet, but he never came visiting when he was flush, did he?' Sensing her growing hostility, he softened his tone. 'Just think for a minute. You don't really want to force your mother to see him again, surely? He hurt her very badly, you know.'

Laura turned from him to Fay, appeal in her eyes. 'He asked if you were still as lovely.'

Patrick abruptly tipped his head back and emptied his glass. Then, with a challenging look at them all, he strode out of the room to refill it. No one spoke until he returned with two glasses, one of which he handed to Fay. He put an arm round her.

'All right, darling?'

'Not really, no.' Her hand was trembling so much she had difficulty holding the glass, let alone lifting it to drink. She let him lead her to the table and sit her down opposite her father.

'Well?' Laura demanded. 'Are you going to invite him, or not?'

'Not,' said Patrick.

Tears welled up in her eyes. 'I think you're all vile! You can talk to *your* father, Mum, whenever you like – and so can you two,' she

191

flung at her half-sisters, who were listening wide-eyed. 'You can't have any *idea* how I've longed to meet mine. No one even *speaks* about him – it's as though he never existed!'

'That's enough, Laura!'

'It's *not* enough! You can be as stuffy and unforgiving as you like, but *I'm* going to see him, as often as I can, and you can't stop me!'

She turned and ran out of the room, and they heard her footsteps on the stairs. So much for Ellie's love-hate theory, Fay thought numbly. Holding her glass between both hands, she finally managed to drink, feeling the spirit sear her throat. At least it dispelled the numbness, which was the intention, and she rose unsteadily to her feet.

'I'll go after her,' she said. 'Patrick, would you start serving the meal? The table's laid and you must all be hungry.'

He reached out to detain her, but she evaded his hand and went quickly from the room.

Laura was standing at her bedroom window, her arms across her chest, hugging herself. She didn't turn as the door opened, but her reflection was painted on the darkness outside. Fay went to her in silence and put her arms round her.

After a minute, still facing the window, Laura said, 'I wouldn't speak to him at first.

It was such a shock seeing him at last, and actually *smiling* at me, as though nothing had happened. I started to walk quickly away, but he caught hold of my arm and stopped me. So I ... let fly, demanding to know what right he had to walk back into my life without any warning and ... and turn everything upside down.'

Fay waited motionless, her arms tightly round the trembling body.

'But finally he broke into my ranting and more or less made me agree to go for a coffee. That was when he ... explained, or tried to.'

'What did he say?' Fay asked aridly.

'That he'd been young and irresponsible and terrified of commitment. That he'd loved you, and would have loved me too, in time, but I cried all night and he couldn't take it. And ... I can't explain it. He just kept holding on to my hand – wouldn't let me pull away – and in the end we both had tears pouring down our cheeks.'

Laura turned at last in the circle of her arms, looking at her with Jeremy's eyes. 'But I didn't mean to hurt you, Mum, and he doesn't, either.'

So the old charm still worked. Aloud, she said, 'I know, darling. Daddy's just being ... over-protective.' Or jealous.

'You will see him, won't you? We have to give him a chance.'

'I'll speak to Daddy once he's over the shock.'

'But—'

'Leave it there for now. I promise we'll consider it very carefully. Now, come down and eat. Yes' – as Laura moved in protest – 'you must. No one will say any more on the subject for the moment.'

They descended the stairs together. Jenny was carrying the plates through to the dining room. She glanced up at them, smiling at Laura. 'It's steak-and-kidney pie, your favourite,' she said.

Somehow, the meal passed. No one had much appetite and conversation was forced. When it was over, Jenny and Claire returned to their homework and Laura helped clear the table before going out to meet a girlfriend. Gordon, aware of the weighty silence between Fay and Patrick, made his excuses and returned thankfully to his flat.

Patrick had taken coffee through to the sitting room. He was in his usual chair and the television was on, but she could tell by his rigidity that he wasn't watching it. She knelt beside his chair and put her arms round him, and he convulsively pulled her closer.

'This is what I prayed would never happen,' he said against her hair.

'I know, I know. But it *has* happened, and we have to face it, for Laura's sake.'

'I've tried to be a good father to her,' he said, his voice still muffled. 'It hurts, that she hasn't thought of me as one.'

'Oh darling, of course she has! But she's always felt a bit different, I suppose, looking so unlike the others. It's only natural she should want to establish her own identity. When she was little, she used to ask questions about Jeremy all the time, until I ... more or less stopped her. I shouldn't have done.'

She paused as a memory, long-forgotten, came to her of Laura aged four or five, crimson with rage, shouting: 'You wouldn't make me do it if my *real* daddy was here!'

'If I'd talked about him more,' she ended, 'she might not have felt so desperate now.'

Patrick raised his head. 'Desperate?'

'Ellie thinks this is what's behind her moodiness, and never being quite one of the others.'

'Oh come on, you're exaggerating. I know she and Christa fight, but so do most siblings, and she gets on fine with the younger two.'

Fay sat back on her heels. 'Patrick, will you do something for me?'

'Anything in the world, you know that.'

'Will you let me invite Jeremy round?' He stiffened, and she went on quickly. 'Don't you see, it would take all the heat out of the situation? If we ask him for a meal, say, and you and Dad and the girls are all here, he'll see we're a complete and happy family. I honestly don't think he means any harm. If he's down on his luck, he'll have come home to lick his wounds, and what more natural, once he's back in the neighbourhood, than wanting to see his own daughter?'

'But how would *he* feel,' Patrick asked, 'being back here with you at Sandford?'

'Hardly with me. And if he doesn't want to come, he can say no, can't he?'

'I don't like it, Fay. He might try to worm his way in somehow.'

'Look, we're all twenty years older, and things have changed. We're not the same people we were then. He can't do anything to hurt us.'

Brave words. Fay, pleading on behalf of her daughter, was far from certain what her own reaction would be to seeing her former husband. He still invaded her dreams on a regular basis, an enigmatic figure always on the fringe, never coming completely into her field of vision.

'Just a meal, Patrick? Please?'

He sighed. 'If you really think it's necessary.' He paused. 'Will this satisfy Laura, do you think, or is she liable to keep popping off to see him all the time?'

'We'll have to wait and see. He might not be intending to stay down here for long.'

'Do you know how to contact him?'

'Laura will. I'll ask her in the morning.'

Laura flung her arms round her mother's neck. 'Oh, thank you!' she cried. 'Thank you, thank you, thank you!'

Fay smilingly disentangled herself. 'Where is he staying, do you know?'

'At the Royal. That's what made me think he was hard up.' The Royal was one of the seedier Caverstock hotels, notorious for loud discos on Saturday nights. 'Here's the number.'

She handed over a scrap of paper, and Fay's heart jerked at the familiar scrawl.

'Right,' she said, striving to sound calm. 'I'll see what we can arrange.'

She waited till they had all left the house before, for some obscure reason, going up to her bedroom and closing the door. With absurdly pounding heart she sat down on the bed, the scrap of paper in her hand, and pulled the phone towards her. Since it was still before nine, she reasoned, he was un-likely to be out. A voice answered, she asked for Jeremy, and was put through to his room.

The phone was lifted on the first ring. 'Yes?'

'Jeremy?' she said hesitantly.

'Fay?' His voice rose delightedly. 'My God, Fay – is it you?'

She moistened dry lips. 'How are you, Jeremy?'

'I never expected ... I mean, I thought I'd get a call from Laura, saying I was *persona non grata*.'

The sound of his voice after all these years vividly brought back the last time they'd spoken, that furious exchange as he'd stamped out of this very room, when she'd brought Laura back to bed in the early hours of her birthday. The memory of it clogged her throat and for a minute she couldn't speak.

Possibly he realised what she was experiencing, because he went on, 'She's a lovely girl, isn't she, Fay? A credit to you. But tell me, how are you? And Patrick? Bit of a surprise at the time, you two getting together so quickly.' There was actually amusement in his voice, damn him.

She pulled herself together. 'We're all fine. Laura will have told you we have three more daughters.' Her fingers tightened on the phone. 'In fact, we were wondering if you'd like to come over and have a meal with us.'

'Have you learned how to cook? When Laura wrote that she was attending catering college, I wondered if it was in self-defence!'

'Come and see for yourself.'

'Fay...'

His tone had altered, the teasing suddenly gone. She waited, and after a moment he went on.

'I want you to know I'm not proud of the way I behaved. It was despicable, I know. At the very least, I could have told you what I was doing, not just disappeared without a word. If it's any comfort, I've often regretted that.'

He waited for her reply, but she had none to offer. Did he expect her to say blandly that it was all right, or that it didn't matter? The words would have stuck in her throat.

'Anyway,' he went on after a minute, 'it's water under the bridge now, and I'm sure Patrick's been a better husband than I would have been.'

'You haven't said if you'll come to dinner,' she said steadily.

'How remiss of me.' His voice lightened, losing the wistful note. 'I should be delighted. When do you suggest?'

She wanted – needed – to get it over, to be able to put it behind her.

'How about tomorrow, at seven thirty?'

'That would be perfect. It's very good of you, in the circumstances.'

'We both owe it to Laura.'

'Yes,' he said soberly.

'See you tomorrow, then.' She dropped the phone back on its rest. Her heart was battering against her ribs. Across the room, she could see her reflection, still as a statue, in the dressing-table mirror. Oh God, she

199

thought, please don't let me go to pieces when I see him.

'I want Ellie to be there,' Patrick said, when she phoned to tell him of the arrangement. 'She'll be a stabilising influence.'

'I was just going to ring her,' Fay said numbly. 'Patrick, it will be all right, you know.'

'It had better be,' he said.

Roger put his head round the surgery door as he replaced the phone. 'Not more problems?'

'It never rains,' Patrick said heavily. 'The past has reared its ugly head in the shape of Jeremy Page. He's back in Caverstock.'

'Good grief! I thought he was history.'

'What's more, he's coming to dinner with us tomorrow evening. I hope it chokes him!'

Roger whistled tunelessly. 'Whose idea was that?'

'Fay's. She reckons Laura's been missing him.'

Roger raised his eyebrows. 'All her life? How can she miss what she never had?'

Patrick shrugged. 'It was Laura he contacted. Waited for her outside her college.' He ran his fingers through his hair. 'God, Roger, what am I going to do?'

'Play the host, I assume, with your usual élan. After all, what harm can he do?'

'I don't trust him. I never have.'

'Frankly, Pat, this pathological hatred of

yours has always puzzled me. If anything, you should be grateful to him. He did you the biggest favour of your life by leaving Fay.'

'It's not hatred,' Patrick said dully, 'it's fear. Surely you can see what a threat he is?'

'After twenty years?' Roger scoffed. 'Don't be ridiculous!'

'It's not ridiculous if Fay's still in love with him.'

Ellie stood listening to Fay's halting voice, the receiver clamped in her hand. So it had happened, what in her heart she had always supposed to be inevitable. Jeremy had come back. Why, and for how long, there was no way of knowing. Should she mention the rumour Jess had heard? Better not; no point in worrying Fay still further.

'Well, you were considering getting in touch with him, weren't you?' she said, deliberately downplaying the news. 'He's saved you the trouble.'

'Yes, but if I'd instigated it, I'd have had time to get used to the idea. This way, it's just been sprung on me. Ellie, I can't stop shaking! What should I wear? What can we eat, for heaven's sake? He actually had the nerve to ask if I'd learned to cook! There's a challenge, if you like; but if I go for something too complicated, I'll get in a panic and it will all go wrong.'

201

'Do a casserole,' Ellie advised. 'The preparation will be over long before the meal, and it will simply cook itself in the oven.' Inspiration struck. 'And why not let Laura do the sweet? She'd love to show off to Jeremy, and it would save you the hassle.'

'Ellie, you're a genius!' Fay said gratefully. 'By the way, Patrick insists that you join us.'

'A royal command?'

'Sorry; what I mean is, he'd very much like you to be there. As a "stabilising influence".'

'Nice to know my function in life,' Ellie said dryly. 'Of course I'll come. I wouldn't miss it for the world.'

Fay moved through the rest of that day on autopilot. She changed the projected menu several times, adjusting her shopping list until it was almost illegible. Finally, to end any further prevaricating, she drove to the shops and bought the ingredients.

Back home, she went several times to her wardrobe, surveying its contents and trying to decide which garment would be the most appropriate. She mustn't appear to make a special effort, she told herself, but of course she wanted to look her best. Eventually, after trying on a variety of clothes and discarding them as unsuitable, she selected a green woollen dress with a gold belt which emphasised her still-slender waist. Holding it against herself in front of the mirror, her eyes were drawn to the thin gold chain round her neck, which she never took off: Jeremy's last present to her. Would he recognise it? She considered removing it, then discounted the idea. It might cause comment from the family, who had never seen her without it, and in any case would be emphasising its importance. Of their own accord, her fingers went up to the fine links. Had he been intending to leave her when he bought it?

Impatiently she turned from the mirror, hung the dress back in the wardrobe, and went downstairs to begin preparing the meal.

Laura leant over the dressing table and studied her reflection for signs of resemblance to her father. It was mainly the eyes, she decided, though she'd also inherited his build. Used to Patrick's height, she'd been oddly disappointed by Jeremy's short stature. He was about the same height as her mother, five foot six or so, while she herself, the feminine equivalent, was little over five feet. No wonder her half-sisters towered over her.

She tried, without much success, to consider him dispassionately. Though not as famous as he'd once been, he was still handsome and undeniably attractive. She had noticed the other women in the café looking at him. A father, then, to have been proud of

– if he hadn't deserted them. Could she ever forgive him that? Could her mother? How would the family react to him, Dad in particular? And what, she thought in sudden panic, should she call Jeremy? Patrick had been 'Daddy' all her life. She couldn't snatch it away from him.

Her father was coming, she told herself, still, in this familiar room, unable to believe it. In an hour or so, he would be here. Unable to concentrate on her work, she'd left college early, though the main reason was that she'd still had the mango-and-passion-fruit shortbread to make. Mum had only asked her to do the desserts when she'd arrived home last night, and what with having to wait for the meringues, the banana ice-cream cake had taken most of the evening. All was done now, though, and leaving the shortbread, crisp and golden, to cool on the counter, she had had a long and leisurely bath while she tried to decipher her emotions.

It was as a direct result of her begging that Jeremy was coming this evening. Now, too late, she had reservations, fearful that in her mind Sandford would be for ever stamped with memories of him moving around in it – in the sitting room, seated at the dining table. It was *their* house, not his; he had long since given up any right to it. Yet the fact remained that for seven short months he had lived here, breakfasted each morning in the kitchen, slept with her mother in the main bedroom. She flushed as an unwelcome picture of them together filled her mind.

Suppose the evening went horribly wrong, there was an almighty row and Dad flung him out of the house? It would all be her fault.

Downstairs, she heard the front door open and Aunt Ellie's voice in the hall. Thank God she was here, Laura thought on a wave of relief. Ellie had been her rock throughout her uncertain childhood and difficult teens. She could still be relied on. With a last look in the mirror, Laura went down to greet her.

He had not changed much in appearance, Ellie thought. If anything, the touches of silver at his temples and the lived-in creases of his face made him the more attractive; and of them all, she noted wryly, he seemed the most at ease. Fay was brittle, her father hostile, Patrick stiff, Laura on edge. Giving them time to adjust, Jeremy had turned his attention to the younger girls, and Jenny, at sixteen, was responding, Ellie saw with a tug of the heart, with a woman's awareness, evidenced by her sparkling eyes and glowing cheeks. Even Claire, initially shy, was now laughing and chattering as though she'd known him all her life.

And I, Ellie thought sardonically, the spinster schoolmistress, am like the Greek chorus, observing all from the sidelines. Metaphorically speaking, of course. Heaven forbid there was a tragedy to be played out here. A sudden shiver ran down her back, surprising her.

Patrick turned to her. 'Cold, Ellie? The heating should have come on at six, but—'

'I'm fine,' she said quickly. 'Just someone walking over my grave.' Or someone else's. She shook herself. What *was* the matter with her? She stole another look at Jeremy, seated diagonally opposite her and possibly, she thought with sudden perception, not quite as relaxed as he appeared. His body language indicated that he was very much aware of Fay, next to him at the head of the table; and she, doubtless, of him. Light touch paper and retire.

'The last we heard of you, Jeremy,' Patrick was saying a little too heartily, 'you were running some sort of leisure complex in the Midlands.'

'That's right.' Jeremy toyed with his glass. 'I built the place up for them and ran it for five years. Then there was a disagreement over policy, and I was shown the door. There ain't no justice.'

Not the story Jess had heard. 'So what are your plans now?' Ellie asked. Aware of what this evening was costing Patrick, the least she could do was support him by keeping the conversation going. In any case, she was curious.

'Frankly, I haven't any. It only happened a few weeks ago, and I'm still getting my head round it. Besides, it's not easy finding anything to suit me at my age. At forty-five, I'm somewhat long in the tooth for the kind of work I've been doing. I rather hoped Caverstock Grammar might come up trumps, but they didn't want to know.'

'You can still coach, surely?'

'Of course I can. But I did rather drop them in it, all those years ago, when a better offer came up. Now, they're taking their revenge.'

Claire said suddenly, 'There was a programme on TV a few weeks ago about the Olympics in the '60s and '70s. They showed you winning your medal.'

Jeremy smiled at her. 'Well, perhaps that will jog a few memories.'

'Have you still got it?'

'Somewhere, no doubt.'

'I'd love to see it.' She flushed, suddenly unsure how long this uneasy truce would last. 'I mean, if that's all right.'

'Provided I can find it, of course you can,' Jeremy said easily. 'Remember when I hung it round your neck, Fay?'

Fay's face flamed, and Ellie didn't doubt the comment had sexual connotations.

What a bastard the man was, seated at Patrick's dining table, next to his wife. He was playing with them all, but with what end in view?

Fay stood up. 'Laura provided the sweet course this evening,' she said ringingly. 'Help me clear the plates, darling, and we'll bring it in.'

There was a distraction while the dinner plates were passed down the table.

'Best beef burgundy I've had in years,' Jeremy said, smiling up into Fay's still flushed face. 'Congratulations to the chef.'

She gave him a tight smile and carried the plates out of the room, followed by Laura with the vegetable dishes. Patrick's hands were tightly clenched beneath the table.

'And what about you, Patrick?' Jeremy asked in a drawl. 'Still pulling out the old molars?'

'Among other things.'

'Lucky you. At least no one's likely to tell you you're past it.'

'It's not all plain sailing,' Patrick said shortly. 'For one thing, it's getting harder and harder to treat National Health patients these days.'

'No problem: let them go private. Rushyford residents are pretty well-heeled.'

'Something of an overstatement, I'm afraid.'

Fay and Laura returned, bearing the

spectacular ice-cream cake and the plate of shortbread layered with golden fruit.

'Wow!' Jeremy exclaimed. 'Will you look at that? Are you saying my little girl made these?'

Patrick's correction came like a gunshot. 'She said Laura did.'

There was a taut silence; then Jeremy continued, unabashed, 'I'm spoilt for choice. I hope I can sample some of each?'

'Of course.' Laura was flushed with pleasure, though the look she darted at Patrick was one of apology.

Gordon, breaking a silence that had lasted for most of the meal, evidently decided it was time to make a contribution. 'The England team's not doing too well in Perth,' he commented. Sport had always been a safe topic with his ex-son-in-law.

Jeremy grinned. 'So what's new?'

The change of subject had the desired effect, and discussion of sport in its various guises carried them safely through the remainder of the meal. At eleven o'clock, Jeremy rose to his feet.

'Well, I must be on my way. Thank you all for a very pleasant evening and a delicious meal.' He put an arm round Laura's shoulders and gave her an affectionate squeeze. 'Can I offer anyone a lift home?'

Ellie said, 'I'm the only one who doesn't live here, and I have my car, thanks.'

'Oh?' His eyes went to Gordon. 'I hadn't realised. The landlord has come home to roost, eh?'

'In a manner of speaking,' Gordon said. 'We've turned the top floor into a flatlet. It's worked very well.'

'I'd be interested to see it sometime.'

No one took him up on that, but Jeremy, apparently not expecting them to, was already walking out of the room. Fay went with him, Patrick following behind. As she opened the front door, he reached out a hand and lightly touched the chain round her neck.

'Pretty,' he commented and, leaving her wondering whether or not he had recognised it, walked over to his car, which was parked behind Ellie's. As he opened the door, he looked back.

'Thanks again,' he said. 'I've enjoyed myself. See you.' And he got inside.

Fay felt Patrick's arm come possessively round her, and they stood together watching as the car went slowly down the drive, its headlamps carving a yellow path out of the darkness. Only when its tail lights had turned out of the gate and disappeared did they go back into the house.

Eight

It came as no surprise to Fay, a few days later, to find Jeremy on the doorstep.

'Don't shut the door,' he said quickly, when she answered his ring.

'I wasn't going to.' She waited, her hand still on the doorknob. She was alone in the house – even her father had gone out bowling – and she had no intention of inviting him in. Her racing heart left no doubt of the power he still had over her.

'I wondered if you'd come for a drive with me – for auld lang syne?' He indicated his car at the gate.

'That would set the tongues wagging, wouldn't it?'

His mouth twitched. 'You could wear dark glasses and a wig. Where's your sense of adventure?'

'It's given way to self-preservation. You left me to pick up the pieces once before. I'm not risking it again.'

'I was a bloody fool,' he said softly. 'When I saw you the other night...' He held a hand up as she stiffened and moved to close the

211

door. 'All right, all right, you don't want to hear my problems, and I've already said I'm sorry. But can't we put that behind us and be friends? For Laura's sake?'

'You and I could never be friends, Jeremy.'

For a long moment their eyes held. Then he sighed. 'No, you're right. For one thing, I'd never be able to keep my hands off you.'

She stepped back, and the gap between door and frame narrowed. 'Just one thing,' she said breathlessly. 'If you hurt Laura *in any way*, I'll kill you.'

He raised his eyebrows. 'Why should I hurt Laura?'

'Why, indeed? Just remember what I said.'

The door closed between them. Motionless, she waited, and after a minute his footsteps sounded on the gravel. She sank to the floor and put her head in her hands, as memories she'd tried for twenty years to bury swarmed back to torment her: his first, drunken kiss at the tennis club and its devastating effect; his slow courtship and her growing impatience; the first time they'd made love by the stream, when Laura had been conceived, and all the other times they'd lain together in the bedroom she now shared with Patrick. And here she was, experiencing that same gnawing hunger for him, unalleviated by the passage of time.

Softly and despairingly, she began to weep.

* * *

Afterwards, it seemed to Ellie that the next six weeks were a breathing space, a marking time while they all waited to see what would happen. That something must was beyond dispute. With Jeremy still in the neighbourhood and showing no signs of leaving, it was like living on the edge of a precipice. A strong gust of wind, one loose stone, and they'd all go hurtling over the edge. Nor could she forget her presentiment at the dinner party, a conviction that tragedy lay in wait.

Laura alone seemed untroubled – in fact, happier than Ellie could remember. For some years now, she'd fallen into the habit of phoning every few weeks to invite herself to Ellie's for Sunday tea. Those visits away from the ever-constant presence of parents and sisters provided a much-needed oasis, and had in fact become precious to both of them. Many confidences had been shared as Laura progressed awkwardly from childhood to rebellious teens, and now they met as equals.

It was on one such Sunday that Ellie learned she was meeting Jeremy regularly for lunch, sometimes as often as twice a week. 'We've so much catching up to do,' Laura said artlessly. 'And I've offered to try to help him find a job.'

'Here?' Ellie asked sharply.

'Wherever one's going. The location's not important; we won't lose touch again. Anyway, once I've qualified, I'll be off to London.'

'Isn't he capable of finding something for himself?' Ellie heard the acid in her voice, and Laura reacted defensively.

'Of course he is, but he was getting a bit discouraged – you heard him at dinner – and with two of us working at it, we can speed things up.'

Typical of Jeremy to let someone else do the groundwork. 'So how are you going about this job-hunting?' Ellie asked after a minute.

'*Yellow Pages* mainly, but I've one or two contacts. I've already been through all the schools, sports clubs, leisure centres and so on. Nothing positive yet, but there are several hopefuls. He's going along for a couple of interviews next week.'

'What do your parents think of all this?'

'They're not interested – or pretend they're not. My father invited us to dinner, but they made excuses. I think he was rather hurt.'

Laura always referred to Jeremy as 'my father'. Dad, or Daddy, was reserved for Patrick, and she couldn't bring herself to use his first name. With all the divorced families around, Ellie thought impatiently, some standard form of address should have evolved. 'Daddy Jeremy', for instance? Heaven forbid!

'Actually,' Laura was continuing, 'they don't seem interested in anything at the moment. They went to Roger and Pammy's anniversary party last night, and you'd have thought they were off to a funeral.'

The next morning, during break, Ellie phoned Fay. She was not breaking confidences – Laura had told her parents she was seeing Jeremy – and she wanted to share her concern.

Cutting through Fay's greetings, she came straight to the point. 'You do know Laura's trying to find Jeremy a job?'

'She mentioned it, yes. I don't think she's having much luck.'

'And that she's meeting him regularly for lunch?'

Fay said waspishly, 'Well, this is what you wanted for her, isn't it?'

'Suppose she *does* find something – or he does himself – and he stays in the district?'

There was a brief pause, then Fay said tightly, 'We'll have to face that when and if it comes.'

Ellie gave up.

She had seen Patrick twice since the dinner party, on each occasion when he dropped in on the way home from work – though since her house was over the river, it was hardly 'on the way'. He seemed increasingly stressed, and she thought he'd lost weight.

'What's wrong, Patrick?' she asked eventually. She had poured them both a whisky and they were sitting by the fire in her cosy little room, while the November rain lashed the glass behind the drawn curtains.

He took a sip of his drink. 'Everything, since you ask. Everything's absolutely bloody.'

'Specifically?'

'Well, for a start things are going from bad to worse at the practice. Ron – one of our dental mechanics – fouled up an expensive job and it's had to be done again; and even more serious, there seems to be some money missing. The receipt books aren't numbered, and it looks as though some stubs have been pulled out and the money pocketed. There's even the suggestion that signatures on cheques have been forged.'

'Who could be responsible for that?' Ellie asked worriedly.

'The receptionist on the front desk handles the cash and cheques. She's been with us a couple of years – it's the hell of a delicate situation. Quite honestly, Ellie, I've had enough. For two pins I'd throw the whole thing up.'

'You don't mean that,' she said gently.

'But I do. Work has become a slog recently, with pretty little satisfaction at the end of it. Then, when I get home...' He broke off.

'Yes?'

'Well, let's just say it's not a bed of roses there at the moment – hasn't been for some time.'

Ellie frowned. 'When did this start?'

'Oh, Fay's been touchy for a while now, jumping down my throat for no reason.' He shot her a glance. 'I feel guilty saying that – I wouldn't to anyone else, but ... oh God, I don't know. It's hard to tie down, because it's not consistent. Sometimes we're OK for weeks on end and I think I must have imagined it, but overall things have been going downhill for a year or two.'

'I'm so sorry, I didn't realise.' And she should have done, Ellie thought furiously. At least Jeremy's reappearance wasn't to blame, though it couldn't have helped.

'She's been worrying about Laura, I know,' Patrick was going on. 'Well, that at least is over. She's a different girl, now she's found her beloved father.' There was bitterness in his voice.

'She said he invited you to dinner.'

He slammed his hand on the arm of the chair. 'If Jeremy Page thinks we're embarking on a social round with him, he can think again. I can't stop Laura seeing him, but I'm damned if I'm going to give him a seal of approval.'

He ran a hand over his face, and Ellie

ached to comfort him. 'He won't stay long,' she said soothingly. 'He can't find work – there's nothing for him here.'

As soon as she said it, she could have bitten her tongue. Patrick immediately took her up on it. 'There's Laura,' he said heavily. 'And Fay.'

'Fay?' Ellie looked at him in dread.

'She still loves him, Ellie. She always has. Now he's come back, perhaps I should just get the hell out and leave them to it.'

'That's nonsense,' Ellie said sharply. But was it? There had been that electric charge between the two of them over dinner. Yet even Fay couldn't be so completely addle-brained as to get involved with Jeremy again.

She leant forward, clasping her hands. 'You're going through a bad patch, that's all, and it's getting you down. What you need is a break. Can't you get away for a weekend, just the two of you? That might be all it takes to set things right.'

'There's still the practice.'

'Talk to Roger about it – thrash it out between you. For heaven's sake, you've known him long enough. Surely you can be frank with each other.'

He looked at her for a moment, then gave a brief laugh. 'I should have married you,' he said. 'If I hadn't met Fay, I might well have done.'

Ellie forced a laugh. 'For want of anything better?'

He smiled wearily. 'You know I didn't mean that. I've always found you easier to talk to than Fay.'

'That's because your emotions aren't involved,' she said matter-of-factly.

'Whatever the reason, I value your advice, Ellie. Come to that, I value *you*.'

Enough. He was in danger of becoming maudlin. 'Well, that's nice to know. I value you, too, but that's not going to stop me packing you off home. Fay will be wondering where you are. And remember what I said about a weekend away.'

They both stood up. 'I'll see what I can do. Bless you, Ellie.'

'You too,' she said.

It was Dominic Marshall's eighteenth birthday and, following a disco party the previous evening, a more sedate lunch was being held on the Sunday for family and godparents. The latter were represented solely by Ellie and Mark, one godfather having emigrated to Canada some ten years previously. He had, however, sent a handsome cheque in final discharge of his duties.

Ellie always enjoyed her visits to the Marshall household, feeling herself to be almost a member of the family. The house was comfortably shabby and untidy, with piles of veterinary magazines on the floor, together, as often as not, with saucers of water or milk, a potential hazard to the unwary, for the benefit of some orphaned or recuperating creature that was being given temporary residence.

The Marshall boys, Dominic and Matthew, were, like their father, several inches over six feet, with shocks of brown hair and loose-limbed frames. Ellie always feared for their heads when they came through the door, but at the last minute they unfailingly ducked.

She was admitted on this occasion by Lucy, the youngest member of the family, who was in Jenny's class at Rushyford High and who now looked very much as her mother had when Ellie first met her.

'Come through,' Lucy invited. 'We're all in the sitting room.'

Ellie submitted herself to the usual Marshall greeting, involving enthusiastic bear hugs and exclamations of delight, after which, dextrously avoiding several pitfalls on the carpet, she joined Alice Ridley, seated in an armchair by the fire.

'Ellie, my dear!' Alice raised her face for Ellie's kiss. 'It seems an age since I saw you.'

'*Mea culpa*, I'm afraid. I was saying as much to Jess.' And that, she realised guiltily, was over a month ago.

'So tell me the news. I hear about school

from Lucy, but how's the family?'

Ellie hesitated. 'Fine,' she said cautiously.

'Ah – wait a minute – I remember now. Hasn't your sister's first husband put in an appearance? That must be rather awkward for you.'

'Actually we've only met him once, when Fay and Patrick invited him to dinner, and it all passed off well. Laura's seen more of him, of course. It's wonderful for her to have a chance to get to know him at last.'

Alice looked concerned. 'I shouldn't have thought that was necessarily a good thing, in the circumstances.'

Ellie looked at her in surprise. 'What circumstances, Alice? She *is* his daughter, after all.'

'Yes, my dear, but if what they say is true—'

'Mother, I'm sorry to interrupt, but I could do with Ellie's assistance in the kitchen.' Jess stood over them, face flushed, and Ellie, puzzled, caught the warning glance she flashed her mother. What had Alice been about to say?

She followed Jess out to the large, rambling kitchen. 'If she was going to mention about Jeremy being sacked,' she said mildly, 'I already know. You told me yourself.'

'What?' Jess still appeared flustered. 'Oh, no, it wasn't that. I meant it – I really could do with some help. Would you mind

221

watching that pan? It's caught once already, and I need to see to the vegetables.'

And she turned away, leaving Ellie, unconvinced, to do as she was asked. She was still stirring when, minutes later, Mark came breezing in.

'Sorry I'm late, everyone; I'm on call this weekend. How's my favourite teacher?'

He put his arms round Ellie from behind and kissed the back of her neck.

'All the better for seeing you,' Ellie replied. And meant it.

During lunch everyone cheerfully talked at once, and Ellie had no chance for a private word with Alice. In fact, the old lady seemed a little subdued – chastened, perhaps, by her daughter's silent reprimand. As usual, the meal was substantial, catering for the four large men in Jess's life, and Ellie was amazed, as always, at the amount they managed to consume. It was at such times that she most regretted not having married and had a family of her own. Today, the sense of loss was especially strong, and an unaccustomed wave of sadness came over her.

Dessert followed, lashings of apple pie with cream, a pavlova, and a sherry trifle, all of which disappeared like snow in summer. Unusually, though, despite the laughter and companionship, Ellie's depression did not lift. It was Alice's hastily suppressed comment that had triggered it, serving to underline her own uneasiness at Laura's growing closeness to Jeremy. In addition, there was Patrick's unhappiness, previously unsuspected, and the worry about Fay and how all this was affecting her. It seemed suddenly that the foundations of her world were shifting and all was not as it seemed.

'You're very quiet today, Godmother,' Mark commented over coffee, and Ellie flushed as they all turned to look at her.

'Sorry,' she murmured, embarrassed. 'I've rather a headache, that's all.'

'In which case,' Alice said sympathetically, 'this is definitely not the place to be!'

'Would you like me to take you home?' Mark enquired.

'No, no, I wouldn't dream of breaking up the party. But I think perhaps, if you'll all excuse me, I will be making a move. It's been lovely, and I've really enjoyed it.'

'I'll walk you back,' Mark said firmly, and this time she didn't protest.

The Marshalls lived less than half a mile from Ellie, and as it had been fine when she left home, she had come on foot. Now, however, a mist was drifting in and the after-noon was already darkening. Mark tucked her arm through his and they set off briskly down the pavement.

'Amazing to think Dom's eighteen,' he commented. 'I remember the night he was born. I'd been attending a difficult delivery of eight piglets, and Jess wasn't best pleased when I said it had been harder for the sow!'

'I shouldn't think she was!'

Their footsteps rang in the deserted street. Lighted windows glowed through the mist, offering glimpses of families spending Sunday afternoon together. Ellie had seldom felt more alone. When they reached her gate, she turned to Mark with a bright smile.

'Thanks for seeing me home, Mark.'

He stood looking down on her. 'Are you going to tell me what's wrong?'

'I did tell you, I...'

'A diplomatic headache, yes. But I mean the truth?'

Her eyes dropped and he said quietly, 'May I come in?'

She nodded, and he followed her up the path, waiting while she unlocked the door. A wave of warmth came to meet them, and Ellie felt her usual surge of affection for the small hallway and the welcoming room that awaited them.

Mark followed her into the kitchen, watching as she filled a kettle and put out cups and saucers. 'Coffee always makes me thirsty,' she said. 'I need a cup of tea.'

When it was ready, he carried the tray through and put it on the low table in front of the gas fire. 'Now,' he said, 'no more prevarications. What's the matter?'

She was silent as she poured the tea, wondering how much to tell him without breaking any confidences.

'Family problems?' he asked shrewdly. 'To do with Jeremy Page's return?'

'Partly,' she said on a sigh.

'Would it help to talk about them? You know my lips would be sealed.'

'There's not really much to tell – just an overall feeling that something awful's lying in wait.'

He smiled. 'Been reading the tea-leaves?'

'It's ridiculous, really; I'd been telling Fay Laura should have contact with her father, but what I had in mind was regular letters and phone calls, with the occasional meeting in London or somewhere neutral. I certainly didn't envisage this ... this total immersion. He's a pretty ruthless character, for all his laid-back, easy-going manner, and I'm terrified he'll let her down in some way.'

'But he's not back here permanently, is he?'

'I don't know. Laura's trying to find him a job.' She put her cup down and looked across at him. 'Mark, do you know why he left the Midlands?'

'Trouble with a member of the leisure club, wasn't it? I only heard about it third-hand. Why? What relevance can that have to anything?'

'I don't know. But I think your mother was going to say something before lunch, and Jess stepped very smartly in and swept me off to the kitchen.'

'I wondered what you were doing there. Jess doesn't usually enlist visitors' help.'

'I'm sorry I was such a damp squib. I just suddenly felt it was all ... getting on top of me.'

'Poor Ellie – always taking the world's troubles on your shoulders.'

And he knew only a fraction of it. There was also Fay, and Patrick...

'Mark...'

'Um?'

'What are your plans for the rest of the day?'

'Well, I'm on call' – he patted his mobile – 'but I'm not expecting any emergencies, so most probably an evening slobbing out in front of the telly.'

'Could you possibly slob out here?'

He looked at her enquiringly. 'Yes, of course, if you'd like me to.'

'I think I'd like some company tonight.'

'Tonight?' A grin spread across his face. 'Are you by any chance propositioning me, Miss Marlow?'

She smiled back at him, her spirits suddenly lifting. 'I rather think I am,' she said.

Caverstock looked its best at this time of the

year, Laura thought, as she hurried along the pavement. There were Christmas decorations strung across the road and the shop windows had turned into Aladdin's caves, piled high with gold, jewels and crystal. It had turned suddenly colder, and frost still lay in the shadows.

She smiled to herself, thinking of the gold cufflinks she had just bought for her father. It was too bad their lunch had had to be cancelled again, though great he was going for another interview, and at least it had given her the chance to shop. She'd asked him what he was doing for Christmas, but he'd been vague, saying only that he'd been in touch with 'a couple of guys' he used to share a flat with. She'd gathered both were married, and doubted whether any hospitality would stretch to Christmas dinner. She wished passionately that he could come to Sandford, but knew it to be out of the question. Her parents' attitude had hardened since the dinner party, as though they felt they'd done all that was required of them, and admittedly the atmosphere had been strained ever since.

She turned into one of the department stores, emerging through the swing doors adjacent to a coffee bar, where muffled shoppers sat on high stools, clasping hot mugs to warm their hands; and there at the far end, to her bewilderment, was Jeremy.

She hurried over to him. 'Hello! Was the interview cancelled?'

He turned quickly, and she caught a flash of what looked like alarm before he smiled at her. 'Hi there, cherub! What are you doing here?'

'I might ask the same of you. You stood me up for lunch, remember.' She hitched herself on to a vacant stool beside him.

'Sorry about that; the interview was postponed till this afternoon, but it was too late to contact you.'

'Well, I can at least join you for coffee.'

He glanced over her shoulder towards the door. 'Actually, I'm just going. I have to get across town by two.'

She stifled her disappointment. 'Who is it you're seeing today?'

'Oh, just someone Danny Martin put me in touch with – that guy I was telling you about.'

'Who you used to share with?'

'That's right. Sorry, love, I really must go. I'll let you know how I get on.'

And before she could reply, he had kissed her cheek, slipped off the stool, and disappeared into the crowd of shoppers.

'Coffee?' asked the sullen girl behind the counter.

'No, thanks.' Laura in turn slid to the floor and, feeling oddly deflated, made her way back to college.

* * *

Gordon sat staring morosely at his daughter across the kitchen table.

'Not in any better mood, I see,' he commented.

'I've a lot on my mind,' Fay snapped, spearing a tomato with her fork, 'and you're not helping, with your constant nagging.'

He ignored her. 'It's that scoundrel Page, I suppose.'

'Father, really!'

'It's no use "Father, reallying" me. I might be old, but I'm not blind and I'm not a fool. You've been like a cat on hot bricks ever since he reappeared.'

'That's not true! It's Patrick I'm worried about; he's having a bad time at work.'

'And at home too, judging by what comes floating upstairs. I can hear you rowing, you know, night after night.'

'We're not rowing,' Fay began, then came to a halt. What was the use? Why bother denying everything he said, when he was right, and knew it. 'Oh God!' she said rockily, putting down her fork.

He reached a scrawny hand across the table. 'I'm not getting at you, girl. I'm worried, that's all.' He paused. 'You never got over him, did you? Not really?'

Mutely she shook her head.

'I said as much to your mother, when you married Patrick. "On the rebound," I said,

229

"that's what it is. She doesn't love him."
And you didn't, did you?'

'Not then,' Fay admitted, fumbling for a
handkerchief.

'And now?'

'Oh, I love him now, of course I do.'

'But not the way you loved Jeremy?'

She didn't reply.

'Trouble is, the poor devil knows it. That's
why he's on hot bricks too. Not going to do
anything foolish, are you?' he added anxiously.

She shook her head, not looking at him.

'Even though you want to?'

She looked up then, her eyes wide, and he
smiled.

'I might be an old codger, but I've been
there in my time. I know all about the lusts
of the flesh, as they put it in the Bible, and
how strong they can be.'

He saw that he had surprised her, and
smiled inwardly. She was not to know he
was thinking not of her mother but of a girl
he'd met during his National Service, a
young WRAC who'd been in the same
camp. God, it was an age since he'd thought
of Molly, but she could still make his heart
race, pathetic old fool that he was.

Fay slipped off her chair, went round the
table and laid her cheek on his grizzled
head. 'I do love you, Dad,' she said.

Nine

Jenny looked up from her cereal to see Patrick standing uncertainly in the doorway.

'I thought you'd gone, Dad. What have you forgotten?'

'I'm not sure. I came back for something, but I'm damned if I can remember what.'

'Your briefcase?' she suggested, catching sight of it propped against the fridge.

His face cleared. 'Thanks, love.'

He retrieved it and hurried out of the room.

'Alzheimer's!' Claire said flippantly, but Jenny was frowning.

'Don't joke about it,' she said sharply. 'I don't like to see him like this. That's the third time this week he's forgotten something. He missed the parents' evening, and he was going out in his slippers yesterday, till Mum stopped him.'

Claire wasn't interested. 'Oh damn!' she exclaimed, clapping a hand to her forehead. 'It's Wednesday and I've not done my French homework. I'll be shot!' She looked at the clock on the wall and pushed back her chair. 'Come on, Jen, snap out of it! We'll miss the bus at this rate.'

Cramming the last piece of toast into her mouth, Jenny hurried out of the kitchen after her.

Christa took a sip of her cocoa. She was in the common room at the halls of residence, and they'd been discussing their plans for the coming holidays. So far, she hadn't joined in.

'You're very quiet, Chrissie,' Linda Barber commented. 'Have you anything lined up?'

'Not really; I think I'm going to have to play it by ear.'

She hadn't told anyone about Jeremy Page's return, but it had been very much on her mind, and she wished vehemently that she'd been there to meet him. What did he look like? How had Mum been with him? She'd tried to imagine how she would feel if someone she'd loved all those years ago suddenly reappeared, and felt a prickle of unease. Life at home was so safe and predictable; she didn't want any stranger disrupting it. And what about poor Dad? He must have thought he'd heard the last of Jeremy Page long since.

'How do you mean, play it by ear?' That was Sally Frost, her freckled face curious.

Christa hesitated. As the time for going home approached, her apprehension was

232

steadily increasing. It might be good to talk it over, somehow defuse it in her mind.

'There have been ... developments at home in the last few weeks.'

Instantly she had everyone's attention. 'What kind of developments?'

'Why, what's happened?'

She looked round at their expectant faces. 'My mother's ex has reappeared on the scene.'

'So?' Sally again. '*My* mother's ex is always popping up, and my father's, too.'

'This is different,' Christa said with difficulty. 'Nothing's been heard of him for twenty years, except the odd card to my half-sister.'

'He's not your father, then?'

'No, no relation at all, which is odd, really, considering *my* father is *his* daughter's step-father.'

'You've lost me!' Jane Birdsall said comically.

'Actually,' Christa added, 'he was quite famous in his day. His name's Jeremy Page; have you heard of him?'

Nobody had.

'Well, he won a medal in the '68 Olympics, and played cricket for his county, and Lord knows what else. But he was injured in a car crash and that scuppered his sporting career.'

'Oh, yes,' Linda broke in. 'I remember

now; there was something about him on TV a few weeks ago. He looked quite dishy!'

'That was then,' Jane said dampeningly.

'So you've never met him?' Linda pursued.

'No, none of us had – not even Laura. He left when she was a baby, and she's been bitter and twisted about it ever since.'

'I don't blame her,' someone muttered.

'Then why has he suddenly reappeared?' Sally demanded. 'Is he planning to seize your mother and ride off with her into the sunset?'

Someone giggled with embarrassment, and Christa flushed. 'All I know is that he's out of work. Mum played the whole thing down on the phone; it was my younger sister who filled me in. She said Laura made them invite him to dinner.'

'Will he be spending Christmas with you?'

'I don't know,' Christa said, hating the thought. 'That's what I meant about playing it by ear.'

'Well,' Jane remarked, standing up and collecting their mugs, 'we'll be waiting with bated breath to hear what happens!'

Which, Christa reflected as she went up to bed, hadn't really helped much after all.

'I bumped into Fay at the shops,' Pammy Hastings remarked to her husband over lunch. 'We had a coffee together.'

'How was she?' Roger asked, helping himself to more pie.

'Nervy, I think, is the best description. She wasn't really concentrating on what I was saying; her eyes kept flicking about all over the place.'

'Well, you can go on rather!' Roger said with a grin.

'Seriously, I think this business with Jeremy is getting her down.'

'What business? As far as we know, they've only seen each other once.'

'But Laura's really hooked on him, isn't she? She can hardly speak of anything else.'

'Only natural, I suppose, meeting him after all these years.'

Pammy flashed him a glance. 'How's Patrick coping?'

'Not well, since you ask.'

'I thought he looked very strained at the party – they both did. Has he said anything?'

He hesitated, and Pammy said impatiently, 'For God's sake, Roger, you can tell *me!*'

'He said he thinks Fay still loves Jeremy.'

Pammy let out her breath on a sigh. 'And do you?'

'Good God, how should I know? I've never seen them together. In fact, I've only seen Jeremy once in my life, in the pub that time, when he was married to Fay and had his arms round another blonde. But as you know, I was very apprehensive about Pat stepping in so soon after he scarpered. He didn't give her a chance to get over him. And I'll tell you something else: he's still got one hell of a hang-up about Jeremy. He can hardly mention him without foaming at the mouth.'

'It's rotten timing,' Pammy said worriedly, 'added to the problems you're having at the practice. No wonder the poor love is cracking up. Is there anything we can do?'

'I can't see what, other than be supportive while they work it out for themselves. The best thing that could happen is for Jeremy to get the hell out and go back to wherever he's been these last twenty years. The longer he stays here, the worse things are likely to get.'

It was half past six. Laura, home from college, was upstairs washing her hair, Jenny and Claire were closeted with their homework and, as it was late night at the surgery, Patrick had not yet returned.

Fay put the cheese pie into the oven, set the timer for forty-five minutes, and started to wipe the surfaces clear of onion peelings. The sound of the doorbell made her jump. Probably more carol-singers, she thought; they'd started even earlier this year. She took a fifty-pence piece from her purse and went to open the door, totally unprepared to see Jeremy, illuminated by the hall light, standing on the step. Her knees literally buckled and she held on to the door for a minute before instinctive caution took over.

She said swiftly, 'You can't come in!' and with one movement pushed up the latch and stepped outside, pulling the door closed behind her. The evening air was bitter and she shivered.

'I thought you'd come back,' she said.

'Thought, or hoped?' The old teasing note was in his voice.

'Don't play with me, Jeremy,' she said harshly. 'I deserve better than that.'

'Dearest Fay, you deserve all that is bright and good.'

With the light gone, his face was in darkness, the outline of his body a denser shape against the obscurity of the garden. She blinked, waiting for her night vision to adjust, and he reached out and tentatively drew her towards him. As though a spring had been released, she gave a shuddering gasp and, pulling his face down to hers, began kissing him feverishly, straining against him with growing urgency as his hands moved insistently over her.

Long minutes later, as she moaned against his mouth, he gently put her from him, reaching out to steady her as she shivered convulsively from cold and desire. His own breathing was ragged, but he gave a low laugh.

'Oh Fay, Fay, it's really too bad you always come so encumbered.'

'What do you mean?' It was an effort to speak.

'House, husband, family. Trappings to weigh down a free spirit.'

She didn't understand, but had no time to question him. Patrick might be back at any minute. 'You should have phoned,' she said through chattering teeth. 'It was madness to come at this time, when the girls are home.'

'Actually,' he said, 'I came to see Laura.'

It was as though he'd punched her in the stomach. The breath was driven from her body, to be replaced by the icy air that seeped into her very soul.

'You...?' Her lips felt like rubber and she couldn't go on.

'I need to talk to her. I knew she'd be home by now.'

Her voice was shrill. 'Then for God's sake why did you let me ... why didn't you *say* so?'

'You didn't give me a chance,' he said, and laughed. 'Not that I'm complaining, and if you'd like to come behind a bush, we can finish off what we've started.'

She gasped, and her hand went stingingly across his cheek.

'Fair enough. I suppose that means I can't see Laura?'

'Go to hell!' she choked and, stumbling

back inside, slammed the door and let down the catch with a rattle. As on his last visit, she waited for his footsteps to move away, though this time they were harder to make out above the tearing wrenches of her breath. Opening her clenched hand, she saw she was still holding the fifty-pence piece.

Patrick said, 'I have to go up to London next week, and it'll mean a night away. Guy and I have been summoned by the solicitor – a query concerning some property our parents owned.'

He glanced at Fay, but she sat white-faced, staring into the distance, as, come to think of it, she had been doing all evening. 'Fay? Did you hear what I said?'

'No ... sorry?'

'I have to go to London next week, for a meeting. As it's for nine o'clock, it'll mean going the day before and staying overnight.'

She was aware of relief. A reprieve, then, from his worried face and unhappy eyes, which were beginning to unsettle her.

'Which night?'

'Wednesday.'

'Christa comes home on Thursday. Could you meet her at the main-line station and bring her back with you? It would save her having to get a connection.'

He shook his head. 'I'd really rather not be tied down. I don't know how long the meeting will go on, and I don't want to be worrying about the time.'

Fay nodded acceptance. 'It was just a thought,' she said tonelessly. 'She wouldn't be expecting you, anyway.'

He frowned. 'Are you feeling all right?'

She turned her blank eyes on him. 'I suppose so,' she said.

But she wasn't – oh God, she wasn't! Those few minutes outside had chilled her with a deep, penetrating cold that numbed her very being, and despite turning up the thermostat – in the face of Patrick's protest – she was unable to get warm. In addition, she was buffeted by the most debilitating of emotions: self-loathing, humiliation, shame, and a deep, bitter hatred directed at the man who had caused them. Time and again the scene replayed in her head, and each time this destructive self-abasement intensified.

If only – oh God, if only! – she'd waited to hear what he wanted, instead of pre-empting him. If only she could put back the clock, be as cool and formal as she had been the last time he'd called.

But in the weeks since the dinner party tensions had grown between herself and Patrick, and Laura's incessant chatter about Jeremy had kept him in the forefront of her mind. Night after night she'd woken from disturbing dreams of him, and her body ached with the need that seeing him again had revived.

Patrick was still staring at her, a crease between his eyes. 'Is there anything I can get you?'

'I'm just so cold!'

'Good God, woman, it's nearly eighty degrees in here! Have you got a temperature?'

Registering for the first time that he was in his shirtsleeves, she pushed herself to her feet. 'Perhaps I have. I think I'll go to bed. I might be able to get warm there.'

She walked unsteadily from the room, aware of his frowning gaze, and, pulling herself up by the banisters like an old woman, went upstairs. Never, she vowed to herself, would she lay herself open to the remotest possibility of seeing Jeremy again.

Laura had been delighted by Jeremy's phone call on Monday morning. The cancelled lunch dates had made her wonder if he was tiring of her, but she'd told herself she was being stupid and that of course it was more important to attend the interviews. It was just a shame that several times they'd overlapped the lunch hour.

She was surprised, too, by his choice of venue. They usually met in a little Italian café for a pizza or a plate of pasta. Though she had diffidently offered to go Dutch, he would not hear of it, and she'd assumed that it was his finances that limited their choice. That day, however, he suggested the grill room of one of the better hotels.

'My goodness!' she exclaimed. 'What are we celebrating?'

He had merely laughed and said, 'Twelve thirty? I'll see you there.'

And now they were sitting opposite each other in the beautifully appointed room, with candles on the table, since the day was dull and overcast, and fresh flowers in a little vase, and a bottle of red wine.

'Why are we here?' she asked again.

'I thought it was about time I gave you the kind of food you cook yourself, instead of an eternal diet of carbohydrates. Anyway, today is rather a special occasion. I'll explain when we've eaten.'

Her eyes widened. 'You've been offered a job? Oh, come on, tell me now!'

But he wouldn't be swayed, so under his prompting she told him what she'd been doing, how the family were, and what was planned for Christmas.

'I do wish you could join us,' she added impulsively, but he laid a hand quickly over hers.

'Don't worry about me, Laura. I'll be fine.'

They had smoked salmon, and fillet steak crisply brown on the outside and pink

242

within, and sautéed potatoes and a green salad, and Jeremy kept asking if the food was up to standard. The dessert trolley was wheeled round, and Laura, who had glimpsed the prices on the menu, waved it away, but he insisted she choose.

'I think I'll go for the rum baba,' he said.

'A speciality of mine!' Laura told him laughingly, as she indicated the meringues chantilly. With a burst of joy, she realised that she was suddenly, completely, happy, warmed by the wine and good food and above all delighting in the company of the man opposite her, her father, whom she had missed and longed for all her life. After all these years he was here with her, and all was right with the world.

The waiter brought coffee and, despite her protests, Jeremy insisted on liqueurs.

'I'll never be able to do any work this afternoon!' she demurred.

'Think of it as our Christmas treat,' he said. 'It is December, after all.' He reached into his pocket and took out a small parcel wrapped in gold paper. 'Put this under the tree, from me,' he said.

'Oh ... thank you,' she stammered. 'I wasn't expecting ... I mean, I have something for you, too, but I was going to wait till nearer the time.'

'We won't be seeing each other nearer the time, Laura,' he said gently. 'That's what

243

I've brought you here to tell you.'

She stared at him, a clutch of fear obliterating her new found happiness. 'What do you mean?'

He was smiling, but his eyes were serious, intent on her face, and she realised this wasn't easy for him. He reached for her hand again, and she let it lie in his, praying incoherently – for what, she didn't know.

'I have to tell you that you needn't put up with your reprobate of a father any longer. It's time for me to move on.'

She sat motionless, her eyes unblinking on his face. Then she moistened her lips. 'But you mustn't just give up. There'll be more interviews – we'll find something suitable.'

'I haven't been to any interviews, Laura.'

Her eyes dilated and she tried to snatch her hand away, but he tightened his grip.

'Sweetie, don't look like that. I can't tell you what it's meant to me to get to know you at last, and you've been so sweet, trying to help me. I know I've been a damned nuisance.'

'But you haven't!' she burst out. 'Of course you haven't! It means everything to me, having you here.' She broke off at the pain in his eyes.

'You're not making this easy, are you?' he said wryly. 'Look, I'll put my cards on the table. When I lost my job, I really hit rock bottom. I tried to put a good face on it, but

I was short of cash and my self-esteem was non-existent. I thought no one would ever bother with me again.'

He paused, but she made no comment.

'But you took pity on me, bless you, and I can never thank you enough for that. And now – I just can't believe my luck – I've met someone who knows all my weaknesses but is still able to love me. Her name's Georgia Prentiss, and she's the best thing that ever happened to me. The icing on the cake is that she has enough money for both of us! So we've decided to set up home together, and I'm leaving on Wednesday. Be happy for me, sweetheart.'

Silence stretched between them. Eventually Laura said with difficulty, 'Are you saying this is the last time I'll see you?'

'Well, for the foreseeable future,' he said awkwardly. 'We can still write, of course, and I'll phone you from time to time, but—'

'In other words,' she broke in, 'just when I've got to know you, you're going away and leaving me. Again.'

'Oh now, Laura, love, I don't think that's quite fair.'

'No!' she said ringingly. 'It isn't! I'm sorry I ever met you!' She stumbled to her feet and, leaving the gold parcel lying on the table, turned towards the door. He rose quickly to go after her, then, thinking better of it, stood watching as she threaded her way rapidly between the tables. After a minute, aware of turning heads, he sat down and lit a cigarette.

Well, he thought philosophically, he'd done his best. He couldn't be expected to kick his heels around here all his life, just so that he could see Laura now and then. She was only a kid – she'd get over it.

Conscience assauged, he slipped the little parcel into his pocket and signalled to the waiter for the bill.

Ellie's secretary stood in the doorway, looking embarrassed. 'I'm sorry, Miss Marlow; I know you asked not to be disturbed, but there's a young lady outside who's insisting on seeing you. I suggested she wait until school finishes in an hour or so, but she became quite agitated.'

Ellie sighed. 'Is it one of the old girls?' She was used to ex-pupils coming to ask her advice on a variety of subjects, but they normally made appointments.

'I didn't recognise her. Her name's Laura Nelson.'

Ellie looked up quickly. 'Laura? She's my niece. It's all right – you weren't to know. Yes, of course I'll see her.'

Whatever had brought Laura running to her at this hour of the day? She'd never come to the school before, and in any case she should be at college. Ellie felt a coldness in the pit of her stomach. This could only be to do with Jeremy.

She stood up as Miss Handley showed her in. The girl's face was white and pinched. She made no move to come further into the room and, as Ellie went towards her, she said simply, 'He's leaving.'

Ellie stopped and frowned. 'Jeremy?'

'Yes. He's going off with some rich woman.'

'Come and sit down, dear. I'll send for some tea.'

Having done so, she sat back in her chair. 'Now tell me. When did this come up?'

Laura raised her head, and Ellie was appalled at the hopelessness in her eyes. 'At lunch time. We went to the Swan Grill. I thought it was to celebrate something – he'd said it was a special occasion – and after the meal he just ... came out with it.'

'What did he say exactly?'

'That he was grateful for me having tried to help him – but it turned out he hadn't been to any of the interviews I'd fixed for him. And I went to so much trouble to find something suitable.' Her lips trembled and Ellie leant forward.

'I know you did, darling.'

There was a tap on the door and the secretary reappeared with a tray. Ellie poured two cups of tea and pushed one across to her niece. 'Drink it, Laurie. It'll help. Who is this woman? Anyone we know?'

'Her name's Georgia Prentiss. He said she was the best thing that had ever happened to him.' Her voice cracked and she hastily lifted her cup and drank. 'She's got loads of money,' she continued then, 'and they're going to live together. He's leaving on Wednesday.'

'He actually told you she had money?' Ellie asked incredulously.

'Yes. He said it was the icing on the cake.' Laura's voice rose. 'I thought he really liked me – might even come to love me. We've spent so much time together these last two months – got to *know* each other. At least, I thought we had. But at some stage he must have met this woman – which, no doubt, was why he started cancelling our lunches. I bumped into him in Henderson's a couple of weeks ago. He was pretty jumpy, couldn't get away fast enough. I suppose he was meeting her there, and panicked when I turned up.'

'Laura, darling, I'm so very sorry.'

'It was bad enough that he left me once. At least he didn't *know* me then, so it wasn't really personal. But this time...' Tears came at last. Laura put her head down on the desk and sobbed broken-heartedly.

Ellie came round and laid a hand on her shoulder, waiting for the storm to pass.

Tears were better than that frozen composure when she arrived. For the first time, her thoughts turned from her niece to her sister. How would Fay take the news of Jeremy's departure? And Patrick? At least he'd be able to breathe more easily. It wasn't, after all, Fay that Jeremy had come back for. But why the hell, she thought in exasperation, had he come back at all, upsetting all their lives?

Gradually Laura's sobs lessened. Ellie passed her a box of tissues. She blew her nose and finally looked up.

'I bought him some gold cufflinks for Christmas,' she said. 'They cost a bomb. Pity I had his initials engraved on them.' She gave a wan smile. 'Do you happen to know any JPs?'

'I'm afraid not. Finish your tea, darling, then I'll take you home.'

'There's no need,' Laura said. 'I've interrupted you enough, and it's only half past three.'

'No point in being a headmistress if you can't leave early occasionally. I thought you might like me to be there when you tell your mother.'

Laura's eyes widened, and Ellie saw that she hadn't seen past her own sense of betrayal. Then she said, 'It won't make any difference to her. She refused to see him after that first time.'

'All the same, it's been unsettling for her, having him so close. You must see that. You told me yourself your parents haven't been very communicative lately.'

Laura drained her cup. 'Right. Let's go and tell her, then.'

'Good!' said Fay. 'Now, perhaps we can all get on with our lives.'

Laura made a small sound, and Fay looked stricken. 'Oh darling, I'm sorry – I wasn't thinking. He's really hurt you, hasn't he, letting you down like this?'

'But you expected it, I suppose,' Laura said bitterly. 'For God's sake don't say, "I told you so".'

'I wasn't going to. So ... he's leaving Caverstock. Where is he going, or didn't he deign to say?'

'Actually, Fay,' Ellie put in, 'you interrupted before hearing the whole story. He's going to live with some woman he's met – Georgia Something.'

Fay's face blanched and Ellie caught a flash in her eyes of something she couldn't interpret before the shutter came down again. 'I see.'

'She's loaded,' Laura said viciously. 'Come to think of it, she probably subsidised lunch today. Oh God!' She put her hand to her mouth.

Fay put her arms round her and pulled her

250

close. 'Never mind, darling, we're all still here for you; and at least you met him and got to know him, which was what you always wanted.'

'It's not enough,' Laura said in a muffled voice.

Watching them, aching with pity for them both, Ellie remembered how Fay had been when Jeremy had left the first time. At least, she thought, things couldn't be as bad as that again.

Ten

Ellie phoned Fay the next morning.

'I'm ringing to see how Laura is.'

'I don't know,' Fay said flatly. 'She spent yesterday evening in her room. I went up once or twice, but she wouldn't let me in. And this morning she'd left before I came down. The girls always get their own breakfast.'

'She *has* gone to college?' Ellie asked sharply.

'Yes, she's there – I phoned to check.'

'And what about you?'

'How do you mean?'

'Come on, Fay. You've been on edge ever

since Jeremy came back.'

'Well, I don't need to be any longer, do I?'

Ellie said hesitantly, 'Look, I know it's none of my business, but did he ever contact you, after the dinner party?'

'You're quite right, it isn't any of your business.'

Which probably meant he did, Ellie thought worriedly. 'I should think Patrick's glad he's gone, anyway.'

'No doubt, but he didn't say much. Look, is there anything else, because I've got better things to do than spend the morning talking about Jeremy Page.'

'Then I won't detain you any further,' Ellie said stiffly, and hung up.

'Damn!' she said aloud. That was rude and stupid. Whatever Fay might say, it was obvious she was churned up about Jeremy, and she should have had more understanding. She considered phoning straight back, but Miss Handley came in with some letters to sign, and the opportunity passed.

Nevertheless, her family remained on her mind. Fay, Patrick and Laura all had their problems, and she couldn't help worrying about them. It was a relief, at the end of the school day, to walk back to the haven of her own little house, where, unusually, she poured herself a stiff drink. It was as well she did, for the traumas of the day were far from over.

She had had her meal and was watching an anodyne programme on television when there was a shrilling of the doorbell, followed immediately by hammering on the door. She ran to open it, and was shocked to see Patrick standing there, his face distraught. The thought flashed through her head: *Fay's gone with Jeremy after all!*

'Patrick! Whatever—?'

He pushed past her. 'I need a drink. Now.'

'Yes, of course.'

Useless to question him in this state. She went to the cupboard and poured him a large whisky, which he downed in one draught and held out the glass for a refill.

'Only if you promise not to drink it all at once,' she said.

He stared at her for a moment, then his mouth twitched. 'You sound like a damned schoolmistress!' he said. But he took the glass from her and moved over to the fireplace.

'Are you going to tell me what's happened?'

'Yes, I'll tell you. I've killed someone.'

Ellie froze. *Jeremy?* 'What...?'

'At the surgery. I gave a patient an injection, and ... he died.'

Her heart steadied a little. 'Oh Patrick, how terrible! But ... it wasn't your fault, surely?'

'Cause and effect, Ellie. Cause and effect.

I injected him, and he died. QED.'

'But ... was he allergic or something?'

'That's for the post-mortem to decide. He'd said he wasn't. Ellie, he was only forty-five. He'd a wife and four kids. They're all my patients – I *know* them; I've been treating them for years.'

'But what happened, exactly?'

'Well, he was in a bit of a state when he came in. Then unfortunately the injection was intravenous – it happens sometimes, causing a rush of adrenalin. Normally the patient comes out in a cold sweat, feels faint for a minute or two, and then it passes.'

'But this time it didn't pass?'

'No, he went into a full-blown heart attack. We used the emergency drug kit, which almost always works, but we couldn't bring him round. The ambulance arrived within minutes, but he died on the way to hospital.'

'What infernal luck,' Ellie said softly. 'So what happens now?'

'The post-mortem and coroner's enquiry. As far as was known, he'd no health problems.'

'Perhaps he'd a weak heart that no one suspected.'

'Or perhaps it was negligence on my part.'

'I'm sure it wasn't,' she said stoutly. 'Had you given him an injection before?'

'No. As I said, I've been treating his wife

254

and kids for years, but he himself signed on only about a year ago. It's not been necessary before.'

'What does Roger say?'

'He's as poleaxed as I am. To add to the complications, I'm supposed to be going to London tomorrow and staying overnight. I offered to cancel it, but he said there's no point and it would do me good to get right away. I'd intended working in the morning and driving up after lunch, but in the circumstances I think I'll take two full days off – give things a chance to settle. There's nothing urgent booked in, and in any case I doubt if my patients will want to see me until this has been cleared up.'

'Now you're being ridiculous. I'm quite sure no one—'

'Are you? I'm not.'

'Does Fay know?' Ellie asked after a moment.

'Not yet. With all due respect, she's not the kind of person you turn to in a crisis – too emotional. She was crying in bed last night; she thought I was asleep, but I heard her. You know, I suppose, that Jeremy's leaving?'

Ellie nodded, praying that that last sentence was a non sequitur.

'Having broken little Laura's heart,' he went on tightly. 'God, Ellie, what's wrong with him? He seems to have a knack of making women love him, then kicking them in the teeth. I'd like to knock his own teeth down his throat.'

Ellie put a hand on his arm. 'Sit down, Patrick. I suppose you haven't eaten?'

'No, but I couldn't.'

'I think you need something in your stomach before driving home. Those whiskies weren't the first, were they?'

He shook his head, not looking at her. 'I went to a pub with Roger. We were both in shock.'

'Then phone Fay – she'll be expecting you. Tell her the position, and ask if it's all right if I give you supper. Don't worry; it'll be light and easy to eat.'

'She probably hasn't even noticed my absence.' But at her instigation, he went to the phone, and she heard him say briefly that there'd been trouble at the practice, Ellie was scrambling him some eggs, and he'd be home shortly. Then he came into the kitchen and stood watching her in silence as she swiftly prepared the meal.

The food – or perhaps the whisky – seemed to help, because the glazed look left his eyes. As soon as he'd finished, he stood up. 'Thanks as always, Ellie. At least I feel a bit more in control now.'

'It'll work out,' she said softly. 'It's a terrible tragedy, but I'm convinced no blame will attach to you.'

'I wish I could be as sure.'

'Believe me. By the time you get back from London they'll have the results of the post-mortem, and you'll be in the clear.'

At the door, he took her in his arms. 'I always come to you with my troubles, don't I? I don't know what I'd do without you.' And to her surprise he bent down and gently kissed her mouth.

'Good night, Ellie. God bless you.'

'Good night, Patrick.'

She watched as he went down the path to his car, as, years before, she had stood watching him from her parents' doorway. Only when he had driven off and the sound of the car had died away did she slowly shut the door.

The following morning, Ellie again phoned Fay.

'I wanted to apologise for hanging up on you yesterday.'

'It's all right; no doubt I deserved it. I hear Patrick's been crying on your shoulder.'

'In a manner of speaking. What a ghastly thing to have happened.'

'God knows, we could do without it. He's off to London later, to some business meeting.'

'How's Laura?'

'All right, I suppose, but it's hard to tell. As you know, she's always pretty self-contained.' Her voice brightened. 'Christa's coming home tomorrow. How about coming round to supper, to welcome her back?'

'I'd love to. It seems ages since I saw her.'

'Come at seven, then. Patrick's sure to be back by then.'

But he wasn't. At first, no one really noticed; Christa was the centre of attention as her younger sisters plied her with questions about university life, and even Laura joined in. It wasn't till after seven thirty that Fay glanced at the clock and remarked, 'Patrick should be here by now; I wonder what's delayed him.'

'The traffic's horrendous in London,' Christa said, 'with Christmas shoppers adding to the chaos. Has he got his mobile with him? Try him on that.'

'It's switched off,' Fay reported, after a vain attempt. 'We'll give him till eight, then we'll eat.'

Ellie felt a coldness in the pit of her stomach, remembering across the years a similar comment of Fay's on the night Jeremy had left. If she went up to the bedroom, would there be a note waiting there?

She glanced at her father, wondering if the same thought had occurred to him, then shook herself. She was being ridiculous. As Christa said, the traffic was bad, and Patrick seldom bothered to tell Fay when he was going to be late.

Accordingly, at eight o'clock they went into the dining room and Fay served the meal, leaving Patrick's portion in the oven. At nine, the telephone rang.

'That'll be him,' Fay said. 'About time – I was beginning to get anxious.'

But her relief was short-lived. It was Guy Nelson on the phone, asking to speak to Patrick.

'He's not back yet, Guy,' Fay told him. 'We were just—'

'Back from where?'

'Well, from meeting you. He—'

'Fay, that's what I'm ringing about. He never showed up.'

'But ... that's not possible. He left here after lunch yesterday. Oh God, do you think he's had an accident?'

'Has he phoned you at all since he left?'

'No, but I wasn't expecting him to.'

She turned to Ellie, who had come to stand beside her. 'Patrick didn't go to the meeting. What can have happened to him?'

Ellie's heart jerked sickeningly. 'Do you know where he was staying?'

'At the Belvedere – where he always does.'

'Then let's call them and see if he was there.'

Fay said into the phone, 'We're going to ring his hotel, Guy.'

'Right. I'll call back in half an hour, to see if there's any news.'

Fay put down the phone and glanced into the dining room. Her father and daughters were still seated at the table, their white faces turned towards her.

Claire said unsteadily, 'Has something happened to Daddy?'

'I don't know, darling. I'm just going to try his hotel. Perhaps he was taken ill in the night.'

The cool voice of the receptionist informed her that Mr Nelson had checked out that morning.

'Then he was there? He did spend the night at the hotel?'

'Yes, madam. He had breakfast and checked out at eight thirty this morning.'

'How did he seem? I mean, was he all right?'

'I'm afraid I can't help you there; I wasn't on duty.'

Defeated, Fay relayed the report. 'So we know he got to London all right and spent the night at the hotel. But where did he go from there? Why didn't he turn up at the meeting? That was the whole reason for going.'

'Did he mention any other business he wanted to see to while he was there?' Gordon asked.

Fay shook her head. 'Anyway, he'd have gone to the solicitors first. They were meeting at nine.'

Ellie said tentatively, 'He's been under a lot of strain. Perhaps at the last minute he felt he couldn't face it.'

'But then he'd have come home.'

Suppose he couldn't face home, either? 'He may even have amnesia,' she suggested. 'In which case, he'll probably report in at a hospital or police station.'

'But he's got identity on him – credit card, driving licence, things like that. If he'd forgotten his name, he'd only have to look in his pockets.'

The phone rang again, startling them all, and Fay snatched it up; but it was only Guy, ringing back as promised. Fay related what they had learned.

'Try not to worry, Fay; there must be a logical explanation. He might well turn up later, but if not, I'll go to the hotel in the morning and see if I can trace his steps from there. For one thing, I'll check if his car's in the car park.'

Fay shivered. 'And if it is?'

'Well, with luck we might be able to trace a taxi he took. The police have ways of doing that.'

'You think we should inform the police?'

'Not yet; there's really nothing to tell, and they don't usually worry if an adult disappears for a couple of days. It happens all the time, usually after a domestic tiff.' He paused, but when Fay made no comment, added, 'They nearly always turn up again.'

Promising to phone in the morning, he rang off.

'In the meantime, we carry on as normal,' Ellie said firmly. 'Probably by this time tomorrow, we'll be wondering why we were so concerned. So – Jenny and Claire, off to do your homework, and Laura and Christa can help me clear the table. You go into the sitting room, Dad. We'll bring some coffee in a few minutes.'

They did as they were told, and somehow the evening passed, but the feeling of déjà vu persisted. Ellie was almost expecting to be asked to stay the night, as she had before; but when at last she said she must be going, Fay made no demur, merely accompanying her to the door.

Ellie put her arms round her. 'Try not to worry. I'm sure he'll turn up soon, wondering what all the fuss was about.'

Fay gave her a tight little smile. 'Thanks for all your support, Ellie. I'll phone you when I've spoken to Guy.'

Patrick's car was indeed still in the underground car park at the Belvedere, but there was nothing in it to explain his disappearance, merely a few sundries in the glove compartment and a road map stuffed in the side pocket.

Guy had further established that his

brother hadn't eaten at the hotel on Wednesday evening but had handed in his key around eight thirty and gone out. According to the night porter, he had returned soon after eleven and, under Guy's prompting, the man admitted cautiously that 'the gentleman had seemed a little under the weather'. Pressed further, he went so far as to say that Patrick had appeared agitated; he couldn't remember the number of his room, and had had to be guided in the direction of the lifts. The porter had surmised that he'd had 'a drop too much to drink'.

All this Guy reported to Fay when he drove down to Rushyford to see her.

'He might have been drinking,' she said doubtfully, 'but over the last few weeks he'd become very forgetful, even here.'

'What could have happened on Wednesday evening that made him skip the meeting and take off somewhere?' Guy mused. 'Unless, of course, he'd never intended coming in the first place. Can you think of any reason why he might have gone off for a day or two without saying anything?'

She shook her head, staring at him with wide, frightened eyes.

'He hasn't taken his passport, by any chance?'

'Oh God – I never thought to look.' She jumped up and ran to the old bureau that had belonged to her grandmother; but

Patrick's passport, together with her own, was in its usual place in one of the drawers.

When she sat down again, Guy took hold of her hands. 'Fay, I hate to ask this, but I have to know: were things ... all right ... between you?'

'Not brilliant, to be honest,' she said in a low voice. 'For one thing, my first husband turned up last month, and has been seeing a lot of Laura. Patrick hated that. And he's been having problems at work, too. In fact – it was awful, Guy – on Tuesday someone died at the practice, after Patrick had given him an injection. He was out of his mind with worry.'

'Poor devil, he *has* been through the mill. The death could have been the last straw. You say he's been forgetful lately; that's often a sign of mental disturbance. I think with all this build-up we could get the police interested after all. Would you like me to get on to them?'

'Please. Do you think something's happened to him?'

'The best-case scenario is that he's simply had as much as he can take for the moment, and gone to ground for a day or two; but it could be more serious, and we have to make sure he's OK.'

So Patrick was reported as a missing person and the wheels began to turn, and two days later Guy, white-faced, reappeared at

Sandford. He took Fay's arm.

'Now, I don't want you to panic, but some-one's been found answering to Patrick's description.'

Fay stared at him. 'Found? Dead, you mean?' Her voice rose.

'Yes, but there's no saying it *is* Patrick. There must be thousands of people with the same build and colouring – we just need to eliminate the possibility. Will you come, Fay?'

She drew back. 'Couldn't you go?'

'I thought you'd want to come with me. You needn't actually ... view the body if you don't want to, but I think you should be there.'

Fay said in a whisper, 'Can I bring Ellie?'

'Of course.'

It was a Sunday and Ellie was at home when the call came. She felt herself sway and sat down quickly on the chair by the phone.

'Fay would like you to come with us,' Guy Nelson ended.

'Of course I will.' Her voice was a croak. But it's not him, she assured herself urgent-ly. It isn't Patrick. It can't be.

The journey up to London was a night-mare. Guy drove, and Fay held Ellie's hand tightly in the back seat. Previously, Ellie had met Guy only at Patrick and Fay's wedding and subsequent christenings, and had never spoken to him at length. She had, however, liked him on first acquaintance, and his calm dependability in these difficult circumstances confirmed that liking. Thank God he was accompanying them on this harrowing journey. In the rear-view mirror, she searched his face for resemblances to Patrick, but Guy took after his mother, Patrick, his father.

At the mortuary, they were treated with kindness and consideration. For as long as she lived, Ellie would remember standing gripping Fay's hand while Guy, accompanied by a sombre-faced policeman, went to view the body. Minutes later he emerged, ashen-faced, but shaking his head.

'It's not Patrick,' he said. 'The man has quite a look of him, but that's all, thank God.'

'What did he die of?' Ellie asked, when, over a cup of reviving coffee, she was able to think more clearly.

'Natural causes,' Guy replied. 'Someone found him collapsed in the street and phoned the police. They told me there was money in his wallet, but no credit cards and no means of identifying him. Must have had a heart attack, I suppose.'

'Someone, somewhere will be worrying about him,' Fay said soberly, 'but thank God – oh, thank God – it wasn't Patrick.'

During the next few days there were no

reported sightings, nor had any taxi-driver in the vicinity of the hotel recognised Patrick's photograph. After leaving the Belvedere at eight thirty in the morning, he seemed to have vanished into thin air.

Then, during a routine police check on his financial affairs, some news did emerge, but it was a worrying development. At nine thirty on the Thursday of the previous week Patrick had visited the West London branch of his bank and withdrawn ten thousand pounds from his personal account.

'It was all done according to the book,' the worried bank manager assured the police. 'Mr Nelson had proof of his identity, he knew the password, and, naturally, we checked with the Rushyford branch as to the state of his account. It was a little unusual to take out such a large sum in cash, though of course, in a branch this size in central London, it didn't pose any problems.'

'I don't understand,' Fay stammered, when she was informed. 'What would he want with all that money?'

'It certainly puts a different complexion on things,' Guy admitted gravely. 'It's beginning to look as though he intends to be away for some time.'

'But why?' Fay wailed. 'And where has he gone? Someone, somewhere, must have seen him?'

Christmas was only ten days away, but they made no preparations for it. Ellie's school broke up, and she missed the structure it gave to her days, leaving her with too much time to worry and wonder. Over and over she repeated to herself the last conversation she had had with Patrick. He'd spoken of taking 'two full days off', which surely meant, at that stage at least, that he'd intended returning? What could possibly have happened to make him act as he had, and without even letting them know he was all right? That was the least he could have done; a phone call from a public call box would have been scant help in tracing him, but would at least have eased the worst of their fears.

Roger and Pammy, stunned by developments, proved staunch friends to Fay, Pammy in particular calling at Sandford most days and sitting with her for hours on end. The cause of the surgery death had been confirmed as a violent reaction to the injected drug, allied to a congenital weakness of the heart, not previously diagnosed. Patrick in his absence had been cleared of all blame.

They were existing in this unreal time warp, rushing for the post each morning, never moving far from the phone, when, a few days before Christmas, the final, annihilating blow of that terrible month hit them. It came via a phone call. Fay, her nerves by now as taut as wires, flew to pick it up.

'Hello, yes?'

'Rushyford 49062?' It was a woman's voice, calm and expressionless.

'Yes?'

'Is that Mrs Nelson speaking?'

'I'm Fay Nelson. Who's that?'

'My name is Georgia Prentiss.'

Fay tensed, and the voice continued flatly, 'Perhaps you've heard of me. I'm ... a friend of Jeremy's.'

She paused, but Fay, whose entire mind had for days been concentrated on Patrick, was having difficulty switching it to Jeremy.

'I'm afraid I've some bad news,' she went on, and now her voice wavered. 'I thought you should know that Jeremy ... died two weeks ago.'

Fay gave a little groan and slid to the floor, and Pammy, who had come hurrying into the hall fearing the worst, knelt to support her and took the phone out of her hand. 'Hello, this is Pamela Hastings, a friend of Fay's. Who's speaking, please?'

'Georgia Prentiss. I found her number in Jeremy's diary.'

Not about Patrick, then, Pammy thought with a surge of relief. 'Yes?'

'I'm ringing to tell her that Jeremy's dead. In fact, he was murdered here in London

269

two weeks ago, but I've ... only just found out.'

'God in heaven!' Pammy breathed. 'How ... why...?'

Georgia Prentiss said rapidly, 'His body was hidden in a skip and it's only just been discovered. I ... thought she'd want to know.'

Pammy found she was trembling violently. She was unsure how much Fay had heard, but she was lying back in the circle of her arm, her face like paper and her eyes closed.

'I'm ... I'm so sorry. Is he – was he a friend of yours?'

'We were going to live together.' The voice shook again. 'It must have happened the day we moved in. While I started on the packing cases, he went out to buy a take-away. He ... never came back. I was frantic – I couldn't think what had happened. I went out in the car looking for him.' Her voice broke, but Pammy could think of nothing to say, and after a minute she went on: 'The next morning I phoned the police, but they didn't want to know. Said people were always going off for no reason, but they usually showed up again. I *knew* it was nothing like that. We were just starting out together.'

She stopped abruptly and Pammy repeated helplessly, 'I'm so terribly sorry. Was it a mugging, do they think?'

She heard the other woman blow her

nose, and when she spoke her voice was steadier. 'No, he wasn't robbed, just ... just stabbed once, through the heart. There doesn't seem to have been any motive. Anyway, it'll be in all the papers tomorrow, so I thought I'd better warn Mrs Nelson.'

'That's good of you.'

'Also, I've found a present he bought for his daughter. I'd like to forward it, but I haven't her address.'

Automatically, Pammy gave it. 'Miss Prentiss, I'm so very, very sorry. The awful irony is that Fay's husband has...' She broke off as a terrible, terrifying thought occurred to her, and she instantly crushed it.

'But you don't want to hear anyone else's troubles,' she ended swiftly. 'Fay's ... too shocked to speak to you, but I know she'd want me to pass on her very deepest sympathy. Thank you so much for letting her know.'

Fay's total collapse dated from that phone call. For weeks she lay in her darkened room, uninterested in anyone or anything. At Gordon's urgent request, Ellie moved to Sandford and took charge of the household. Christmas came and went, barely noticed. Roger and Pammy continued to call. Laura, stunned and appalled, was inconsolable.

'The last thing I said to him was that I was sorry I'd met him!' she sobbed in Ellie's arms; and Fay, earlier, had cried: 'My last words to him were "Go to hell!"'

In all the trauma and tragedy, one good thing emerged. Laura and Christa, rivals all their lives, came together in their grief. The desertion of her own father brought home to Christa what Laura must have been suffering all her life. Now, Jeremy was dead, and Laura would never see him again. Dully, Christa wondered if it would be twenty years before her own father came home.

Part 3 – The Present Day

Eleven

Despite her resolve before the dinner party, Ellie had not put her plans to return home into effect. Legally, since their father's death four years ago Sandford had been as much hers as Fay's, though her sister's possession of it for over twenty years was nine points of the law. Overall, she'd enjoyed her stay there. She loved the house and enjoyed its family atmosphere, though the latter had dissipated over the years, as one by one the girls had left home.

And there were undeniable drawbacks. She missed the little house across the river, the convenience of being able to walk home from school, and the freedom of spending the evening as she chose, eating as much or as little as she wanted, and at a time to suit herself. When she had first come to Sandford, it had been to cook for the entire family, as well as paying the bills and running house and garden, since Fay was incapable of doing so. Even now, she cooked the evening meal as often as not, which involved having to shop in her precious lunch hour.

Also, her times with Mark had lost their spontaneity, since they must be planned in advance. No longer could he phone on the spur of the moment and invite her – or himself – to supper, nor, after a trying day at the practice, call round to unwind with her over a drink. There were compensations, though: they had instead fallen into the habit of spending at least part of every weekend together, and as a result their lovemaking was now more regular than it had ever been.

Fay's breakdown, characterised by acute depression and excessive tiredness, had lasted six months, and it was considerably longer before she was back to full health. The double shock of Patrick's defection and Jeremy's murder was horrific enough, but when the police, having learned of the family involvement, had begun enquiries as to a possible connection, she'd gone completely to pieces.

Ellie had been stunned to learn that Jeremy's body was found only a few streets from the Belvedere Hotel, where Patrick had spent the night of the murder. Of course it was a coincidence, but his withdrawal of a large sum of money and his subsequent disappearance took on a new significance, and the police, too, had learned of his distressed condition when he'd returned to the hotel. Questions were asked about the relationship between the two men, and whether they had been on good terms. Fay being protected by her doctor from further questioning, it had fallen to Ellie to insist that they had met only once since Jeremy's return, at a family dinner party.

'Was Mr Nelson anxious about the re-appearance? Jealous, perhaps, of his wife's former relationship with Mr Page?'

'Of course not,' she'd repeated time and again, the more doggedly since she knew she lied. 'Anyway, Patrick knew Jeremy had met someone else and had already left the district – he could hardly have considered him a threat.'

But what *had* happened that evening, to upset Patrick so much? As she lay awake night after night, a disturbing scenario presented itself. Suppose he had, as the porter hinted, been out drinking, and by pure chance had run into Jeremy on his way to buy a take-away? What then? Might words have flared between them? Might Patrick have lashed out?

But each time, as panic escalated, the thought of the knife consoled her. Jeremy had been stabbed, and it was ludicrous to imagine for a moment that Patrick would be walking the streets of London armed with a knife.

For weeks it had been a nightmare existence. The press, scenting a scandal, had set up camp outside Sandford, photographing and calling questions to everyone going in or out, and the newspapers were full of speculation and surmise. Jeremy's obituary belatedly appeared in the nationals, and Ellie, thinking that at a later date Laura might like to have a copy, had torn it out and put it away in her desk.

Eventually, with nothing to fuel it, interest waned and they were able to regain their privacy. The police questioning also ceased, mainly, Ellie suspected, for lack of evidence; but she knew to her disquiet that the investigations into both Jeremy's murder and Patrick's disappearance remained open.

When the body was finally released for burial, neither Fay nor Laura had been fit to attend the funeral. Ellie, accompanied by Mark and Jess, represented the family, though Georgia Prentiss was the chief mourner, a striking figure with her tragic face and Titian hair. The church was full, but whether of people who remembered Jeremy's fame, or just the morbidly curious, Ellie neither knew nor cared, and her mind during the service had been on Patrick as much as Jeremy.

So life had gone on – or, in the case of her father, ended – and after six and a half years, they were no nearer a solution. Perhaps they never would be.

★ ★ ★

Adrian said, 'I have a proposition for you – or rather, my parents have.'

He was perched on a stool in Laura's tiny kitchen, watching her prepare their evening meal.

She glanced at him over her shoulder, eyebrow raised. 'I'm used to *your* propositions, but your parents?'

He smiled. 'You can say no – my mother insisted I make that clear, also that you needn't give an immediate reply.'

She turned to face him, leaning against the counter with folded arms. 'Suppose you tell me what it's all about?'

'We-ell, their fortieth wedding anniversary's coming up in July. They're going to throw a fairly large party, and ... are wondering if you'd be prepared to cater for it?'

Laura's eyebrows lifted as she took in the various implications.

'Price no object,' Adrian hurried on. 'They want to push the boat out, really have something to remember. What do you think?'

'I thought I was to weigh it up before replying?'

'Well, yes, but what's your immediate reaction? You're not insulted, are you? Ma was afraid you might be.'

'Insulted?'

'She's worried about "employing" you, when you might soon be a member of the family,' Adrian said slyly. 'And she's afraid

279

you'll think she's making use of you. In fact, I might as well confess, it was my idea. When they were discussing it, I said I could think of no one who'd do it better.'

'Well, thank you for that.'

'She knows you'd need to bring up extra staff, and that's no problem. There's bags of room for as many as you like.'

'When you say a fairly large party, *how* large, exactly?'

'About fifty, I think. They're having a marquee in the garden. Anyway, if it isn't a downright "No", Ma suggests we go up one weekend, and you can discuss it with her and ask any questions that come to mind. Are you up for that, at least?'

'I'll have to speak to Beth,' Laura said slowly.

Beth Kingdom, whom Laura had met at catering college, was a partner in Page Laura.

Adrian frowned. 'We don't want a weekend *à trois*.'

'I appreciate that, but I'd have to discuss it with her before we go up. If we decide to go ahead, I must have some ideas to put before your parents, and that's where Beth comes in. We go through the menus together, and then she does the costing.'

'Say we go up in a fortnight, then? Will that give you long enough?'

'Should do,' Laura said and, as the timer

280

began beeping, bent to take their supper out of the oven.

At Page Laura, every spare moment over the next ten days was spent in their office, poring over ideas for the Crawfords' ruby wedding celebration and making provisional plans.

Beth Kingdom, with her fair hair and round blue eyes, looked considerably younger than her twenty-seven years, but her appearance was deceptive. Not only was she an excellent cook with a flair for originality, but she had a business woman's brain and was able to work out the most complicated logistics and costings in her head.

'You're sure you want to do this?' she asked astutely, when, after broaching the subject, Laura had vetoed a third suggestion in the space of ten minutes.

Laura smiled ruefully. 'Not really, no, but I don't see how I can refuse.'

'Why the reservations?'

'Because once I'm up in the family enclave, I'm pretty sure pressure will be brought to bear.'

'What kind of pressure?'

'To get engaged.'

'Ah! And you don't want to?'

'I want to go on as we are, being together when it suits us...' She broke off and grimaced. 'Perhaps I should say, when it suits *me*

– and then being able to go off and do my own thing. I couldn't do that if I was married.'

Beth put her pen down. 'Well, if that's how you feel, is there any point in going through all this?'

'Yes, there is,' Laura returned sharply. 'It's not our wedding we're talking about; it's his parents' anniversary. Sorry,' she added after a minute, 'I didn't mean to snap. But of course we must do it. It'll be good publicity, even if most of it will be up in Scotland; and it's a challenge, too.'

'OK then.' Beth picked up her pen again. 'If there's really no limit on costs, we can choose some of the fancy dishes beyond the usual price range. It could be quite exciting. What are the facilities like up there?'

'Haven't a clue; that's what I'll be sizing up this weekend. As always, the great unknown is the kitchen itself, and how much space we'll have.'

She sat back in her chair. 'Come to think of it, you know, apart from the distance, which admittedly is a bit daunting, it won't be much different from what we do all the time. I mean, we always take our own things – table linen, cutlery, crockery and so on – so we'll just load the van as usual. We can even take ready-prepared dishes. Thank heaven for refrigeration.'

'How long will it take us to drive up?'

'About six hours, I should think. We'll probably have to go two days in advance, to set things up and do the last-minute buying. That'll be the main problem: laying our hands on dependable local suppliers of fish, fruit and veg and bread. Still, I imagine Mrs Crawford has pretty high standards; she'll be able to advise us.'

'Right,' Beth said, 'let's start on thoughts about the food. Nothing too heavy for summer. Salmon, I suppose, but we'll have to do something different with it – the Scots probably have it coming out of their ears.'

'We could suggest starting the evening with champagne cocktails and canapés in the garden,' Laura said, interest at last quickening in her voice. 'Adrian says there are large grounds. Filo pastry is lighter than short, and we can do a selection of fillings – caviar, shrimp, curry – and tiny chicken kebabs with one of your special sauces drizzled over them. Everything bite-sized, so no plates required.'

'We need to know if they're thinking of an anniversary cake, and if so, whether they want us to make it,' Beth said. 'Personally I'd go for a light gateau – St Honoré, for instance.'

'It would have to be put together in situ,' Laura pointed out. 'I shouldn't fancy driving up the M6 with a fully assembled St Honoré in the back.'

Beth's mind had moved on. 'What about Dawn and the others? Will they have to go up when we do?'

Page Laura had six people on their books whom they employed on an hourly rate, as and when required. The men worked as bartenders, while two of the women were waitresses and the other two did the washing-up.

'Might as well, then they can all travel together. The boys can do the heaving around of tables and chairs and the girls can help set things up, unload the shopping and generally make themselves useful. They'll be glad of the extra cash, and the Crawfords aren't going to quibble. The sky's the limit, apparently.'

Beth smiled. 'And this is the family you have doubts about joining?'

'Don't you start!' Laura protested. 'I have enough hassle as it is!'

Adrian's sister Moira met them at the airport. She was small, like her brother, but there the similarity ended. Adrian was squarely built, chunky, and congenitally untidy, his hair constantly standing on end from his habit of running his hand through it. This morning, under an old tweed jacket, he was wearing a black T-shirt down which he had managed to spill something on the plane, and his trousers, as ever, looked as

284

though he'd slept in them. Moira, on the other hand, was slight and fine-boned and her smooth hair, more red than brown, was caught back neatly in a tortoiseshell slide. Though it was a Saturday morning, she wore a tailored blouse and skirt.

Laura had been told she was recently divorced and still coming to terms with it, but there was no hint of vulnerability in the eyes she turned on Laura, which were frankly assessing.

'I've heard a lot about you,' she said, shaking her hand and leaving her to wonder what, exactly.

They walked to the car and Adrian showed Laura into the front. A good half-hour's drive lay ahead of them, during which brother and sister kept up a constant exchange, only occasionally remembering to explain to Laura who or what they were discussing. The late-May morning was several degrees cooler than it had been in London, the sun struggling to penetrate heavy clouds, and without its beneficence the grey stone of the buildings looked dour and unwelcoming. Laura, for the most part excluded from the family chat, felt increasingly apprehensive about the visit ahead of her.

She had met Jean and Duncan Crawford only twice, both times in London, when they had taken Adrian and herself to the theatre and on to supper afterwards. On neither occasion had there been the chance of any in-depth conversation, and the prospect of spending the three-day bank holiday in their company was daunting, especially since Moira was showing no overt signs of friendliness. Even Adrian, who in London had no noticeable accent, had unconsciously reverted to that of his childhood, and in the process subtly changed from the man she knew into a relative stranger.

Having previously seen him only in the context of their life in London, Laura realised how little she knew about his home, his family or his childhood – everything, in fact, that had shaped him into the man he had become. This weekend should prove enlightening; it might even help her to decide whether or not to marry him.

The Crawfords' home was in a wealthy suburb to the west of Edinburgh, on rising ground that afforded views of open country in one direction and the towers and steeples of the capital in the other. Laura's first impression was of a sprawling, comfortable-looking house, solid in the ubiquitous grey stone which, providentially, lit with sudden gold as the sun finally broke through – a good omen, perhaps.

As Moira swung the car into the drive, the front door opened and Duncan Crawford came out to greet them. He was a sandy-haired man with narrow shoulders and a pale, freckled face, which broke into a smile of welcome as he helped Laura out of the car.

'Come away in,' he said heartily. 'It's good to see you.' And he shook them both by the hand. His wife Jean came hurrying down the steps.

'Welcome to Scotland, Laura,' she said, kissing her lightly on the cheek and hugging Adrian. The two men retrieved the cases from the boot and, with Jean asking perfunctory questions about the flight, they moved in a body up the steps into the house.

The hall was large and oblong, with a handsome staircase just off-centre. There was an open fireplace, now screened with what must, Laura decided, be a professional flower arrangement, and rugs lay on the parquet floor in a scattering of jewel-like colours: red, green, deep blue and amber. An open door straight ahead showed a large and pleasantly furnished room with open French windows giving on to a terrace, and, beyond it, a lawn as smooth as a bowling green.

Jean Crawford took her arm. 'I'll show you your room so you can freshen up; then we'll have a drink before lunch.'

The bedroom in which Laura found herself was a pale duck-egg blue, the carpet thick and luxurious. Beside the handsome wardrobe and double bed – which doubtless she'd sleep in alone – there were an easy chair and a desk complete with writing materials. A door in the corner led to a private bathroom, and on the dressing table a bowl of lilies of the valley scented the air with their heady fragrance.

'I hope you'll be comfortable,' Jean Crawford said, 'but please let me know if there's anything you need. Come down when you're ready.' She gave Laura a quick smile and bustled out of the room.

Laura walked to the window and leaned on the sill, looking out. Her room was at the front of the house, overlooking the road they'd driven up and, beyond it, other houses falling away down the hill to the distant city. Well, she was here. She could only hope that when the initial strangeness wore off, she would feel more at home with Adrian's family.

Pre-lunch sherry was served in the room she had glimpsed from the hall. On entering it for the first time, Laura was aware of disappointment, an awareness that the room hadn't been allowed to fulfil its potential. The furniture was expensive, carpets, rugs and curtains of the highest quality, but it conspicuously lacked the character which, lovingly built up by her family over the years, made Sandford so special. There were no personal touches here – no photographs, no books, and even the flowers had been formally arranged by professionals. It could have been an illustration in a glossy magazine for all the homeliness it conveyed.

She wondered if Jean Crawford, lacking confidence in her own sense of style, had simply turned over the decoration of her home to the experts, and left the results unembellished. Certainly she displayed no great colour-consciousness in her own appearance; though her clothes and shoes were of excellent quality, the overall impression was of a study in beige, hair, face, eyes, even her blouse and skirt, all being the same pale, indeterminate colour, with nothing of contrast to enliven them.

Belatedly aware that she was waiting expectantly, Laura hastily admired her surroundings, commenting on the precisely positioned ornaments and the rich brocade of the curtains.

'It was featured in *Ideal Home*,' Jean said complacently. And if it was indeed an 'ideal home' for them, Laura upbraided herself, who was she to criticise?

After lunch, taken in the equally resplendent dining room, Moira returned to her Edinburgh flat and Adrian and his father went to play golf. 'Which,' Jean commented, 'leaves us free to discuss the purpose of your visit. Where would you like to start?'

'With the kitchen, please. It would be really helpful to know how much space we'd have.'

As she'd anticipated, the kitchen was fitted with every modern device, though obviously on a domestic scale. It would be necessary to bring their portable oven and various other essentials with them. There were, however, plenty of surfaces on which to lay out food, a fairly large fridge and freezer, and a long central table.

'We use all our own glasses, plates and cutlery,' Laura explained, 'so you needn't worry about breakages. I thought perhaps you might like to start with canapés and champagne cocktails in the garden?'

The next couple of hours passed quickly and pleasantly. Jean was gratifyingly enthusiastic over all her suggestions, exclaiming with delight at the choice of dishes, and Laura found herself warming to her. Costs were discussed, including the hiring of the six extra staff, but Jean agreed with everything. Laura enquired about local suppliers and was assured they were of the highest quality. If she was given a list of everything they needed, Jean would place the order for them in perfect confidence.

'Does this mean you'll do it?' she asked at the end.

'If you'd like us to.'

'Then this will be the party to end all

parties!'

They went out into the garden to discuss the siting of the marquee. Since the dining room was at the front of the house, it could not be used as an approach.

'I'd prefer it in the middle of the lawn,' Jean said worriedly, 'but that could be a disaster if it's wet. Do you think it would be safer to have it against the house outside the drawing room?'

'Don't worry about the weather,' Laura reassured her. 'We've frequently had receptions where the guests have had to be escorted across the lawn under golf umbrellas. If the forecast is doubtful, we'll bring special flooring to lay over the grass, so people won't dirty their shoes.'

'You're a marvel, my dear!' Jean said admiringly. 'You think of everything!'

'In my job, I have to.'

Returning indoors, they had a cup of tea, seated companionably at the kitchen table.

'Adrian's very fond of you,' Jean said suddenly.

'And I of him.' Laura, on instant alert, kept her voice neutral. 'You know,' she hurried on, 'I was thinking earlier how little I really know about his childhood and everything. I'd hoped there might be photographs around, but...'

'My dear, if it's photos you want, I've several drawers full! I just didn't want to clutter up the house with them, that's all. Would you like to see them?'

'I'd love to,' Laura said.

Jean hurried upstairs and returned with an armful of albums, over which the two of them pored for the next hour or so. There were pictures of Moira as a baby, and as a toddler holding the infant Adrian. There were snaps of family pets, of Adrian as a serious-faced two-year-old sitting on a donkey at the seaside. Laura studied the small face for similarities to the one she knew, but in vain.

'It's hard to recognise him without the beard!' she laughed.

The next album produced school photographs, and the faded writing underneath them proclaimed: 'Moira starts at Lismore', and: 'Adrian's first term at Braeburn'. There were Sports Day photos and snaps of school plays and, finally, the more formal graduation portraits, before coming to Moira's wedding, which Jean passed over hastily.

As they had gone through the albums, she'd chatted incessantly about her children, their likes and dislikes, their love of dressing up, the heartbreak when pets died, and by the time the sound of voices in the hall proclaimed the men's return, Laura felt she knew a great deal more about the man who wanted to marry her. What she had still not ascertained, however, was whether or not she wanted to marry him.

'We really needn't worry,' Laura reported back to Beth the following week. 'They're not hard to please; they'll be delighted with everything. Incidentally, Jean jumped at the thought of a gateau St Honoré, so on your own head be it. As regards the kitchen, it has more space than many we've worked in, but we'll need to take some of our own equipment.'

She took out the notes she had made during her discussion with Jean, and they went through them together, adding other ideas as they occurred.

'The house has been featured in *Ideal Home*,' Laura said. 'I wonder if we could get it or some other glossy to cover the party?'

Beth whistled. 'That's a thought. Talk about publicity!'

'I'll mention it next time I speak to her. I think she knows quite a few influential people up there, and she's so proud of the house she'd probably jump at it. Incidentally, there are enough bedrooms for everyone, though it will mean a bit of doubling up.'

'Bags I with Stephan!' Beth said with a grin.

Their chief barman was a handsome Dane, who handled with good-humoured stoicism the advances of slightly inebriated ladies at every function he attended.

'And how did the weekend go in general?' Beth asked, when they finally closed their files.

'Fine, after an uncertain start.'

'No pressurised engagement, I presume?'

Laura smiled. 'The question did arise obliquely, but I was able to bypass it.'

'And what of your own feelings?'

'Unchanged.'

Beth shook her head wonderingly. 'I despair of you,' she said.

Twelve

When Ellie returned to her study after lunch, the phone on her desk was ringing and she lifted it as she sat down, her mind already on the afternoon timetable.

'Yes?'

'There's a call for you, Miss Marlow. A gentleman. He didn't give his name, just said it was personal.'

Ellie frowned. 'Very well, Stella, put him through.'

It must be important, she thought with a ripple of unease; Mark never phoned her at school – it was one of their unwritten rules

294

– but if a call was essential, withholding his name was likely to arouse more interest than giving it.

'Ellie?' said a voice in her ear, and it was not Mark's.

A wave of heat washed over her, accelerating her heartbeat and drying her mouth. She said sharply, 'Who is that?'

'I'm sorry – I didn't mean to startle you. I—'

'Who's speaking?'

There was a pause. Then he said quietly, 'It's Patrick.'

Briefly, she wondered if she was going to faint, but that was ridiculous. She had never fainted in her life. Was this a practical joke? Yet she had recognised his voice immediately he'd spoken. Thoughts whirled round her head, colliding with each other. Fay – Roger – *Jeremy!*

'Ellie?'

She moistened her lips. 'Where are you?'

'In London. Would you – is there any chance of our meeting?'

'Patrick, have you any *idea*...?' She broke off helplessly. The phone was slippery in her sweaty palm; she transferred it to her other hand.

'Please, Ellie. You know I always come to you when I'm in trouble.'

She said forcefully, 'You can't just phone like this, after nearly seven years! Where have you been? Why did you never get in touch?' *Did you kill Jeremy?*

'I'll explain everything when I see you. Don't turn me down, Ellie. You're my only hope.'

She was silent.

'If you tell me to get lost afterwards, fair enough, I shan't bother you again, I promise. Just meet me this one time.'

Still she didn't speak. The minutes ticked away. Finally he said resignedly, 'Very well. I can't blame you, but it was worth a try.'

Yet how could she let him disappear again, without answering the questions that had haunted her for years? She owed it to Fay, to the girls, most of all, perhaps, to herself.

She said tautly, 'All right, Patrick; I'll meet you this one time.'

She heard him release his breath, indication of the strain he'd been under. 'Bless you. How soon can you make it?'

The following day's scheduled flicked through her mind. There was nothing that could not be handed to someone else. In any case, delay was now unthinkable.

'I could manage tomorrow,' she said.

'Wonderful! Twelve thirty at Claridges?'

She raised an eyebrow. 'You're not exactly penniless, then.'

'Not exactly.'

'Very well, Patrick. Twelve thirty at Claridges.'

She put down the phone and pressed her hands to her burning cheeks. Had that really happened? Was it possible that she was actually meeting Patrick tomorrow? He hadn't asked her not to tell Fay – hadn't, in fact, mentioned Fay at all – but she knew she would not. No point in upsetting her, until she knew the facts.

The phone rang again, making her jump. She snatched it up and waited. Stella said hesitantly, 'Miss Marlow? The Chairman of the Governors would like a quick word, if you have a moment?'

Ellie drew a deep breath, composing herself. 'Of course, Stella. Put him through.'

After the brief hiccup, normal service was being resumed.

She had barely slept the previous night, and on the train coming up the magazine lay unread on her lap as she gazed out of the window, wondering what possible explanation Patrick could have for his abrupt departure and more than six years' silence.

Deciding the tube would be unbearable in this season of heat and tourists, Ellie took a taxi to Claridges. By the time it pulled up outside the imposing building, her heart was beating high in her chest and she was trembling. She went directly to the ladies' room, where she washed her sticky hands in cool water and gazed critically at her reflection. A touch more powder and lipstick, perhaps. Then she made a *moue* of derision at her reflection. It was not a lover she was meeting, for God's sake; it was the man who'd deserted her sister and precipitated her breakdown, who had disrupted her own life and necessitated her moving to Sandford, who had let down his daughters just as surely as Jeremy had Laura – and who might, just might, have murdered his rival. But that, she didn't really believe.

Steeling herself, she walked out of the cloakroom and made her way to the restaurant. At the door she paused, but before she could speak the maître d' approached her and said smoothly, 'Miss Marlow? The gentleman is waiting for you. Please come this way.'

Almost fearfully she followed him, threading her way between the tables, and then she saw, just ahead of them, a man rising to his feet. He was by the window and his face was against the light, but she knew him with every fibre of her body. He came round the table and, taking both her hands, kissed her on the cheek.

'Ellie,' he said. 'You don't know how good it is to see you.'

The maître d' pulled out her chair for her and, with a flick of the thick damask napkin, laid it tenderly over her lap. Then he glided away and they were alone. The last time they'd been together, Ellie thought numbly, was when he'd called round in such distress over the death of his patient – the night before he went to London.

She looked at him across the table, noting the inevitable changes the years had brought. He was deeply tanned and looked well, damn him. A few more creases were evident around his eyes, but they were the type acquired from screwing them up against a bright sun. There was more grey in his hair and his jaw-line was a trifle less firm. Other than that, he was just ... Patrick.

A tall glass full of ice-cold gin and tonic was placed in front of her. 'I hope that's still your tipple,' Patrick said.

She nodded, and sat waiting. He raised his own to her but gave no toast, and they both drank. She set her glass carefully down, her hand numb from its coldness, and met his eyes.

'What happened, Patrick?' she asked unsteadily.

'Give me a moment, Ellie. First, how is everyone – Fay and the girls? And why are you living at Sandford? I tried ringing your house, but the people who answered said they were tenants and gave me that number, which, obviously, I recognised. That's why I rang you at school.'

'I'm at Sandford,' Ellie said deliberately, 'because when you disappeared and Jeremy was murdered, Fay virtually collapsed and I had to take over. She was ill for over six months, and it took even longer for her confidence to come back.'

She looked at him challengingly and saw that he had paled beneath his tan.

'God, I never thought – but I should have, I suppose. It was ghastly news about Jeremy; I only heard of it months later, by way of an English newspaper.'

From the host of questions that clamoured at her, she asked the last first. '*English* newspaper? Where were you?'

'In Argentina. I've been there all the time.'

She stared at him, but there were other, more important points he'd raised. 'You're saying you didn't know about Jeremy?'

'That's right, with being out of the country and everything.'

'But Patrick, he was killed the night you were in London, not far from your hotel.'

Watching him closely, she saw the dawning horror in his eyes. He'd been about to take a drink, but he replaced the glass with a suddenly trembling hand.

'God in heaven,' he said slowly. 'You're not saying they thought *I* did it?'

'What were they supposed to think?' Ellie demanded, playing devil's advocate. 'The next morning you took out a large sum of money and disappeared off the face of the earth.'

'And they're ... still looking for me? The police?'

'Quite probably.' She was determined not to lessen the blow. He deserved to pay for all the heartbreak he'd caused.

After a minute he said flatly, 'And I thought all I had to worry about was travelling on a false passport.'

A waiter materialised beside him and handed them each a menu. Neither of them looked at it. Patrick stirred himself enough to say, 'Could you bring two more gin and tonics, please?' then, as the waiter moved away, 'God, this changes everything.'

Ellie leaned forward urgently. 'Patrick, I can't stand this a moment longer. For God's sake tell me what happened. From the beginning.'

He sat back in his chair, still looking blanched despite his tan. 'Yes, of course. That's why I wanted to see you.' He took a deep breath and began to speak, and Ellie had the impression this was a speech he had rehearsed carefully, perhaps over years, knowing that the time must come when he would have to deliver it.

'When I drove up to London that day, I was fully intending to attend the meeting with Guy and the solicitor, but I was out of my mind with worry about that patient dying.' He broke off. 'What happened about that? Was I held responsible?'

'No. The basic cause was an adrenalin rush caused by the intravenous injection, added to the fact that he was stressed out anyway at the thought of having treatment. It all combined to give him a heart attack. As the coroner said, not uncommon in a man of his age.'

'Well, that's a relief, at least. I've often felt bad about leaving Roger to carry the can.'

He paused, but Ellie was not ready to talk about Roger, and after a moment he went on. 'Well, I checked into the hotel, but I couldn't face dinner and decided my best bet was to go out and get blind drunk. I hadn't gone drinking with that intention since I was about eighteen, but I must say I made a pretty good job of it.' A humourless smile tugged at his mouth.

'I went from pub to pub, and eventually settled down at one and struck up a conversation with the man sitting next to me. He was about my age, and told me his wife had died a year previously. He had no ties of any kind, so he'd decided to up sticks and emigrate to the Argentine – in search of some sunshine, he said. He was intending to tour South America and possibly move on to the States or Canada.

' "So," he said, "I'm booked on the evening flight tomorrow. This is my last night in dear old Blighty for God knows how long – perhaps for ever." He fished in his breast pocket and took out his passport and airline ticket. "I have to keep looking at these to convince myself it's really happening." He opened the passport and we laughed over the photo. "No one would recognise me from that in a million years!" he said. "It could just as easily be you!" And it was true. We were both tall, with nondescript features and light-brown hair. Like a thousand others, really.'

He took another long drink, and wiped his mouth on his napkin. 'Well, we drank steadily for a while, and when we decided we'd had enough, we left together. He still hadn't booked anywhere for the night; he'd left his things in a left-luggage locker at Paddington and after collecting them he was going to find somewhere near the station. Then, the next day, he'd get the train direct to Heathrow.'

Patrick stopped speaking and Ellie sat unmoving. The waiter approached and asked if they were ready to order. Patrick waved him away, but Ellie said, 'Perhaps we should choose something?'

'You're right.'

She could see that, now he'd embarked on his story, he resented having to break off. They ordered spinach soufflé, followed by Dover sole with duchesse potatoes and a bottle of Muscadet. Then she sat back in her chair.

'Go on,' she said.

But he remained silent for several more minutes. Then he said heavily, 'They say things go in threes, don't they? Well, thank God there were only two.'

'Two what?'

'Heart attacks. First Mr Temple in the surgery, then this guy.'

Ellie's eyes widened. 'He had a heart attack?'

'Yep. At least, I imagine that's what it was. He suddenly gripped my arm and went down like a sack of potatoes, pulling me with him. I think he was dead when he hit the pavement. I loosened his collar and pulled his jacket open, and his passport fell out of his inside pocket. I slipped it into mine for safety; then I got to work pumping his chest. I even tried the kiss of life, all the things we'd learned to do in an emergency, though of course I had no drugs to hand. I doubt if they'd have saved him, anyway. After a while I saw that it was hopeless, so I ran to the nearest phone box and dialled 999. There was a street sign opposite, so I knew where we were, but I didn't give my name when they asked for it, or wait for them to arrive. I don't know why. Anyway, I was pretty shaken, as you can imagine, and I don't remember making my way back to the hotel, though I must have done, because I woke up there hours later, with a mouth like the bottom of a birdcage.

'And all my worries came flooding back: Temple's death, the missing money, Fay, even bloody Jeremy. And I thought, I wish I could just get the hell out of it, like Paul meant to. Paul Nolan, his name was. Same initials as mine. Quite a coincidence, that. Then later, when I put on my jacket, I found his passport with the airline ticket and various papers tucked inside. His photograph was staring up at me, and I remembered what he'd said: *It could just as easily be you.*

'I told myself it wouldn't be stealing; Paul had no more use for them, poor devil, and he'd no relatives in the world to benefit from his estate. The odd thing was that I didn't make any conscious decision, just accepted it. It seemed like providence.

'So ... I checked out of the hotel, arranged to draw out a substantial amount of cash, and ... flew out to Argentina as Paul Nolan.'

There was a long silence. Ellie started on her second gin. Then she said expressionlessly, 'We were asked to go and identify him.'

Patrick's eyes widened in disbelief. 'You *what?*'

'We'd reported you missing, and a body answering your description – you were right there – was found with no identity on it. So Fay and Guy and I had to view it. Or rather Guy did, but Fay and I went with him.'

'I never dreamed...'

'There were a lot of things you didn't dream about, Patrick.'

'Yes,' he said soberly.

'So what happened when you got to Argentina?'

'By that time I was getting cold feet, and had decided to own up and come straight back. In any case I was pretty sure they'd suss me straight away; but the papers were all in order and I sailed through Immigration, so I just ... went ahead. I reckoned it would be wise to avoid the big towns, so I took a train and got off at a little place out on the pampas, where I got a job working on a gaucho ranch, with no questions asked. I gradually dug myself a little niche in the community, and there I stayed for quite a while. It was a pretty good life, all things considered.'

'Of course, you speak fluent Spanish – Fay told me that. But I hope you're not asking me to believe that working as a ranch hand netted you enough to buy that expensive-looking suit, or to eat at Claridges?'

He smiled. 'No, I'm not asking that.'

'You didn't rob any South American banks, I trust?'

'No, but the truth might strike you as equally implausible.' He'd been toying with his fork, but now he looked up and met her eyes. 'Have you ever heard of Carl Clifford?'

'The best-seller writer?'

'The same. Well, you're looking at him.'

She gazed at him blankly. 'You're Carl Clifford?'

'I am indeed. Which explains why I'm not short of the readies.'

'But I don't understand. I mean, you'd never done any writing...'

'Ah, but I had. Ask Fay. I'd tried my hand at several short stories without success, but it's always been there at the back of my mind. You know, the usual thing: some day I'd like to write a novel. So, with time on my hands, I did, and everything took off from there. I left the ranch, bought a flat in BA and started to live the high life, and for a while it was great. But as time went on, I began to feel homesick. I thought a lot about Fay and the girls and you.'

He twirled the stem of his wine glass, not looking at her. 'The girls especially,' he added in a low voice. 'You might find it hard to believe, after the way I behaved, but I began to miss them terribly. One day I saw a man walking along the street carrying a little girl, with two more clinging to his coat, and I just began to weep – then and there, in the middle of the Avenida Corrientes.'

He took a long drink of wine. 'The crunch finally came,' he continued, 'when my publishers increased the pressure on me to do a publicity tour in the UK. I'd been nervous enough in the States, but I knew I couldn't come back here without clearing up the mess I'd left behind. Though I must say, it never entered my head I was suspected of murder.'

He paused. 'They never found who did it, then?'

'No.'

'What the hell was Jeremy doing in London, anyway?'

'He'd moved up there, to start a new life with Georgia Prentiss.'

'Of course. I remember now, poor Laura being upset about it.'

'That was my strongest card in defending you,' Ellie commented, leaning to one side as the waiter set a ramekin containing the soufflé in front of her. 'The fact that he'd found someone else, so didn't pose a threat to you.'

'My God, Ellie, I'd no idea what I was putting you all through.' He picked up his spoon. 'How is Fay, by the way?'

'Fine,' she said briefly.

'Ellie ... this is tricky, but ... I don't want to go back to her.'

'I doubt if she'd have you.'

'No, probably not. As you know, I was infatuated with her from day one, but in South America, almost without my being aware of it, it gradually faded away. I'm still fond of her, of course, but I don't love her any more; and I doubt if she ever really loved me.'

'You met someone else out there?' Ellie asked steadily.

'Oh, one or two now and again, but nothing serious. It's not that; it's simply that at long last I've grown out of Fay.' He paused. 'What about her? Has she found someone else?'

'One or two, like you, but in any case she couldn't think of marrying for another six months, when you could legally be assumed to be dead.'

He winced. 'Put like that...'

'That's how it is.'

'Is there anyone she might *want* to marry, then, when she's free?'

Ellie crumbled the roll on her side plate. Then she said quietly, 'There's Roger.'

He put down his spoon and stared at her. 'Roger? God, you're full of surprises, Ellie, and I can't say they're pleasant ones. But ... what about Pammy?'

'Pammy died two years ago, of cancer.'

'Oh, my God.'

'They'd both stood by Fay through thick and thin when you ... defected. They were really good friends. And Fay stood by him through Pammy's illness and death. There wasn't anything else between them until about three months ago.'

'I never thought it would be easy, coming

back, but I certainly hadn't anticipated this nest of vipers. And you're still living at Sandford?'

'Yes. Well, Father died and the girls all left home, and Fay seemed to need me, so I stayed on. But I've been thinking of moving back soon.'

'When Fay and Roger get married?' he asked levelly.

'Nothing definite has been decided.'

'And now I'm the cat among the pigeons. Perhaps I should never have come back.'

She put her hand quickly on his. 'No, don't say that. For one thing, you must clear your name over Jeremy's death, and then you'll be free to do your tour.'

'Did *you* think I'd done it – killed him, I mean?'

She met his eye. 'No,' she said honestly, 'I never did. And I'm sure none of the family did, either.'

'Well, thank you for that. What I was going to ask, before all these ramifications came to light, was whether you'd go round and see my solicitor? He's James Brannon at Brannon, Maybury in Rushyford. Explain the position and say I'd be grateful if he would accompany me to a police station when I go and make a clean breast of things. Could you do that?'

'Why don't you just phone him?'

Patrick gave a harsh laugh. 'Can you

imagine explaining all this over the phone? Anyway, I wanted him to have a little warning, that I'm back and so on. Would you mind?'

'I suppose not. What do you want me to tell Fay?'

'Whatever you like.'

'By the way, Jenny's married and expecting a baby.'

'Little Jenny? God, that makes me feel old! Who's the lucky man? That Oliver chap she had a crush on?'

'The same. As for the others, Laura has a top-notch catering business here in London, Christa is self-employed doing translation work, and Claire has set up house with some young man in Oxford.'

He was silent for a while; then he said, 'Funny, when you're away you somehow expect things at home to go on being exactly the same. But my daughters have all grown up and I wasn't there for them, not even to give Jenny away. I let everyone down, but myself most of all.'

'Have you thought about where you would live, if you came home permanently? I mean, now you're writing, you presumably don't want to return to dentistry – or Rushyford, come to that, if you've finished with Fay.'

'No, I've another life now, and a highly satisfying one. I'd thought of buying a place nearer London, but I wanted very much to mend bridges, get to know the girls again, and be on a friendly footing with them. Do you think that would be possible?'

'I don't know, Patrick. You hurt them very badly – worse, if anything, than Jeremy did Laura. You were the head of the family, you'd been there all their lives, and then suddenly, without any explanation, you weren't. Claire particularly fretted for a long time. She kept expecting you to write.'

She glanced at him and saw there were tears in his eyes. 'However,' she went on more gently, 'you're still their father, and if you explain to them as you have to me, perhaps they'll understand. They're not children any longer.'

'And Fay? I guess she was grieving for Jeremy more than for me.'

'It was the combination of things that was too much for her.'

'I'm shocked to hear about Pammy. I was at her wedding, damn it. She was ... great. Was she ... in a lot of pain?'

'It all happened very quickly.'

Their plates were removed, and they sat in silence until the next course was brought. Then Ellie stirred. 'Well, it's all been doom and gloom so far, but I think we've covered the essentials. So now tell me about your life in the Argentine, how you got the idea for your first book, and how it all took off.'

He smiled and some of the tension left his face. He began to talk of the long evenings at the ranch when there was no work to do, and he wasn't interested in sitting drinking and smoking with the others. 'We had TV, of course, but it wasn't very inspiring, and I grew tired of reading books in Spanish. So, I decided to write my own.'

Ellie smiled. 'Just like that.'

'As you say. I can't explain it, but when I'd tried to write back home, my mind had been ... hobbled in some way. It was like jumping over hurdles and I couldn't really get going.'

'Very gaucho-like similes,' Ellie remarked dryly, and he laughed.

'Anyway, it was quite different there. One night I was lying awake listening to all the night noises, and quite suddenly the idea came to me, for *The Interloper*. And – I'm not spinning a line, Ellie – it just seemed to write itself. I could hardly keep up with it. Whole sentences were forming in my head all day, and I had to jot them down on odd scraps of paper. Then, when I got to my room after supper, it was like releasing the dam and I was ... swept away with it. It was most exhilarating.'

'I'm sure.'

'There was an old computer in the ranch house, and I worked away on that. Nobody minded. When I'd finished, I packed it up and sent it to a London publisher under the name of Carl Clifford. Don't ask me why I didn't opt for New York – it was certainly nearer, but I was already beginning to think of coming home.

'Well, it was accepted straight away for an incredibly large advance, and after that there was no looking back. So I packed in my job and, as I said, took a flat in BA to write the next two. It seemed as good a time as any to "ditch" Paul Nolan, and though that name still appeared on all official documents, my publishers and everyone in BA knew me only as Carl Clifford. And there, basically, you have it. Now, what about you? No wedding ring, I see, so Mark Ridley hasn't talked you round yet!'

'Not yet,' she confirmed quietly. 'Oh, I've been busy doing the usual things. Nothing out of the ordinary, but I've had some good holidays. One year I went to Peru. I didn't realise you were so close – comparatively speaking.'

By the end of the meal they were almost at ease with each other, but both were aware there were many things to be resolved before they could draw a line under the past.

In the train going home, Ellie's mind was full of the things he'd told her, but there was something else, too, which had equal claim on her attention. After those first minutes of panic in the cloakroom – occasioned, she now realised, by fear of what she might learn – she had been able to sit and talk to Patrick without any of the heart flutterings that had previously plagued her. Tentatively, she prodded her emotions and received no response. Patrick was her brother-in-law and an old friend. And, for the first time in her life, nothing else.

What had he said about Fay? That his feelings for her had gradually faded without his realising it? The same must have happened to her and, also without her being aware of it, Mark had imperceptibly slipped into his place.

Ellie smiled to herself and, at last opening her magazine, settled down for the rest of the journey home.

Thirteen

By chance, Ellie's birthday fell two days after her meeting with Patrick and, since Jenny had invited the whole family for a celebration meal, she decided to wait till they were all together before breaking her news. In any event, she needed time both to digest what she had learned and also to think of the best way of telling them. In the meantime, she phoned the solicitor and made an appointment to see him after school.

James Brannon had represented the dental practice since Patrick and Roger first set it up, but he was not the Marlows' solicitor and Ellie had never met him. He rose from his desk with outstretched hand as she was shown into his office, a tall, thin man with a high domed forehead and tortoiseshell spectacles.

'Miss Marlow, this is a pleasure. Please sit down and tell me what I can do for you.'

Ellie perched a little nervously on the chair. 'It's a somewhat delicate matter, Mr Brannon.' She squared her shoulders and took the plunge. 'Yesterday, I went to London and met my brother-in-law, Patrick Nelson.'

'Good God! He's still alive, then.' He made a gesture with his hand. 'I beg your pardon; I interrupted you.'

Slowly and carefully, Ellie went through the account as Patrick had detailed it. Brannon sat unmoving, intent on every word. Once or twice she faltered and glanced at him, but he made no attempt to help her, nor to interrupt again, until she came to the end. 'At his request,' she finished, 'I agreed to explain to you what had happened, and ask if you would accompany him to the police station. I must repeat, Mr Brannon, that he knew nothing of Jeremy Page's death for some months, and even then had no idea his name had been linked with the crime. He was expecting merely to own up to travelling on a false passport. You do believe that, don't you?'

'*I* might believe it, Miss Marlow, and I have no doubt you do. What concerns me is whether the police will. Of the other offences, the only one which would concern them is theft of the passport and airline ticket. Thank God we at least know the owner died from natural causes. The Passport Office, I imagine, would concentrate on impersonation and using false documents, although that would seem to be of

317

more interest to the Argentine authorities than those in this country. It would, of course, be a much more serious offence if the passport had been forged, or Mr Nelson had come by it by deception. From what you say, however, that was not the case, nor did he make any attempt to alter it in any way, or to change the photograph.

'Taking all that into consideration, I should say a jail sentence would be highly unlikely. In view of his mental state at the time, which has already been established, we should be able to plead mitigating circumstances and settle for a fine.

'The murder, however, puts an entirely different slant on it, as I'm sure you'll appreciate. Can he provide any back-up for his movements that evening?'

Ellie lifted her shoulders helplessly. 'Even if he knew which pub he'd been in, who's going to remember two particular men drinking together, especially after all this time? We know when he left the hotel and when he returned to it, but that's all that can be verified.' She paused. 'Would it be better not to go to the police after all?'

'I can't advise that, Miss Marlow. He can at least establish the identity of Mr Nolan, who was buried as John Bull or some such, his real name being unknown. For the rest, we must hope that the fact that he's given himself up, so to speak, would work in his favour.'

Not too promising an outlook, Ellie reflected worriedly. However, before she left she extracted a promise that if Patrick contacted him, Mr Brannon would go to London to meet him, and they could take things from there. It was, in the circumstances, the best she could do.

Fay was out when she returned to Sandford, and she made a hurried phone call to let Patrick know the position.

'How's Fay taken it?' he asked, when she'd explained the outcome.

'I haven't told her yet. We're all meeting tomorrow, and I thought it best for everyone to hear it at the same time.'

'Tomorrow? What – oh, of course. The seventh of June: your birthday. I'm sorry, I'd forgotten.'

'Let's say you have more important things on your mind.'

'Could you sound them out for me, Ellie? Find out how they'd feel if I came down? I'm desperate to see them all.'

Downstairs, she heard the front door slam.

'I must go,' she said rapidly. 'Phone me when you have any news, and I'll do what I can this end.'

Adrian was abroad on a business trip, and so unable to be at the dinner. Secretly, Ellie was relieved. She hadn't seen him since Fay's birthday, but what she had overheard at the Watermill had left her with a feeling of unease. Admittedly this was unfair, since it had been based purely on rumour, though if there were any truth in it, she'd a right to be concerned. Adrian's sexual proclivities were his own affair only as long as they didn't impinge on Laura, which they clearly did.

Jenny and Oliver lived in a small house at the far end of Rushyford, just off the main road. Now five months pregnant, Jenny was blooming with health and had refused all suggestions that she should cut down on her busy lifestyle.

'My wings will be clipped once the baby comes,' she said. 'Till then, I'll make the most of my freedom.' So she continued with her job as a garden-designer, which involved driving considerable distances between sites and, once there, standing long hours, often in wind or rain, supervising the execution of her designs. In the evenings she rehearsed with either the local Gilbert and Sullivan company or the choral society. Jenny alone of the girls had a singularly sweet singing voice, which could well have afforded her an alternative career.

'The meal is good, old-fashioned English cuisine,' she informed her family on their arrival. 'I can't hope to compete with Laura, so I don't try.'

'Believe me,' Laura declared, 'after hours of preparing langoustines or duck à l'orange, I frequently sit down to bangers and mash!'

'Drinks outside.' Oliver directed them through the patio doors to the little garden behind the house. Here, Jenny had been able to indulge all her own passions and ideas, and it was crammed full of scent and colour, a secluded haven after the pressures of the day.

Claire and Roy had driven over from Oxford, and were already seated on the terrace when the Sandford party arrived. Claire jumped up to hug Ellie, and presented her with a small packet. 'Happy Birthday,' she exclaimed, 'to the best aunt in the world!'

Oliver opened a bottle of champagne, and they all drank Ellie's health.

'Speech!' called Roy, and everyone clapped.

Ellie braced herself. 'First, thank you, everyone, for my lovely presents, though perhaps the best one is being able to spend my birthday with you all. So special thanks to Jenny and Oliver for inviting us here, and the rest of you for coming.'

There was another smatter of applause and Jenny, thinking she had finished, turned away to return to the kitchen; but Ellie raised a hand.

'There's something else I have to say, and

I don't quite know how to say it.' She looked round at their faces, still half-smiling but wondering at her change of tone. Her nails dug into the palms of her hands. Here goes, she thought. 'On Tuesday, I went up to London and had lunch with Patrick.'

There was total silence. Fay's hand went to her throat; the rest of them simply stared.

'He phoned me at school the day before, and asked me to meet him. Until then, like you, I'd no idea if he was alive or dead.'

Oliver, his arm round Jenny, had guided her to a seat, and Claire was gripping Roy's hand tightly. Still no one spoke, and Ellie went on.

'There's a lot to fill in, obviously, but that can come a little later. The main facts are that he's been in Argentina all this time, and ... that he didn't learn of Jeremy's death until several months later, from an out-of-date English paper. Even then, he didn't realise it had happened the night he was in London. Anyway, he's back now. He's well, but very conscious of the wrong he's done us all.'

'I hope he doesn't think he can turn the clock back,' Fay said in a cracked voice.

'No, he realises we've all moved on. But he very much wants to see you. He's missed you all very much.'

'Then why didn't he write?' Claire demanded, and burst into tears.

'I don't know,' Ellie said honestly. That was something she hadn't asked him.

'And why did he contact you and not me?' Fay asked, her eyes huge in her suddenly white face.

'Perhaps he thought it would be less of a shock to me.'

'And you've known since Monday that he's back?' Fay stared at her accusingly.

'I didn't want to say anything until I'd seen him,' Ellie explained. 'And when I had, it seemed best to wait till this evening, when we'd all be together and I shouldn't have to go through it more than once. One of the reasons he contacted me was to ask me to see his solicitor, explain what had happened, and ask him to accompany him when he goes to the police.'

'The police?' Christa's voice cracked. 'What's he done?'

'He used someone else's passport – if you remember, we found his still in the desk at Sandford.'

'Whose passport?' Christa demanded. 'Did he steal it?'

'Technically, I suppose, but I think you'll understand—'

Jenny rose abruptly to her feet. 'If I don't go to the kitchen, the meal will be ruined. Don't you dare say another word about it, any of you, until we're in the dining room.'

Oliver followed her back into the house

and the rest of them sat in uneasy silence, avoiding each other's eyes.

She'd spoiled the party, Ellie thought in anguish. Perhaps she should have waited until they'd eaten; but then they'd have blamed her for not telling them at once. To her intense relief, Oliver reappeared almost immediately.

'Dinner's ready, if you'd like to come through.'

The Drakes' dining room was an extension off the kitchen, built almost entirely of glass. The pale wood glowed in the last of the evening sunshine but Oliver had already lit candles down the length of the table and their reflections glimmered in the glass walls. Jenny had decorated the table with small posies of flowers that echoed the colours of the carpet – soft mauves and pinks and blues. Ellie, her heart seeming to beat in her mouth, hoped they would all do justice to the meal so lovingly prepared.

During the first course of melon and prawns, Roy came to their rescue with an involved and amusing story about some DIY he was engaged on at the Oxford flat. Everyone was grateful to him, though no one really listened. The main course was trout with almonds, and it was only when they all had their plates in front of them and had helped themselves to new potatoes and vegetables that Jenny looked across at Ellie.

'Please tell us the rest of it now,' she said.

And Ellie did, in detail, up to the point where Patrick had started work on the ranch.

'We mustn't forget that, at the time, he was so stressed out as to be mentally ill,' she emphasised. 'Remember there'd been money missing from the practice, a patient had died, for which he'd convinced himself he was responsible, and on top of all that he'd been under strain for weeks, ever since Jeremy had come back. I'm sorry, Fay, but you must have realised that. He just ... snapped. When, the next morning, he saw the passport photo that was so like him, and that no one else had any use for, it seemed like the answer to a prayer.'

'All right,' Jenny said in a low voice, 'I can just about accept that. But why didn't he at least contact us later, let us know he was all right?'

'I don't know, love. He told me he'd intended to give himself up as soon as he landed; but when, greatly to his surprise, he passed through Immigration so smoothly, he just ... didn't. Perhaps by that time he felt he'd burned his bridges.'

'He could still have written,' Claire protested in a small voice.

'There's one thing more to tell you,' Ellie said rallyingly, 'which I'm sure will come as a considerable surprise. While he was at the ranch, Patrick started writing a novel, and to cut a long story short, it was published and became a best-seller.'

They were gazing at her in disbelief.

'He wrote under the name of Carl Clifford,' she ended.

There was a collective gasp round the table, as they all repeated incredulously, 'Carl Clifford? *The* Carl Clifford?'

Fay said flatly, 'I don't believe it. It's all very well to *say* that. He couldn't *prove* it, could he?'

'I imagine he could if you asked him,' Ellie said mildly.

'It says on the flyleaf of the books that the author lives in South America,' Roy pointed out.

'So do a lot of people,' Fay retorted.

'He said you knew he'd tried his hand at short stories,' Ellie reminded her.

'Which were rejected. That's a long way from out-and-out best-sellers.'

'You have to start somewhere,' Oliver commented. 'Those books are fantastic – I've read them all. I'd really enjoy meeting...' He broke off and flushed.

Fay said stubbornly, 'Well, I for one am not going to forgive him all he put us through, just because he turns out to be the famous Carl Clifford.' She shot Ellie a swift glance. 'Has he been in touch with Roger?'

'I don't think so. I ... told him the position.'

'What position?' Fay's tone was belligerent.

Christa said gently, 'Don't take it out on Aunt Ellie, Mum. It's not her fault.'

Ellie, who had flushed, continued calmly, 'Obviously, he didn't know about Pammy. It was a great shock.'

There was a silence, during which Oliver rose to clear the table and help Jenny to bring in the dessert.

'Strawberries and cream,' she announced, with false brightness. 'Very simple, but I know they're your favourite.'

Ellie rose quickly and put her arms round her, feeling her shoulders shaking as she fought to hold back tears. 'My very favourite dessert,' Ellie confirmed. 'Thank you, darling.'

'Don't cry, sweetheart,' Fay said, in a new, hard voice. 'We won't let him smarm his way back in. He won't have the chance to hurt us any more.'

Jenny extricated herself from Ellie's arms and turned to face her mother. 'But don't you see?' she cried out. 'I *want* to see him, more than anything in the world, and it's got nothing whatever to do with his being Carl bloody Clifford!'

Fay stared at her, aghast. Jenny ran to her, knelt beside her and put her face in Fay's lap. 'Oh, I'm not trying to hurt you, Mum! You know how much I love you – but I love him, too, whatever he's done. And if the police are going to be all stuffy about him being on the scene when Jeremy was killed, he really needs us, doesn't he?'

Fay sat staring down at her, not touching her, and after a minute Oliver went quietly over and lifted Jenny to her feet. Fay looked round the table.

'Is this how the rest of you feel? Christa? Claire?'

Slowly they both nodded. Fay put a hand to her head.

Christa said, 'We're not taking sides, Mamita. He did wrong, and he knows it, and he's come back to face up to it. He didn't have to do that. He could have gone on indefinitely, living the high life over there as Carl Clifford.'

Ellie, thinking of the UK book tour, kept quiet.

Claire turned to her. 'He really does want to see us? You weren't just saying that?'

'He's desperate to,' Ellie assured her, and told them about his tears in the faraway shopping centre.

'You must all do as you think best,' Fay said after a moment, 'just as long as you don't expect me to see him.'

Jenny wiped her eyes and resumed her place at the table, pulling the crystal bowl of strawberries towards her. 'Perhaps now we can get on with dinner,' she said with a shaky laugh.

Odd, Ellie reflected, how many family dramas had been played out round a dining table: Patrick's first, fatal sight of Fay at the Chinese restaurant all those years ago; the discovery of Jeremy's desertion; Guy's phone call which had alerted them to Patrick's disappearance. And now this. Guy, she thought, remembering him for the first time. Would Patrick contact him? If not, she must. No doubt Fay would tell Roger.

By unspoken assent, they did not speak of Patrick again. They were all depleted, emotionally drained, and needed time to gather their thoughts, to go over and assimilate what they'd learned this evening. Ellie, too, was exhausted. It had been more of a strain than she'd anticipated, telling them about him. She was touched that, after all that had happened, his daughters still wanted to see him. She just wished Fay could be a little more forgiving. Perhaps the difference was that Fay had never really loved him.

With the coffee, Jenny brought through a birthday cake, with a solitary candle glowing in the middle of it.

'How tactful of you, darling!' Ellie said with a laugh. 'Only fifty missing!'

Everyone joined eagerly in the laughter,

329

and the evening ended on the same light note with which it had begun. A birthday to remember, Ellie thought ruefully.

In the car going home, no one spoke. Laura was spending the night at Sandford, sleeping in her old room, which was always kept ready for her. They said their goodnights in the hall and made their separate ways upstairs, Christa to the flat, the others to their bedrooms. Ellie was sitting up in bed with a book she was not reading when, as she'd expected, there was a tap on the door and Laura looked round it.

'May I come in?'

'Of course.'

Ellie patted the edge of her bed and Laura settled herself on it. 'Quite a night,' she commented.

'Indeed.'

'How did he seem, really?'

'Surprisingly unchanged. Very sunburned, a little greyer.'

'I loved him too, you know. He was always very good to me.'

'I know, sweetie.' Ellie had noticed that Fay, when ascertaining reactions, had not questioned Patrick's stepdaughter.

'That wasn't why I came to see you, though,' Laura went on. 'I think we're probably talked out on that subject, at least for the moment. It's just that I haven't had a chance to talk to you since I arrived, and I

330

wanted to tell you about the Scottish trip.'

'Of course – to the Crawfords'. How did it go?'

'Very well, actually. Mrs C fell in with everything we suggested.'

'So you'll do the party?'

'Oh, yes. Adrian would never forgive me if we didn't!'

'How is Adrian?' Ellie asked carefully.

'Fine, as far as I know. He's in Europe for another ten days.' She gave a light laugh. 'He surprised me by going quite Scottish while we were up there, but it's worn off again now.' She glanced down, smoothing the edge of the duvet. 'I met his sister for the first time, and I don't think she liked me particularly.'

'Why ever not?'

Laura shrugged. 'Stealing her baby brother, perhaps. Still, we only saw her the day we arrived, so it was no problem.'

'What else did you do up there?'

'Oh, explored Edinburgh, which I loved; visited the Castle, walked the Royal Mile – all the usual things. And on the Monday we drove over to Loch Lomond, which was glorious, and went on a boat trip.'

Ellie reverted to the purpose of the visit. 'Won't it be an awful hassle, having to cart everything all that way?'

'Not all that different, actually. There'll only be the last minute things to buy up there. Beth and I have cooked up a veritable feast between us – or, I should say, we plan to!'

'Tell me,' Ellie invited, and listened raptly as Laura listed the various dishes that would be on offer. What a talented girl she was, she thought proudly. Please God Adrian won't hurt her in any way. Watching the dark, animated face – and God, how like Jeremy she was! – she ached with the fierceness of her love for this child, who from her birth had been closer to her than the others.

Because Jeremy was in her thoughts, she suddenly remembered his obituary, still lying undisturbed in her desk drawer. Consequently, when Laura came to the end of her account and they had discussed the preparations and logistics of the proposed party, Ellie said tentatively, 'To change the subject completely, I wondered if you'd like a copy of your father's obituary?'

Laura's face lit up. 'You've got one? That's wonderful! I was in such a state at the time I never even thought about it; but afterwards, I wished very much that I'd kept one. In fact, I was going to write to the papers and ask for a copy, but never got round to it.'

Ellie swung her feet out of bed and padded over to her desk. Opening a drawer, she extracted a slightly yellowed sheet of newsprint and handed it over.

'Thanks so much; I'll take it up to read in bed. Talking of which, you must be exhausted and here I am, chatting away and keeping you awake. I won't see you in the morning – I'm leaving at the crack of dawn – so I'll say goodbye now.' She leaned over to kiss her. 'Lovely to see you again, despite the bombshell you dropped!'

'Goodbye, darling,' Ellie said fondly. 'Come down again soon.'

When the door closed behind her, Ellie laid her book aside and switched off the light. She wasn't looking forward to the morning; Fay had been cool when they returned home, and wouldn't lightly forgive her for reintroducing Patrick into the family. Well, she hadn't asked for the role of mediator, she thought, tucking her pillow under her chin.

What would happen when Patrick and James Brannon went to the police? Would they believe his story? How would Guy react to his return? And Roger? Especially Roger.

Ellie sighed. If she was to be any use at school tomorrow, she had best put all such thoughts out of her head and go to sleep. Turning on her side, she resolutely closed her eyes.

Fourteen

The next few days passed without any word from Patrick, but the atmosphere at Sandford was still strained. On the Saturday, after Fay had refused to discuss the matter, Ellie took it on herself to phone Guy Nelson and, in view of Patrick's previous attitude towards his family, was not surprised to learn that he hadn't contacted them.

'And he swears it was some time before he learned of the murder?' Guy demanded, when she'd repeated everything Patrick had told her.

'Months, he said.'

'You'd have thought he'd have contacted the family at that point, if not before.'

'I don't think I agree,' Ellie said slowly. 'What, after all, could he have said? That he was sorry? No one would have believed him.'

'Perhaps you're right. I really don't know him any more. How's Fay taking it?'

'Not well. She doesn't want anything to do with him.'

'I can't say I blame her. Quite a turn-up,

this book business, though. I didn't know he had it in him. I've read them myself, and they're damned good. So ... we just wait and see how the police react?'

'That's about the size of it. I'll let you know as soon as I hear anything.'

That evening, Roger called round to collect Fay and, since she was still upstairs, it was Ellie who opened the door to him.

'Ellie.' He kissed her cheek. 'I've been wanting a word with you. I still can't get my head round the fact that Patrick's reappeared.'

'I know,' Ellie replied, leading him through to the conservatory. She had a sudden vision of her grandmother, sitting there in her wheelchair, and felt a spasm of sadness. Oh Gamma, she thought, what a mess we've made of things!

'Have you heard from him?' she asked Roger.

'Lord, no. I gather you told him about Fay and me?'

'He wanted to know if she was seeing anyone.'

'Why?' Roger asked sharply. 'Does he want her back?'

'No, I'm sure not.' She forbore from telling him Patrick no longer loved her.

'All the same, it's put me in the hell of a position. Damn it, he was my closest friend. And I'm worried about Fay, too; she's reacting very strangely.'

'It's only the shock, Roger. It was Jeremy, not Patrick, who was the love of her life.'

He nodded. He looked drawn, Ellie thought with a stab of sympathy. She'd known Roger almost as long as Patrick, and was fond of him. He was a decent man, and he didn't deserve this.

'He was very upset to hear about Pammy,' she added.

They both turned at the sound of footsteps on the stairs, and Fay came quickly into the room. She looked lovely, Ellie thought, but also vulnerable. There were hectic spots of colour on her face and her eyes glittered almost feverishly.

'I thought I heard the door,' she said, going to Roger and lifting her face for his kiss. 'I suppose you've been discussing me?'

He smiled his slow, attractive smile. 'Only in the nicest possible way.'

Fay flung a look at her sister. 'Really? Ellie thinks I'm behaving badly, and she's right, of course.'

Ellie said quietly, 'Fay, darling, I'm not the enemy. I'm on your side.'

Fay's face crumpled, and for a moment Ellie feared she might cry. But almost immediately she regained control and searched in her bag for a handkerchief. 'I know you are, sis,' she said contritely, reverting to the childhood name. 'Take no notice of me; I'm not a very nice person.'

'You're good enough for us, isn't she, Ellie?' Roger asserted, putting an arm round her.

'Warts and all!' Ellie replied, feeling the atmosphere needed to be lightened, and they were both laughing as they left the house.

It was a relief, once they'd gone, to get into her car and drive across the river to Mark. He was still living in the little cottage near the veterinary clinic. It was cosy and charming, and over the years Ellie had grown to love it.

She had spoken to him only once during the past week, when he had phoned on her birthday, and there had not been time, then, to tell him about Patrick. Now, she needed to pour out the story without having to hold anything back or slant it to avoid delicate sensibilities. When he opened the door to her knock, she went straight into his arms and leant against him with her eyes closed, grateful for the enveloping sense of support she always felt in his presence. After a minute she reached up, cupped his face in her hands, and kissed him.

'Well!' he said teasingly as, slightly embarrassed, she moved away. 'What have I done to deserve this?'

'Just been you,' she said, with a catch in her voice. Her realisation on the train was still new and precious, a sustaining comfort underlying all the traumas that had occupied her over the last few days.

'Come and sit down, my love, and tell me what's happened.'

So, with a glass in her hand and Mark's concerned eyes on her face, she went yet again through the story of Patrick's phone call, their subsequent meeting, and his account of the last six years.

'I saw his solicitor as he requested,' she finished, 'but I haven't heard anything since. God knows what happens now.'

'And no doubt Fay's had another attack of the vapours, and everything's landed on you again?'

'Well, she's refusing to see Patrick, which isn't really surprising; but she wouldn't phone Guy, either, so I rang him this morning.'

'They all lean on you,' Mark said tersely, 'Patrick included. They always have. It's high time they stood on their own feet and let you have a life of your own.'

Since he insisted she needed a break from the family, they didn't mention the matter again. They ate lamb chops and new potatoes – Mark's cuisine not being particularly adventurous – and finished with ice cream and chocolate sauce. Then they sat close together on the sofa over coffee and brandy, listening to his CDs.

Finally, as had become their habit, they went up to the little bedroom under the eaves for an hour, before it was time for Ellie to return home. His love-making was gentle and tender, but her response took them both by surprise, being swifter and more passionate than usual, and sweeping them away in a maelstrom of sensations that climaxed with such force that they remained clinging breathlessly to each other for some time after it was over.

'Oh God, Ellie!' he said shakily into her neck. 'That was ... unbelievable.'

Beyond the uncurtained windows, the summer night had darkened into blue luminosity and the first stars were pricking through. She couldn't see his face – only the warm, comforting shape of him – and she wondered how it could possibly have taken her so long to see where her affections really lay.

'I love you, Mark,' she said softly, for the very first time, and felt his sudden stillness. He raised his head, urgently trying to make out her features in the semi-dark.

'Say that again?'

'I said I love you. Thank you for being so patient with me.'

'God, Ellie, I was beginning to think I'd never hear you say that. Oh, my love!' He started to kiss her again and it was some time before she was able to interject breathlessly, 'Can we keep it to ourselves for just a little while longer, until this business with Patrick has been resolved? After that...'

'Yes?' he prompted, continuing systematically to kiss her throat and ears.

'After that, if you still want me, I'll be proud and happy to marry you.'

At the beginning of the following week, Christa received a letter forwarded from her London address, which clearly unsettled her; but she volunteered nothing, and Ellie left for school, hoping yet another crisis was not about to descend on them.

That morning, at break, the awaited call came.

'Patrick! At last! What's been happening?'

'Sorry not to have been in touch,' he said gruffly. 'The truth is, I was putting off hearing the girls' reactions. Are they refusing to see me?'

'No. After the initial shock, they said they wanted to.'

'God, that's wonderful!' he said jubilantly. 'Much more than I deserve.'

'Patrick, did you see Mr Brannon?'

He sobered. 'Yes. He came with me to the station that had been handling my ... disappearance.'

'What happened?'

'Well, I told them more or less the full story, but what really interested them was the murder. They kept asking whether I could prove where I was that night, which, of course, I couldn't. God knows if they believe me, but I took up your point about Jeremy having left the district, so no longer being in our hair. Thanks for that lead.'

'At least they didn't lock you up!' Ellie said fatuously.

'Not yet; I've been bailed to appear in three weeks, but in the meantime I'm free. Though what can come up in three weeks that hasn't in six years defeats me. Still, it gives us a breathing space.'

'Yes,' Ellie said doubtfully. Foolishly, she'd been hoping for an instant exoneration. 'Patrick, I phoned Guy. I think he'd appreciate a call.'

'Yes, yes, I suppose that's the least I can do. But how soon can I see the girls?'

'Well, it's up to you to arrange something.' She hesitated. 'It is all four you're thinking of?'

'Naturally.' He sounded surprised. Then: 'Oh, you mean Laura? Of course I want to see her. I've always been fond of her, and now I'm the only father she's got.'

'That's great, because she's fond of you, too. All the same, it might be politic to contact Christa in the first instance. She's back at Sandford at the moment, after breaking off a relationship, but if you phone early in the week, Fay will be at the book shop.'

'What book shop?'

'She works part-time at one.'

'Fay goes out to work? I can't believe it! And don't tell me she's been engaged in flogging my books for the last four years?'

Ellie laughed. 'I suppose she must have been. By the way, Roger was round on Saturday—'

'Don't rush me, Ellie,' he interrupted. 'The girls are my first priority. I can't charge round mending bridges right, left and centre until I know what's in store. For all I know, I might be behind bars by the end of the month.'

She was silent, and after a minute he added, 'I was thinking of inviting them up for lunch.'

Another fraught meal, Ellie thought resignedly. It was as well they all had strong stomachs.

'A good idea,' she said.

'I suppose ... you wouldn't like to join us? As moral support?'

'No, Patrick, I would not. This is something you have to do by yourself.'

She heard him sigh. 'I was afraid you'd say that.'

On the Tuesday evening, Laura phoned, and it happened to be Ellie who took the call.

'Sorry to be a nuisance,' she said, 'but I think I must have left my travelling clock in my room. I've searched for it here and can't find it.'

'Hang on,' Ellie said, 'I'll go and check. Keep talking, I'm on the cordless.'

'Any news of Daddy?'

Ellie relayed what Patrick had told her.

'Doesn't sound too good, does it?' Laura said worriedly.

'I'd hoped for something more positive, admittedly.' She had reached the room, and even from the doorway she could see the small clock on the table by the bed. 'Your clock's here,' she added. 'I'll put it in a jiffy bag and post it off to you.'

'Thanks. Oh, and thanks again for the obituary. Do you know – it's the oddest thing – it says that after leaving Caverstock Grammar, my father took a post at Brae-burn Lodge, near Edinburgh.'

'Yes, that's right.' Ellie picked up the clock with her free hand and started back downstairs.

'Well, that's where Adrian went to school.'

Ellie stopped abruptly, an unaccountable coldness stealing over her. 'Are you sure?'

'Yes, isn't it a coincidence? Specially since I'd never even have known if I hadn't been up there that weekend. Mrs Crawford brought down some old albums and there was a snap of Adrian in school uniform. Underneath, it said, "Adrian's first term at Braeburn".'

343

When Ellie didn't speak, Laura added, 'It didn't actually say "Lodge"; do you think there could be two of them?'

'I doubt it; it's quite a well-known public school.'

'I worked out that they must have been there at the same time. Isn't it odd that Adrian never mentioned it?'

'It is, rather. Perhaps they never came across each other.'

'But you always know the staff, don't you, even if they don't teach you? You of all people should know that!'

'Yes,' Ellie agreed aridly, 'I suppose you do.'

'I'll ask him about it when he gets back. Must dash; we've a bridge party to do this evening. Thanks for seeing to the clock. 'Bye.' And without waiting for Ellie's reply, she broke the connection.

Very slowly, with a heavy sensation in the pit of her stomach, Ellie continued down the stairs.

'I want you to tell me I'm being paranoid,' Ellie said, later that evening. Having phoned Jess and been invited round, she was sitting with her friend in the comfortingly untidy sitting room. A golden retriever lay on the rug and Jess had one of her lodgers, a Siamese, on her knee. It had been fretting badly and was receiving extra loving care which, to judge by the volume of its purr, was much appreciated.

'You're being paranoid!' Jess said obligingly.

'I hope you'll still think that in ten minutes.' Ellie paused. 'I'm about to break the rule of a lifetime and repeat some completely unsubstantiated gossip that I overheard. Obviously, this is in confidence.'

'Go on.'

'It was at Fay's birthday party, at the Watermill. A man stopped to speak to Adrian on the way to his table, and later, when I was in the loo, two women came in and started talking about him.'

'About Adrian?'

'Yes. One was the wife of the man who'd spoken to him. She said her husband had been at school with him, and – I think the phrase was, "had doubts about his orientation".'

'Good heavens!' Jess exclaimed. 'Well, obviously that was off-beam.'

'Hold on a moment. She went on to say it looked as though he was wrong, since Adrian was there with his girlfriend; but – this is the nasty part – the other woman said if that was the small dark girl, she looked like a boy, which might have been the attraction.'

Jess's hands stilled on the soft fur. 'Oh God, Ellie, how horrible.'

'Yes. I tried to put it out of my mind, but without much success. Admittedly Laura doesn't seem to be head over heels – we've always joked about Adrian's patience with her – but she's happy enough, and I couldn't bear her to be hurt. I've done my darnedest to discount it, but I've had reservations about him ever since.'

'But all this was two months ago. Why the panic call this evening?'

'Because when Laura was down last week, I gave her a copy of Jeremy's obituary, which I'd saved for her and kept forgetting to hand over. She left early the next morning, so I didn't see her after she'd read it; but she phoned this evening about something else, and mentioned Adrian had been at that school in Scotland at the same time as Jeremy.'

'Oh my God!' whispered Jess.

Ellie glanced at her, mildly surprised by her reaction. 'The point is that he never mentioned it. Wouldn't you expect him to, having been at school with his girlfriend's father, specially one as famous as Jeremy still was at that time? It might just be that I'm a bit chary of Adrian at the moment, but it struck me as a strange omission.'

'Are you absolutely sure about this – that they were there together?'

'I haven't checked myself, but Laura says so.'

'Then we must find out as soon as possible.'

Ellie stared at her. 'Heavens above, Jess, you're making me nervous, and you're supposed to be reassuring me!'

Jess didn't smile. She resumed her slow, even stroking of the cat's fur. 'Do you remember at Dominic's party, when Mother started to say something, and I swooped down and bore you off to the kitchen?'

Ellie drew her brows together. 'It was about Jeremy being sacked from that complex. I don't see the connection.'

'She was about to say just *why* he was sacked.'

'But you'd already told me: he was messing about with one of the members.'

'What I *didn't* tell,' Jess said whitely, 'was that it was a *male* member – a boy of seventeen.'

Ellie closed her eyes for a moment. Then she opened them and said firmly, 'No, that can't be right. Not Jeremy. He was a ladies' man if ever I knew one. Damn it, he married Fay and fathered her child. And before that—'

Jess raised a hand. 'I know all that. But as you can imagine, there was a lot of talk when Jack was up in Worcester that time, and what emerged was that Jeremy was a bit ambivalent in that direction. No one questioned that he preferred women – and

347

there'd been plenty of them – but occasionally, if there were none around or he was feeling jaded, he dabbled in the other direction.'

There was a loud buzzing in Ellie's ears. Huge implications hovered on the edge of her consciousness, and she dreaded having to confront them.

'You see what I'm getting at?' Jess went on, leaning towards her. 'If both Jeremy *and* Adrian are rumoured to be bisexual, and they spent several years together at the same school – well, you know what they say about boys' schools.' She dropped her eyes to the cat on her lap. 'It's even possible the association continued, after they both left.'

Ellie spoke above the pounding of her heart. 'Why did you never tell me this before?'

'Like you, I don't like repeating gossip and it didn't seem relevant. Jeremy was no longer part of your lives. All right, he did come back later, but you said he and Fay met only that once.'

'As far as I know,' Ellie qualified. 'I did have my doubts, later.'

'When exactly did he go to Scotland?'

Ellie thought back. 'Soon after they split up. I should say August seventy-four, and he stayed quite a while – over ten years.'

'How old is Adrian?'

'Thirty-two, I believe.'

'So he was born in sixty-eight or nine, and would have gone to public school at the age of – what? Twelve?'

'Yes, and stayed till he was eighteen.'

'In all likelihood, then, Jeremy was at the school for the whole of Adrian's time there.'

'But Adrian would have left in eighty-six or so. I can't see them staying in touch afterwards; but even if they did, what of it? All I care about is protecting Laura now.'

'Exactly,' Jess said succinctly. 'And Laura is about to ask Adrian why he never mentioned knowing Jeremy, a question I doubt if he'll want to answer. OK, it might be no big deal; I dare say he's prepared himself for the eventuality and has an answer ready. But as you said at the beginning, the fact remains that they almost certainly knew each other, and he's kept quiet about it, when the most natural thing in the world would have been to mention it.' She glanced at Ellie, and swiftly away. 'Which, in view of what happened to Jeremy, I think warrants further investigation. Now who's being paranoid?'

Ellie stared at her, white-faced, incapable of speech.

'I think we should bring Mark in on this,' Jess said suddenly. 'Ed too, if you wouldn't mind. They'd be able to advise us.'

Ellie nodded mutely, and ten minutes later the two men were being put in the picture.

'When is Adrian due back?' Mark enquired.

'In about a week, I think.'

'Is there any way to stop Laura seeing him till we've got to the bottom of this?'

'Not without giving her a reason.'

Ed spoke for the first time. 'How did she meet him, Ellie, do you know?'

Ellie tried to collect her distracted thoughts. 'I can't remember. They've been together for a good five years. He keeps asking her to marry him, but she keeps prevaricating.'

'Sounds familiar!' said Mark with a grin.

'You'd never had any suspicions about his sexuality until you overheard those women?' Ed pursued.

'Never.'

He sat back, shaking his head. 'At the moment, you know, there's no basis to this at all. We're only *assuming* they knew each other at school. Even if they did – even if they had some kind of relationship there, which I can see no way of verifying – there's nothing at all to suggest they were in touch afterwards. Did Adrian go to university?'

'Yes, Durham.'

'Then it doesn't seem very likely they *could* have been, does it?'

Ellie felt a surge of hope. 'Then we've built all this out of nothing?'

'It's not even circumstantial. Even in the

worst case scenario – that there was something between them and they continued
meeting – it's no big deal. A lot of men,
especially those who went to public school,
might well have had the odd experience they
wouldn't like their wives or girlfriends to
know about. Adolescents experiment, but
ninety per cent of them grow out of it. In
all probability Adrian's been completely
straight for the last fifteen years.'

'So you think there's nothing to worry
about?' Ellie repeated, beginning to climb
out of the nightmare.

'I'm not saying that, exactly. For one
thing, if they *were* still in contact, Adrian
should have been interviewed at the time of
the murder. For all we know, of course, he
might have been.'

'That's a bit far-fetched, surely?' Mark
objected.

'The leisure club crowd were,' Jess put in.
'I read about it at the time. They were all
cleared.'

Ellie said shakily, 'Do you think we should
go to the police?'

Mark leant forward. 'And tell them what,
darling? That Adrian *might* be homosexual,
that Jeremy might have been, that they *might*
have known each other at school – which
Adrian left eight years before the murder?
There could even be a perfectly logical
reason why he never told Laura: perhaps

because speaking of her father still upsets her.'

'But if there's the faintest chance she might be in danger,' Ellie said with quiet desperation, 'I can't just sit back and do *nothing*. Suppose he panics when she mentions the school connection? He's a lot to lose, even these days, if the story got out.'

'We'll need a lot more hard evidence before we can go to the authorities,' Ed warned her. 'If Adrian hears of this, and we turn out to be way off-beam, he could take us to court and wipe the floor with us.'

'Then how can we get that evidence?'

Jess said, 'Suppose I ring the school tomorrow? Say I'm writing a biography of Jeremy – which is quite feasible – and want to confirm the dates he was there, who his particular friends were, and so on.'

'They're not going to volunteer the information that he was involved with one of the pupils, even if he was, and even if they knew about it, which is extremely unlikely.'

Ed said, 'I'd still like to know how and when Adrian and Laura met. You say five years ago – that's not long after the murder.'

Jess swallowed. 'You mean he might have deliberately engineered it?'

'She does look very like Jeremy,' Ellie said flatly. She gave a shudder. 'God, what am I saying? What are we all?' She looked round their circle of solemn faces.

'Let's just be rational about this,' Mark said. 'All we have to worry about at this stage is Adrian's possible reaction when Laura asks him if he knew her father. Even then, we might be worrying unnecessarily; as I said, there could be a simple reason for not telling her. But in any event, *until* she mentions it, she's in no danger whatsoever, and she won't be seeing him for another week. The irony is that, before we can take it further, we actually *need* her to ask him.'

'No!' Ellie said sharply.

'Well, if not Laura, someone else. They could just say casually, "Oh, I hear you were at Braeburn in the eighties. Did you by any chance come across Jeremy Page?" Then we could gauge his reaction.'

'Whatever you say,' Ellie broke in, 'I'll have to warn her not to broach the subject, and there's no way I can do that on the phone.' She thought for a moment. 'I'll invite myself for the weekend, and somehow bring it up then. It will be easier, face to face; and I can find out how they met, too, since Ed seems to think it's important.'

'I still think it's all a wild-goose chase,' Mark commented, 'but since you're so concerned about it, of course we'll do what we can. Just remember, Ellie, the man *loves* Laura. He's not going to do anything to hurt her.'

'I wish I could believe that,' Ellie said.

Fifteen

First thing the next morning, Ellie phoned Laura on her mobile, to request a bed for the weekend.

'Of course – no problem. But why didn't you mention it when I phoned yesterday?'

'I've only just decided,' Ellie told her. 'I've a rather grand dinner coming up, and I'm going to treat myself to a new outfit. Perhaps you could help me look?'

'Oh, sorry, I won't be able to. In fact, this weekend is rather fraught; we've a wedding reception on Saturday, which will take up the whole day. Could you put it off till next week?'

'I'd rather sort something out now. We can still spend Sunday together, can't we?' She hesitated. 'When did you say Adrian was due back?'

'Next Tuesday, but that wouldn't be a problem. We're not joined at the hip.'

'Talking of Adrian,' Ellie went on with artful carelessness, 'someone was asking the other day how you two met, and I couldn't remember.'

Laura laughed. 'He picked me up! Quite literally, at the V & A. We kept stopping at the same pictures, and catching each other's eye. Eventually he made some comment about a painting, which I agreed with, and he said that, as we seemed to have the same taste, perhaps we should discuss it further over a cup of coffee. And it went on from there.'

Ellie was not reassured. 'How long ago was that?'

'Oh, yonks. Not long after I came to London. Look, I'm sorry, I'll have to ring off. I'm in the car and I've just arrived at a client's house. Will you be coming up Friday evening?'

'If that's all right.'

'I'll give you a quick buzz tomorrow to confirm times. Look forward to seeing you. 'Bye.'

Slightly comforted by having put her plan into action, Ellie continued with her day.

When she returned to Sandford that afternoon, Christa was in the hall, looking flushed and apprehensive. 'Could I talk to you for a moment, Aunt Ellie?' she asked.

'Of course, darling. What is it?'

Christa followed her into the kitchen, where Ellie dumped her shopping bag containing ingredients for that evening's meal.

'I'm going back to London,' she said abruptly.

Ellie turned to face her. 'Back...?'

Her colour deepened. 'Well, back to Neville, actually. I had a letter from him on Monday. He didn't know where I was, and had been ringing the flat till the answer-phone tape ran out. He finally wrote in the hope that I was having mail redirected, which, of course, I have been.'

'And what did he say?' Ellie asked quietly.

'That he'd been a bloody idiot, that the girl meant nothing to him and he'd sent her packing, and that he wanted me back. He sounded pretty frantic.' She looked at her aunt imploringly. 'Oh, I *know* it's awful and none of you approve, and I should never have got into it in the first place. The trouble is, I love him.'

'He's not talking of divorcing his wife, I suppose?'

She shook her head miserably.

'Oh darling, you're only laying yourself open to being hurt again. Who's to say another pretty girl won't take his fancy in a year or so?'

'It's just a chance I'll have to take.'

Ellie's heart melted with pity for her. She was lovely, intelligent, witty, a successful career woman. She deserved so much more, but she was in love, and that blinded her to all else.

'Will you explain to Mum? If I stay and tell her myself, she'll try to talk me out of it, and I can't take that – not at the moment.'

'You mean you're leaving now?'

'Yes. Everything's in the car.'

Ellie looked at her aghast. 'But shouldn't you think it over carefully, before—?'

'I've thought of nothing else for the last couple of days. I finally phoned him last night. It was ... wonderful to hear his voice again.'

'Then all I can say is, good luck.'

'Thank you.' Christa kissed her. 'I knew you'd understand. Oh – with all this going on, I almost forgot: Daddy phoned this morning. He wants the four of us to meet him for lunch.'

'Yes, he told me.'

'If you're speaking to the others, tell them I'll be in touch. It'll be amazing to see him again.'

'He's not out of the wood yet, Christa.'

'I know. But at least I'll be able to see something of him when I'm back up there.'

Ellie walked out to the car with her. 'Do you ever see Laura when you're in town?' she asked suddenly.

'We sometimes meet for a meal.'

'What do you think of Adrian?'

Christa, about to get in the car, turned in surprise. 'Since you ask, he's always struck me as a bit of a creep. Still, *chacun à son goût.*

Why do you ask?'

'Oh ... nothing. But could you keep an eye on her for me, without her noticing?'

'Auntie, what is this?'

'I'm just uneasy about her, that's all.'

Christa held her eye for a long minute; then, seeing she wasn't going to elaborate, shrugged. 'OK, I'll keep an eye on her, though Lord knows what I'm supposed to be looking for.'

'Thanks, darling,' Ellie said and, with a heavy heart, watched her go down the drive, toot at the gate, and disappear from sight.

When Ellie told Fay Christa had gone, she promptly burst into tears.

'Doesn't she realise how much I need her, now of all times? I suppose Patrick's been in touch with her.'

'He has, but that's incidental to her moving back. That letter she had on Monday was from Neville.'

'I knew it! I was in two minds about burning it before she came down.'

'Fay!'

'Well, I didn't, did I? Your influence, perhaps. What did Patrick want with her, anyway?'

'He's invited them all to join him for lunch.'

'Laura too?'

'Laura too.'

'They don't seem to know the meaning of

the word loyalty,' Fay sniffed, wiping her eyes. 'Well, at least I have you.'

Ellie's heart sank. Not for much longer, she thought. 'I'm going up to spend the weekend with Laura,' she said aloud. 'I need a new outfit for the Governors' dinner.'

Fay stared at her. 'But what about the boutique on Riverside Walk? You always go there.'

'I decided to try Knightsbridge, for a change.'

'But ... that means I'll be all by myself!'

'You're a big girl now, Fay. Almost a grandmother, in fact. If you really can't face being alone, get Roger to come and hold your hand.'

'There's no need to be like that,' Fay protested, tears starting again. 'You know I'm especially vulnerable just now, with Patrick reappearing and all the business about Jeremy stirred up again. I really do think Christa might have shown a little consideration, instead of running back to that man the minute he raises a finger.'

Ellie, tired of arguing everyone else's cause, turned back to the cooker and did not reply.

Neville was waiting for her at the flat, and within five minutes they were making love, gasping and clutching at each other in an agony of impatience that convinced Christa that he really had been missing her.

'Bless you for coming back,' he murmured, when he was capable of coherent speech. 'We have about twelve weeks to make up, and I'm going to enjoy every minute of it! Darling, I must have been out of my mind. You do forgive me?'

Her eyes moved greedily over him – the slightly lined face, the hooked nose, the intense blue of his eyes, the lean body that was only here and there beginning to show signs of incipient flabbiness.

'No,' she said, seeing she had surprised him, 'I don't forgive you, but I'm prepared to give you a second chance.'

He smiled, kissing her fingertips. 'Believe me, I don't intend to squander it.'

They showered and dressed and went out to one of their favourite restaurants for dinner, and over the meal she told him of her father's reappearance. 'My sisters and I are meeting him for lunch soon,' she ended.

'I'm very happy for you.'

Unbidden, her aunt's parting words came into her head, and she frowned. 'Aunt Ellie has a bee in her bonnet about Laura,' she said. 'I don't know what it is, but she asked me to keep an eye on her; and she wanted to know what I thought of Adrian. Remember, we bumped into them once, at Covent Garden?'

'I remember. And what *do* you think of Adrian?'

'How did he strike you?'

Neville smiled. 'I'm not going to be drawn into this.'

'Why not?'

'Because if I say something that offends you, you might pass it on to your sister.'

'Didn't you like him, then?'

'Dearest girl, I was in his company for less than three minutes.'

'But you're trained to make snap decisions in your job, form instant opinions.'

'Let's just say I wouldn't like a daughter of mine to go out with him.'

Christa looked startled. 'Why? What's wrong with him? I mean, I don't particularly care for him myself, but he's very bright, and he comes from a good family.'

Neville raised both his hands in mock defence. 'You asked for my opinion, and I gave it to you. That's all that I'm prepared to say.'

Christa said slowly, 'Now you've got me worried. Ellie didn't *say* Adrian was the problem; the question about him just sort of followed on. In any case he's abroad at the moment – he missed the family dinner. All the same, I think I'll give Laura a call later – she doesn't go to bed before midnight.'

As it happened, Laura was at that moment

receiving another call.

'Surprise, surprise! Guess who?'

'Adrian! Where are you?'

'Heathrow – we've just landed. Things went more smoothly than we expected, and as everything's signed and sealed, there was no point in staying any longer. I've missed you, my love. How are things?'

'Fine, though I missed you, too.'

'Well, I've brought you back a little something I think you'll like. Shall I come straight to the flat?'

'Good idea. I presume you've eaten?'

'Yes, on the plane. No great shakes, but it appeased the appetite. I won't want anything else.'

'I'll expect you in an hour or so, then.'

Laura tidied away the recipe charts and schedules she'd been working on and slipped them back in her briefcase. Casting an eye round the large, open-plan room, she plumped cushions, removed an empty coffee cup, and plucked some dying flowers out of the vase. Then she had a shower and washed her hair. Adrian was sure to stay the night.

It was almost eleven by the time he arrived. After he'd given her the present, a gold-link bracelet with a heart as the clasp, they sat drinking companionably while he told her about the trip. She had the impression that he was on edge, still psyched up, perhaps, by his business contacts and the flight home.

As he ended his account, she said, 'I've got some news too. My father's come back.'

Adrian looked up sharply. 'Your father?'

'My stepfather. He disappeared, you know, when ... when my real father was killed, and there's been no word from him since. The police have always been suspicious because of the timing, but he was in South America and didn't even hear about the murder till months later.'

Adrian didn't reply. She glanced at him, but he was staring intently into his glass.

'So do the police believe him?' he asked at last. 'That he didn't know about it?'

'I don't know. He's on bail at the moment.' She paused. 'Why did you never tell me you knew my father?'

He turned blank eyes on her. 'I don't know what you're talking about.'

'You were at Braeburn when he was games master there. You must have known him.'

'Whatever gave you the idea I was at Braeburn?'

'Your mother showed me a photo of you in school uniform.'

After a moment he laughed. It was not a pleasant sound. Then he said, 'It always upset you to talk about him. It seemed better not to mention it.'

'So you *did* know him? Did he take you

for games?'

Adrian drained his glass and, standing up, went to refill it. 'He did,' he said over his shoulder, 'but I was hopeless at sport. I was ashamed to play in front of him, when he'd had such a brilliant career.'

Laura leaned forward. 'What was he like in those days? Was he popular with the boys?'

He returned to his chair. 'You've changed your tune, haven't you? I thought you didn't like talking about him.'

'But I don't know anything about that part of his life, and I'd like to. I just can't believe you never mentioned knowing him.'

Adrian slammed his glass down. 'For God's sake, Laura, I've told you why! Now can we just drop the subject?'

She gazed at him in surprise. 'What's the matter? Didn't you like him?'

His face contorted. 'Will you for God's sake shut up?' he shouted. They stared at each other, both of them startled by his outburst; then he slumped in his chair. 'Oh, what's the use?' He ran his hands through his hair in a characteristic gesture. His face, tired when he arrived, suddenly looked haggard. 'No,' he said deliberately, 'I didn't *like* him; I loved him.'

She gave an uncomfortable laugh. 'Schoolboy crush?'

The light was shining on his glasses, obscuring his eyes. 'Much more than that.

He loved me, too, though he tried not to show it.'

Laura felt suddenly sick. What was he saying? What was the matter with him?

'That's nonsense,' she said sharply. 'I'm quite sure he wouldn't show any favouritism.'

Adrian gave a strangled laugh. 'Since you insist on discussing it, we might as well get the facts straight. I'm talking now about when I was older – sixteen and seventeen. He loved me, I tell you.' He bent towards her. *'He made love to me!'*

Nausea welled in her throat. He was mad – he must be. She said faintly, 'I don't believe you.'

He didn't seem to have heard her. 'I'd hero-worshipped him all my life; all the younger boys did. As I said, I was useless at games, clumsy and uncoordinated. I thought he despised me. One day, when I'd played exceptionally badly and let the house down into the bargain, I broke down in the locker room when everyone had gone. He came in and found me. And I ... well, I suppose I flung myself at him, and he held me and told me it was all right. Then, gradually, he started to caress me, and it was the most wonderful experience of my life. And ... that was how it started.'

Laura sat frozen, staring at this man she had thought she'd known but whom she didn't know at all.

'It didn't happen that often,' he went on. 'Only three or four times in all. That's what made it special. I knew he loved me, and that was enough. Oh, of course he had women – I used to hear the other masters laughing about it – but they were a blind. He didn't want people to know the truth.

'When I had to leave school, it was ... like a bereavement. I wrote to him every week of my first year at Durham. He didn't reply – he'd warned me before he was no good at letter-writing – but it was still a contact. Then I heard he'd left Braeburn and no one knew where he was. I was ... distraught.'

Laura, still staring at him in horrified fascination, couldn't prevent herself asking, 'What happened then?'

He looked up, and she saw there were tears running down his face. 'Fate,' he said simply. 'That's what happened. I started my job with Jameson's, and one day I was on a bus going along Piccadilly, and I looked out of the window and saw him – just saw him, walking along the street.

'I flung myself off the bus – could have been killed – and rushed after him. It was eight years since I'd seen him, but it felt as if it were yesterday. We went for a drink and he told me he'd been working in the Midlands but had had to leave, and was thinking of going down to Caverstock, where he used to live, to find a job. He also wanted to see his daughter – he'd told me before that he had one – and that he'd learned she was attending a catering college there. He thought she'd put in a good word for him, if he could just win her round.'

Adrian's eyes focused on her, seeming to realise for the first time it was to that daughter he was speaking. 'He was very proud of you,' he added, switching to the second person.

Laura said with an effort, 'But you weren't ... you didn't...'

He smiled that strange, unfamiliar smile. 'We did once, yes, at my flat. I was deliriously happy at having found him again, sure this time there was nothing to keep us apart, and that once he'd found a job we could be together permanently; but he said not to contact him in Caverstock, as he didn't want the family to know about me yet.'

'Yet?' whispered Laura. 'He said "yet"?'

Adrian brushed that aside. 'Whether he actually said it or not, it was implied. He was fairly hard-up, and I lent him quite a lot of money over those weeks. He swore he'd pay me back, but I didn't want him to. I'd have given him everything I had.'

He drank more of his whisky. 'So he went off to Caverstock, and presumably renewed his acquaintance with you and the others, and I didn't hear anything of him for six weeks or more. Then, at the beginning of December, he phoned to say he'd be in London on Wednesday the seventh and wanted us to meet, as he had something to tell me. I was sure it was the green light – that at last we could be together.'

His voice changed, flattened. 'So I met him in a pub as arranged, and he handed over a wad of cash, and said we were now quits and he needn't trouble me any more because he was going to get married again, and his fiancée had loads of money. Then, as calm as you please, he said, "Must go – I'm supposed to be getting a take-away. Thanks for your help," and walked out of the pub.

'I was frantic. I went running after him, catching hold of his arm and trying to pull him round to face me. He was embarrassed, I could tell that, and he dragged me down a side alley so people wouldn't see. When I went on crying and hanging on to him, he lost his temper. He said did I really imagine he was interested in an unattractive little squirt like me? That's what he called me: an unattractive little squirt. Can you imagine how I felt? Hurt and rage and desperation just welled up, and I remembered the knife in my pocket, which I'd carried ever since I was attacked by a gang of youths outside a gay bar. Without even thinking about it, I just ... pushed it into him. It was incredibly easy.'

He put his head in his hands and began to weep.

Laura tried to speak, but at first no sound came. Halfway through the account her hands had gone to her face, and now she slowly dragged them down, her fingers leaving red marks on the whiteness of her cheeks.

'I couldn't just leave him lying there,' Adrian went on in a muffled voice. 'There was a skip standing on the pavement, and I hoisted him up into it and covered him over. I suppose I was trying to ... bury him.'

'Why are you telling me this?' she whispered. 'Oh God, why?'

He shrugged. 'I always knew that once you started asking questions, it would be over. I don't care what happens to me; I didn't then. I waited every day to be arrested – I'd almost have welcomed it – but it was two weeks before they even found him.' He looked at her earnestly. 'I wasn't trying to *hide* him, you know, just give him a decent burial. But Patrick Nelson had disappeared and police attention fastened on him. It seemed I was being given another chance, so I switched my love to you.'

'To *me*? Are you saying you knew from the first who I was?'

'Of course I did.' He looked up, wiping a hand across his face. 'I went to his funeral hoping to see you, but only your aunt was there. I saw his red-haired woman though, all grief-stricken. She was the one I should have killed; if it hadn't been for her, he'd have come back to me.'

He blew his nose. 'I noticed her before you did, you know, at that reception. I knew damn well who she was, and why she was staring at you. I tried to steer you away, but she was too persistent. I was desperate to find out how much you knew about her, but you just clammed up.

'Anyway, since you weren't at the funeral, I went down to Caverstock and waited outside the catering college, as Jeremy'd said he was going to. When you came out, my heart almost stopped, you were so like him. It was as though he'd come back to me.'

He picked up his glass, saw it was empty, and put it down again. Laura didn't move.

'After that, I went down to Rushyford every weekend. I used to follow you to the shops, and when you went somewhere for a coffee, I was just across the room. It went on for months, until you went to London. I was terrified I'd lost you; then I saw one of your vans with Page Laura on the side and tracked you down again. So I fixed our meeting at the V & A.

'I do love you, Laura,' he added belatedly. 'For yourself, I mean, but even more because of who you are. When you're in my arms, I feel I'm holding Jeremy as well.'

The nausea returned. She had to get away from him, she thought vaguely, but her limbs seemed paralysed There was a long silence, which was broken, shockingly, by the shrilling of the phone. She half-ran, half-stumbled over to it and picked it up, but her throat was dry and she couldn't speak.

'Laura?' It was Christa's voice.

She didn't reply, imagining her sister in the blessed safety of the hall at Sandford.

'Laura – are you all right?'

She made a supreme effort. 'No,' she said on a croak, and then, 'Adrian's here.'

She heard Christa give a muffled exclamation, before saying swiftly, 'Laurie, I'm back at the flat and Neville's with me. Do you want us to come round?'

'Yes,' whispered Laura aridly. 'Oh, yes.'

'We'll be right there.'

She put the phone down. Adrian hadn't moved. 'Who was that?' he asked casually.

'Only Christa.'

'What did she want?'

'Nothing much, just to say she's ... moved back to the flat.'

His voice sharpened. 'She's not coming here?'

Laura tried to swallow past the lump in her throat. 'Why would she do that, at this time of night?'

'Because you sounded so odd on the phone?' He was standing up. 'We have to go.'

'What do you mean, go?'

'Get out of here. I can't have you repeating what I've just told you.'

'But where would we go? Adrian, I won't say anything...'

He seized her arm. 'Where are the car keys?'

She shook her head, but he scooped up her handbag with his free hand, turned it upside down, and the keys fell on to the table. He caught them up and pushed her ahead of him out of the flat and down the long flights of stairs to the basement car park.

Christa said for the second time, 'He wasn't supposed to be back till next week. God, Neville, she sounded terrified. Surely not of him, though? He's so mild and unassuming. OK, I'm not wild about him, but the one thing you can say for him is that he worships the ground Laurie walks on.'

She glanced sideways at Neville, but his eyes were intent on the road. 'You had reservations, though, didn't you?'

'He struck me as being unstable, that's all.'

'In just three minutes?'

'As you pointed out, I'm used to making snap decisions. You'll have to direct me here, darling. Which way at the traffic lights?'

'Left. Then the apartment building's on

372

the right.'

'Good area,' Neville commented. 'Let's hope there's somewhere to park.'

They turned the corner, and Christa pointed out the large modern building half-way down the road. 'There it is. If you drive just past it, there's usually...'

She broke off as a silver Golf came roaring out of the slope leading up from the car park, its tyres screeching as it skidded round and careened off down the road ahead of them.

Christa clutched Neville's arm. 'That's Laura's car! Where on earth is she going? She knows we're on our way!'

Neville's foot was already on the accelerator. 'There's someone in the passenger seat,' he said, 'but I'd guess friend Adrian is behind the wheel.'

'They could be killed, driving at that speed! It's a built up area!'

'With luck the police will pick them up, but we'll give them a helping hand. My mobile's in the glove compartment; can you reach it?'

She fumbled frantically at the unfamiliar catch and the front fell forwards, shooting the phone on to the floor. Christa swore softly, unbuckling her belt to retrieve it. The car skidded round a corner and she clutched at Neville's knees as she righted herself and refastened her belt. Shakily, she handed him the phone.

'This is Neville Henderson of Grant, Henderson Enterprises,' he said into it. 'I wish to report a car being driven at speed along Hartford Road. A silver Golf, licence plate number...?' He turned to Christa, who shook her head helplessly. '...unknown. I have reason to believe that a young woman is being abducted. I'm in pursuit, but I've no wish for the speed cops to stop me rather than him. Can you head him off? He's driving north, possibly aiming for the M1.'

Christa heard the crackle of a reply, and he switched off.

'They advised me to leave the pursuit to them,' he said grimly, 'but I presume you don't want us to lose them?'

Christa shook her head. She had complete faith in his ability to control the car, but was less sure of Adrian's, particularly in what were obviously stressful circumstances. 'Suppose they...?' She closed her eyes, unable to finish.

Laura clutched at her seat as the car sped through a second red light with undiminished speed, and a startled pedestrian leapt back from the kerb.

'Where are we going?' she shouted, against the roar of its movement.

'Scotland,' he shouted back. 'We'll be safe there.'

'If we don't crash in the meantime. Adrian, please slow down! You'll get us both killed!'

'That might be the best solution.'

She went cold with terror. God, don't let her have put the idea into his head!

He added conversationally, 'I have to keep the speed up; there's someone on our tail.'

'Probably the police,' she said, praying she was right.

'No; they'd have had their sirens on by now. Big swanky car – Merc by the look of it. It's been behind us all the way from the flats.'

Christa? Laura wondered. Christa and Neville? Oh, please!

'Aha!' Adrian said suddenly. 'Now, we *have* got the fuzz.'

A car that had been waiting in a side street with its lights off switched them on and slid swiftly out on to the road between them and their pursuer, sirens suddenly blaring and lights flashing. For several eternal minutes the three cars streaked along in convoy, while other vehicles, horns hooting indignantly, skidded out of their way. Then, some distance ahead of them, Laura saw another flashing blue light and made out a police car parked across the road.

'Slow down!' she screamed. 'Adrian – for God's sake!'

The roadblock rushed towards them with

sickening speed. In desperation Laura grabbed the handbrake with one hand, at the same time wrenching the steering wheel with the other, and the car slewed to the left, feet away from the stationary car. In their headlights, she caught a glimpse of the policeman's white face, mouth open, as, with rapid deceleration, the car mounted the pavement, skittered along it for a few yards, hit a wall a glancing blow with a scream of tearing metal, and finally shuddered to a halt. Laura, flung forwards and then joltingly back against the headrest, lost consciousness for the first time in her life.

Epilogue

It was six weeks after the crash, and life was gradually returning to normal. Laura had spent three of those weeks at Sandford, recovering from her whiplash injuries. The family feared, though, that the mental damage would last longer, as she was forced to come to terms not only with her father's sexuality, but also with the shocking discovery that it was her lover who had murdered him.

Her last thought before passing out had been that Adrian, slumped over the steering wheel, was dead, but this proved not to be so. He'd received a nasty chest wound and severe bruising to the face and head, but that, as Neville grimly remarked, was the least of his problems. The police had remained at his bedside, and when he was able to be questioned, he'd willingly repeated to them everything he'd told Laura. It seemed that, having lost her, he no longer cared what happened.

His parents, horrified and disbelieving,

had flown down to be with him. Occasionally, Laura thought of the wonderful spread she and Beth had planned for their ruby wedding. There would be no celebrations for the Crawfords now. Jean had written her a note, but she'd not yet felt able to reply.

Since the traumas of that night, the family had grown closer together; Claire and Roy frequently drove over to spend a Sunday at Sandford, while Jenny, who, in the seventh month of her pregnancy, had at last agreed to give up work, dropped in most days. One weekend, Christa persuaded Neville to forego his dutiful trip to Cheshire and come down with her. As she'd hoped, his smooth charm quickly dispelled any initial awkwardness and, since Fay considered him instrumental in saving Laura's life, the irregularity of their relationship was implicitly condoned.

Patrick meanwhile, freed from police suspicion and escaping fairly lightly on the passport charges, was in the process of buying himself a small house at Richmond and had already embarked on his latest book. He was in frequent touch with his daughters and had been particularly supportive of Laura, horrified by the ordeal she had suffered.

As soon as she felt well enough, Laura had returned to her flat and Page Laura. There was work to be done, she told her protesting family, and she needed above all to be occupied. She promised, though, to come down at weekends when she wasn't working, at least for the next few months.

It was on one of those weekends, a Sunday in late July, that they were all relaxing in the garden. Roger and Mark had joined them, and for the first time in months the atmosphere was light-hearted, with no underlying stress. Ellie and Mark, having decided they'd held back their news long enough, felt this an appropriate time to break it.

During a lull in the conversation, Mark rose to his feet. 'Ladies and gentlemen, I have an announcement to make. I'm delighted to tell you that I have finally won Ellie round, and she's agreed to marry me in September.'

Amid the general exclamations of delight and congratulations, Fay's voice rose above the others. 'In that case, I think it's more than time that Ellie had her fair share of Sandford. You'll need a home, and I've been hogging this one long enough.'

'Oh, Fay, no,' Ellie protested. 'We couldn't...'

'Why couldn't you? You're part-owner, but in all these years you've never had it to yourself.'

'But where will you go?' Mark asked her.

Roger put an arm round her. 'I can answer

that: she'll move in with me. I'm still hoping we'll eventually follow your example.'

'This calls for champagne,' Mark said, 'and it just so happens that I came prepared.'

Ellie stood up. 'I'll come with you and get some glasses.'

While he went to retrieve the bottles from his car, she turned into the kitchen. Sandford, hers! she thought, literally hugging herself with glee. She couldn't have wished for a more perfect wedding present.

Suddenly, the cool, familiar room seemed peopled with memories: her grandmother, smiling in the shadows as Cook allowed her infant self and Fay to lick the mixing spoons; her mother, brisk and sharp-tongued, always on edge in this house; and her father, grudging and difficult, but loving it as passionately as did his daughters and granddaughters. Ellie was grateful that she'd come closer to him in his last years.

So life would go on, she thought, taking out glasses through a nostalgic mist of tears. And perhaps after her and Fay, one of the girls would take up residence and bring up her own children here. Or perhaps not. That would be in the lap of the gods. In the meantime, she decided, hearing Mark come back into the hall, after their health had been drunk she had a toast of her own to propose, to those who had lived in this house before them: *Sandford and its ghosts!*

Smiling at the fancy, she went out, with Mark at her side, to rejoin her family.